THE LOWLANDS

LAUREL MARTIN

Copyright 2022 Laurel Martin.

All rights reserved. No portion of this book may be reproduced in any form without permission from the publisher, except as permitted by U.S. copyright law.

This is a work of fiction. Names, characters, places, and incidents either are the products of the author's imagination or are used fictitiously. Any resemblance to actual persons, living or dead, businesses, companies, events, or locales is entirely coincidental.

Cover by: Laura Boyle Design

(softcover) ISBN: 978-1-7781836-1-4

(ebook) ISBN: 978-1-7781836-0-7

For Nicole and Kelly

CHAPTER ONE

Riley stared out the passenger window, stewing. *How could he have been so insensitive?* She kept going over it in her mind, getting herself more upset. The weather wasn't helping. They'd been driving through a light but steady rain since leaving Florida that morning.

For as long as she and Jake had been married, a whole four years, they'd been driving to Florida each February to stay with his parents at their winter home. Rob and Wendy Marshall owned an oceanfront house on Sanibel Island. It was beautiful, not too ostentatious—in fact, quite modest considering how well off they were. The bulk of the Marshalls' wealth had come from the sale of their business, Niagara Estate Winery. Several years beforehand, Rob and

Wendy had separated a large portion of the vineyard and Jake had started a spin-off business. His ice wines had become hugely successful.

Riley enjoyed spending time with Jake's family. They were down-to-earth thoughtful people, and they treated her like she was their own daughter. This last two-week stay had flown by, and Wendy had gotten up early to see them off. That was when Riley had overheard her casual comment to Jake about the possibility of grandchildren someday. He'd been quick to shut her down. "I wouldn't hold your breath, Mom. Riley's not ready."

She remembered how shocked she'd been, hearing him say it like that. It felt like he was blaming it all on her.

She debated bringing it up, confronting him now in the car and asking him why he'd said such a thing. They hadn't even *talked* about starting a family—not since that one heated argument when they were first married. But that was four years ago. Clearly, he still didn't get it.

How could someone who's normally so caring and supportive be so blind? What she needed was security, and not the financial security he could easily provide. She needed the security of knowing he'd be an equal partner and take on half the responsibility, half the worrying, half of everything that came with raising children. She wasn't about to sacrifice her career to be a stay-at-home mom.

"You seem awfully quiet today," he said, glancing over with a smile.

She decided not to get into it, not while they were driving. "I'm just feeling a bit down today. Probably the weather."

"Well, it sure is a dreary day, I'll give you that." He reached over and squeezed her hand gently. "It was a wonderful vacation, wasn't it?"

"Yes. Really nice." It had been wonderful. But now, she just wanted to get home. She was anxious to see her own family and get back to work. She was in the final planning stages of opening a second location for her catering business. She'd decided that if the commercial property she wanted was still available, she'd move forward on it. Maybe then, Jake would see that her career was every bit as important as his.

A few large droplets of rain splattered against the windshield. Then, half a dozen more. Then, boom! It was like she and Jake had crossed some imaginary line into a full-blown downpour. The wiper blades launched into high speed, leaving only a shattered view of the road ahead.

Jake was gripping the steering wheel with both hands, leaning forward, straining to see the flickering glimpses through the windshield. "Wow, this sure came out of nowhere." A gust of wind slapped a sheet of rain against the windshield and his head jolted back. "Whoa!"

"Jake, this is unbelievable." She almost had to shout over the boisterous pounding of rain. "Maybe we should pull over or get off the highway at the next exit."

He kept his eyes on the road. "Good idea. Can you check the navigation and see if you can find—"

Her cell phone started screeching. She stared at the emergency alert, her mouth half open. "Oh, my god. It says 'Tornado imminent, seek shelter'!"

"What the hell—where are we supposed to seek shelter? We're in the middle of nowhere," Jake said.

Riley reached forward to the large touch screen centred in the dash and zoomed in on the car's navigation system. "I don't see any exits nearby. What do you think? Should we just pull off to the side?"

Jake stayed focused on the road, his chin practically touching the leather-wrapped steering wheel. "I don't know." He put on the four-way flashers and moved over to the right lane. A transport truck came barrelling past them on the left, leaving an airborne stream of water in its wake. The spray swooshed against their windshield, propelled by another gust of wind. "What a jackass." Jake shook his head. "Riley, I think we should just keep going. For all we know, we could be sitting right in the tornado's path if we pull over here. Plus, we're liable to get hit by one of these stupid trucks."

Four or five miles down the highway, the rain started to ease off. Jake took in a deep breath and blew it out slowly. "I don't want to jinx anything, but I think the worst is over."

Riley tapped her knuckles against the woodgrain trim on the console. "Knock on wood." She twisted in her seat to look out the rear window. "That was pretty intense, wasn't it? I don't think I've ever been in a storm like that." She scanned the sky in all directions. "I don't see any funnel clouds anywhere. I think we're okay."

Jake was still struggling to hold the car steady. The depressions in the pavement were filled with rain water that kept tugging at the car and gushing noisily into the wheel wells. He steered them out of the ruts. "I don't get it," he said. "It still feels like something's pulling at us."

A second later the whole car was shuddering and a loud thumping erupted underneath. "Oh, shit," Jake said.

"We must have picked up something in one of the tires." A warning light popped up on the screen in front of them. *CHECK TIRE PRESSURE.* "Yeah, no kidding. Thanks for the heads-up." He turned the four-way flashers back on. "Riley, we're going to have to get off the highway."

She checked the navigation system again. "We're coming up on an exit. It's just one mile up, and there's a service station there. Do you think we can make it?"

"We're going to try. These are run-flat tires—supposedly you can drive up to a hundred miles with a flat, but I somehow doubt that. This feels bad, like there's some serious damage." The thumping slowed down with them as they got onto the exit ramp.

At the gas station, Jake parked at the far side of the lot near the air pump, grabbed the umbrella and jumped out to take a look. He circled the car, stopping at the rear passenger-side tire.

Riley opened her window and stuck her head out, trying to see. It smelled like burning rubber. Jake squatted down next to it. The tire was totally flat with a hunk of metal protruding near the rim. He gave her a thumbs down. "It's a goner," he said as he got back into the car. He looked at his watch solemnly. "Time of death, three fifteen p.m." He tossed the umbrella behind his seat. "Guess it was just too *tired* to hang on."

Riley groaned and gave his shoulder a light shove. "That was bad, even for you, Jake." She looked at him more seriously. "Now what?"

His smile faded. "Now I feel stupid," he said. "We don't have a spare. I remember the sales guy telling me how great that was, how we'd have so much extra trunk space. Honestly, the guy went on and on about these run-flat tires and how you'd never need a spare. I don't know who's the bigger jerk—him or me."

"Well, I for one, appreciate the extra trunk space, and I think our golf clubs do too."

He smiled at her. "Ah, you're just trying to make your dummy husband feel better." He reached over her legs, pulled the S-Class Cabriolet owner's manual out of the glove box and gave her a quick kiss. "Guess I better call the twenty-four-hour roadside assistance."

The call was answered promptly and connected to the car's audio system. "Thank you for calling Mercedes Roadside Assistance. Our wait times are longer than usual, but your call is important to us. Please stay on the line, and one of our agents will be with you shortly."

"Figures," Jake remarked as the instrumental music commenced. "Why do they choose the worst possible music for these things? Are they *trying* to agitate people?" Several minutes later, a consultant came on the line. Jake answered a slew of questions, after which, the consultant verified their vehicle location on GPS.

"Sir, we have you located just off Interstate 95 North, near Yemassee, South Carolina."

"Yes, that's right," Jake confirmed.

"Okay, sir. The Mercedes dealer nearest to you is in Hilton Head. I'm going to dispatch a tow truck. Can you hold the line, please?" It must have been a rhetorical question, because, without waiting for an answer, the line clicked, and they were thrown midway into an encore of the irritating instrumental music. The trumpets and French horns were leading the charge, taking on a group of persistent piccolos that refused to pipe down.

Jake looked over at Riley and they both rolled their eyes as the music droned through the surround-sound speakers. He started to laugh, then pretended to get into the groove, rocking back and forth in his seat, snapping his fingers to the beat.

Riley burst out laughing. "Oh, Jake. Always the joker." It was one of the many things she loved about him.

A moment later, the line clicked again and the roadside assistance woman was back. "Apparently, they're very busy—some sort of storm in your area. The tow's going to be anywhere from two to three hours."

That would totally throw them off track. She could see the disappointment on Jake's face. "The thing is," he tried to explain, "we're actually headed north, and Hilton Head is almost an hour south of where we are now. Is there no other dealership north of us that we could be towed to instead?"

"No, sir. The closest option would be in Hilton Head. I've already dispatched the tow."

While Jake finished up with roadside assistance, Riley searched online to see exactly where the dealership was and what time they closed. It was already after 3:00 p.m.; the dealer website showed their service department was open until 5:00 p.m. "Well, here's some more good news," she announced. "The dealer's probably going to be closed by the time we get there. There's no way we'll make it to our hotel in Columbia tonight."

"Seriously?" He shook his head. "This day just keeps getting better. Now we'll have to change our plans." Wavy lines appeared across his brow.

"I'll phone the hotel. It'll be fine." She didn't mind changing plans. Improvising was kind of her thing. At work, some of her best dishes were created on the fly. She'd realize she was out of one ingredient and simply substitute something else. Or maybe she'd change the whole recipe and, miraculously, it would turn out to be even more amazing. Jake, on the other hand, preferred things to be orderly and systematic. When it came to harvesting the grapes for his ice wines, the uncertainty of the weather would often stress him out. The temperature had to be a sustained minus 10 degrees Celsius, or it was a no-go and plans would have to change.

Jake opened his door and swung a leg out. "I better go inside and let them know we'll be parked here for a few hours waiting for a tow." She watched him zig-zag around a few puddles as he passed the gas pumps and headed toward the store. That was when she noticed the police cruiser parked along the other side of the building. She took a mental note, figuring the washrooms might be over there. No doubt, she or Jake would need one at some point.

A few minutes later, Jake returned carrying a couple of water bottles in one hand and something hidden behind his back in the other. He swirled the hidden arm around in a grandiose way, as if he were doing a magic trick for her. "Tada," he said, revealing two of Riley's favourite ice cream bars. "Thought we might as well make the best of it."

Riley's eyes widened along with her smile. "Ah Jake, that's so nice." His thoughtfulness and quirky sense of humour had won her over. She set aside her hurt feelings from earlier and gladly accepted the ice cream bar.

As she unwrapped it, she gave him an update, "Listen, I was able to cancel our hotel room for tonight in Columbia, and I'm just looking at some other options in Hilton Head not far from the dealership there." She took a small bite of the ice cream bar and continued to talk out of the side of her mouth. "There's no way we'll make it home by tomorrow night, not now."

Jake licked the bottom of his bar where the ice cream was starting to melt. "I'm just thinking, if we have to change our plans anyway, how about I cancel my Friday morning meeting? Then, there wouldn't be any rush to be home by tomorrow night. We could take our time and spend an extra night in Hilton Head." He looked over at her, wiggling his eyebrows up and down. "Maybe this was fate and we were meant to book a round of golf for tomorrow."

Riley hesitated. It sounded like a great idea, but she'd planned on being at work Friday. Other than that, it did sound fun, and she'd get a chance to try out the new driver they'd bought her in Florida. Taking one more day might be just what they needed.

"Wait," he said, slapping the palm of his hand against his head. "I'm so sorry. What about your catering events? Didn't you have something big happening this Saturday?"

"It's okay. You know what, maybe I can call Lisa and see if she's got everything organized and ready to go. It's time I started trusting her to handle things without me. Afterall, once the new location opens, I won't have time to supervise both."

Jake gave her a skeptical look. "Somehow, I don't believe you're ready to leave everything entirely up to Lisa."

She scrunched her eyebrows together, ready to deny it, then conceded, giving him another light shove to the shoulder. "Okay, fine. Maybe if we're home early enough on Saturday, I might just pop over and see how things are going."

Jake laughed. "Yeah, I thought so. How about golf tomorrow, then? Are you sure?"

"I'm sure. Golf Thursday, then drive most of the way home on Friday. I'll phone my mom tonight and see if she can keep Mister Bingley until Saturday. I'm sure she won't mind. I left plenty of cat food."

"Great," Jake said, opening his golf app to search for tee times.

It had only been about forty minutes since they'd called roadside assistance when the flatbed tow truck pulled in. Jake was impressed with the speediness. "Now, that's what I call, under-promise and over-deliver."

• • •

Riley watched as the driver descended from the cab of the tow truck and headed their way. He was a big guy, probably in his mid-forties, with a long scraggly beard hanging way down over his chest. Jake got out and talked with him for a bit, then came back and poked his head into the car. "Riley, grab your purse or whatever you need and jump out. He's going to drive the car up onto the flatbed and chain it up." He switched to his best imitation of the driver's thick southern drawl. "We'll be raddin' with him in the cab of that thay-er truck."

Riley climbed into the cab, while Jake stayed outside watching Longbeard take the car up the ramp. The rusty hinges grated as she pulled the door open. The cab was filthy—garbage and food wrappers all over and a layer of dust at least a quarter inch deep across the dash. The Hula dancer bobblehead had managed to shake most of the dust off herself, but, even still, she didn't look happy to be there.

An ashtray full of smelly cigarette buts hung open on an angle in front of her. Riley tilted her knees to one side of it, then discreetly took a quick Snapchat video to send to her younger sister. She added some text: "S.C. Posh Tow Truck, LOL". Riley laughed to herself, thinking about how Scotty would crack up when she saw it. Growing up, Riley had been the neat freak and couldn't stand any dust or mess, while Scotty would rarely clean her room.

The door grated again as Jake climbed into the cab. Longbeard was still doing whatever he was doing to chain up the car. Jake scanned the inside of the cab. The sun was starting to break through the clouds, and intermittent rays of sunshine struggled to make their way through the streaks and layers of cigarette scum on the windshield. Jake settled into his seat. "Well, this is special, isn't it?"

When Longbeard got in, Riley edged over toward Jake as much as she could. Longbeard was breathing heavily. "That's too bad 'bout yer flat tire. Where y'all headed?"

"Back home to Niagara Falls, Ontario," Jake said. "We were hoping to make it as far as Columbia tonight, but that's not happening now." Riley was grateful that Jake opened his window a few inches to let in some fresh air. Keeping the conversation going, he asked Longbeard, "Are you a Panthers fan or maybe Falcons?"

"Falcons—sometimes me and the boys go on down to 'Lanta for a game."

Oh, here we go, Riley thought. Jake was a big sports fan and followed the NFL pretty closely. If there was an opportunity to talk sports, he'd be all over it.

"Oh yeah, they've got a great wide receiver, Julio Jones," Jake shared some stats that inspired more discussion.

The conversation went on much longer than Riley would have liked, and she certainly had nothing to add. She didn't pay much attention to American football, although she had a huge amount of respect for Colin Kaepernick. The way the league had treated him made her even less interested in the NFL.

She wondered why Longbeard was signalling to leave the highway when the only sign she'd seen was for someplace called Coosawhatchie. When she'd looked at the map earlier, she'd thought they'd be going much farther down the highway before exiting. "The exits for Hilton Head are still quite a way down I95, aren't they?" she asked politely.

"Well, lem'me tell ya. This time a day, the 95'll be backed right up. This here shortcut will be the quickest route."

They drove down an access road then turned onto a dirt backroad heading into a forested area. The trees were covered with dangling webs of Spanish moss. Riley was feeling uneasy but didn't want to overreact. After all, they were still heading southeast for the most part, so maybe this was some sort of shortcut the locals used.

She looked at Jake. He seemed a bit baffled too. "Hey, man," he said, keeping his tone casual. "Where are you taking us, anyway?"

Longbeard kept driving and smiled showing his yellow teeth. "Now, y'all don't pitch a hissy. This might not look like much of a road, but it'll link us right up with the 462 to Hilton Head. Then, y'all can get yer tire fixed."

Riley wanted to question him on that, but didn't want to seem rude. Jake pulled out his phone, she could see him opening Google Maps. Maybe he could verify their location. A second later, he nudged her and angled his phone toward her. He'd lost service.

The road had become nothing more than a dirt path. Riley was getting scared. It sure didn't seem like this was going to link up with any other road. They were being taken farther and farther into the woodlands, and she could see swampy sections on each side of the path. She elbowed Jake, and this time he spoke in a much more forceful tone. "Okay, listen. I think you'd better turn around and take us back out to the highway right now."

Longbeard slowed the truck down. "Okay, okay, don't get your knickers in a knot. I've been runnin' all over hell's half acre on account a you folk." He brought the truck to a stop and mumbled under his breath, "Y'ain't nothin' but a pair a highfalutin…"

Suddenly he reached under his seat and pulled out a knife. In a second flat, he had his big sweaty arm around Riley's neck and held the knife up next to her face. Riley grabbed onto his arm, trying to loosen it from her throat. It was so tight; she was starting to choke.

"Well, I declare. She sure is a feisty little thing, ain't she?" His hot, stale breath wafted along the side of her face.

Jake clenched his jaw; he looked ready to rip the guy's head off. Instead, he put his hands up, keeping them in Longbeard's view. "Let her go!" he yelled." Riley knew there was nothing he could do—not with a knife held against her. "Please!" Jake pled. "We'll give you whatever you want. Just let her go!"

Longbeard pressed the tip of his knife against Riley's face telling her to hold still. She tried to pull away, wincing as the knife pierced her cheek. She felt a sharp, searing pain. She pressed her head back against his chest, trying to prevent the knife from going in any deeper. Blood dripped onto her blouse. The frantic look on Jake's face only heightened her fear. He was yelling "Stop it! Please—let her go!" She tried her best to hold still.

Longbeard pulled his arm tighter under her chin, lifting her partially off the seat. "Now y'all listen up," he said. "Here's what you're gonna do. Take them batteries and SIM cards out of yer phones and pitch 'em out the window right now.

CHAPTER TWO

It was an unexpected windfall to be getting another vehicle. That would make three this week. Beth-Anne was itching to see it. Caleb said it was some sort of luxury sports car coming in. He was acting all professional-like sitting at his computer, looking up the wholesale values and all. She straddled his lap, blocking his view. "How much longer we gotta wait?"

"He's on his way now," Caleb swivelled his chair, trying to see the computer screen.

"Well, I'm thankin' we'll be dining out tonight." If she had to stay late waiting for Zachary to show up, she'd better be getting a nice dinner out of it. They could certainly afford it considering the good week they'd had.

Caleb's auto redistribution business had become quite profitable as of late. That was likely due to her influence. The barn was near fully renovated inside and beginning to look like a genuine autobody shop. Caleb had got all the proper equipment hauled in and even set up a small office. It overlooked the work area where two men were busy prepping the vehicle that had come in yesterday. She got up and closed the lid on his laptop. "I'm tired a waitin'."

They were standing outside the barn when the tow truck finally pulled in. It came in fast, churning up the gravel in the laneway. Zachary was grinning up in the driver's seat. The vehicle skidded to a stop and the trailing plume of dust drifted back over them. He rolled down his window, letting in a surge of the gritty cloud, then held his hand over his eyes while the dust curled its way around the cab. Beth-Anne took a step back. *Dumb ass.* Caleb was eyeing the vehicle up on the flatbed. *Whistling at it, like it was some sexy babe.*

"Now we're talkin'," Caleb said. "That looks real nice, Zachary." He gave him a nod of approval.

Zachary dragged his hand down the length of his beard and let it settle back onto his chest. "Lem'me tell ya, them young folk must be livin' high on the hog." He started to laugh, and the laugh grew into a hacking cough. He spat a mouthful of sputum out the window.

Beth-Anne gave him a dirty look. She couldn't stand him. Zachary was like an irritation under her skin. He was always acting as though he and Caleb were besties, trying to make it seem like she was the outsider. Caleb hustled over to the barn and opened the wide door.

Zachary backed in the flatbed and brought the car down the ramp. He clutched the key fob importantly as he came around and popped the trunk. "The licence plates and their suitcases are in here," he said. "I ain't never seen plates like these before." He lifted them out, pointing his finger at one. "Says ICE WINE, with this here fancy logo in the middle." He tossed the plates back in the trunk. They clanged together as they bounced off the golf clubs. "Got their wallets in my cab. Hold on while I get 'em."

Caleb pointed at the luggage and jabbed her with his elbow. "I'm thinking there might be somethin' special in them designer bags for you, Beth-Anne. Maybe a sexy nightgown or some fancy jewellery."

She was always wanting more than he could give her. One of these days, she'd move on and find someone who could provide her with all the luxuries in life, like this car. That's what she ought to be driving. Caleb was temporary, and him thinking it could be something more was downright impractical. He need only look at himself in the mirror.

Zachary handed their wallets over and Caleb examined their identification pieces. "Jake Marshall and Riley Marshall." He pulled out their credit cards and forty American dollars.

Beth-Anne cut in. "That all there was?" She looked at Zachary sideways, gauging whether or not he was being truthful.

"That's all. I swear. The young'uns today, they just use them credit cards." He looked to Caleb for approval.

Beth-Anne kept her eyes fixed on Zachary while she whispered in Caleb's ear. "That dog don't hunt. If there was cash in them wallets, he woulda taken it. Likely left forty in there just to make it look good."

"You know Zachary, you're gettin' paid a pretty penny already," Caleb said, rubbing his hand over his unshaven jaw. "Although, looks like this time you done brought us a real money maker. Did you get the GPS locator pulled out?"

"Right after I dumped them." Zachary brushed his hands together. "Found it in less than five minutes, then took my sledge hammer to it. She's all ready for her makeover. Me, on the other hand—my eyeballs are floatin'. I need to go take a piss real bad." He headed for the washroom.

Caleb strutted over to his desk and got back on the computer. He started searching the internet for the ice wine company and typed in "Jake and Riley Marshall." Dozens of articles popped up. Beth-Anne stood looking over his shoulder.

One site had a corporate home page that showed the same logo as the crest on the licence plate. "This is them alright," he said. Other articles mentioned the family's large donations to local hospitals. One was headed "Philanthropists Rob and Wendy Marshall Give Largest Donation Niagara Hospital's Ever Seen."

Caleb scrolled through the article. "Are you seeing this, Beth-Anne? No wonder these young folk are so rich. Their family's got millions to spare."

She leaned in closer, thinking about the possibilities.

Caleb came out with it first. "Maybe Jake Marshall's daddy is gonna want to do another kinda donation."

Normally, she was one to take her time and think things through, but this was like finding a winning lottery ticket. All they had to do was cash it in.

Zachary sauntered back from the washroom, doing up his fly as he approached. "Zachary, where'd ya drop them rich folk?" Caleb asked.

"About 12 miles or so off the highway. Took 'em down one of the old dirt roads into the wetlands. I know that area like the back of my hand." He was looking real pleased with himself. "Back in the day, there used to be a hunting lodge in there. When I was a boy—"

Caleb cut him off. "Can you draw me a map?"

"A map?" Zachary looked puzzled. "Lem'me tell ya, people go in there at night, they'll wind up sunk in a swamp. Ya gotta know where yer goin'. Why do ya wanna know?"

Caleb shut down the computer. "I've got an idea."

CHAPTER THREE

After Longbeard drove off with their car, Riley just stood there in shock. The gouge in her cheek stung, but aside from that she felt relieved—almost euphoric. They were alive and this horrible nightmare was over. Jake was holding her. "It's okay, Riley. We're okay. Let's take a look at your cheek."

Riley tilted her head back. Blood and tears trickled along her jaw line. Jake looked inside her mouth, making sure the puncture hadn't passed right through, then let out a sigh of relief. "Looks like it's just a surface wound. You might need a couple of stitches though." He dug into his pocket and pulled out his one and only Kleenex. "Here, Riley. It's all I have. Hold this up against it."

THE LOWLANDS

She nodded, "I had a whole packet of Kleenex in my purse—a brand-new packet I just bought." She was so annoyed. "He didn't need to throw my whole bag into the marsh." Her sleek Marc Jacobs bag had slipped below the surface of green algae, and the thin layer of pea soup had closed over it immediately, like it had never happened.

The sun was starting to sink behind the trees. Pines and gargantuan live oaks with sprawling branches enclosed them under a canopy as far as the eye could see—each and every limb draped and dripping with gothic-looking Spanish moss. Endless leafy vines latched onto tree trunks, wrapping themselves around and around, slithering up the trees. Riley thought she could hear them moving. "Kind of reminds me of those creepy vines in *Jumanji*."

"Yeah." Jake swatted his hand back and forth in front of his face. "And are these mosquitoes or a swarm from *The Birds*? Honestly, I've never seen such huge ones." He turned toward her, a concerned expression on his face. "Seriously, Riley, we need to get out of here. At best, we've got about an hour and a half of daylight left. How are you feeling? Can we pick up the pace?"

"I'm trying, Jake. Had I known we'd be hiking through hell, I would have chosen socks and running shoes instead of these chunky-heeled sandals." The thin straps around her ankles didn't offer much support. Not only that, she was worried about what she might step on. She had a phobia of snakes.

"Do you want me to carry you for a bit? Jump on for a piggyback ride." He squatted down, his arms out to the sides."

"No, that's okay."

"Why not?"

"Cause my shorts are wet. I peed accidentally when Scumbag-Beardman had his fat arm around my throat."

Jake stood up and embraced her, lovingly holding her head against his chest. "I'm so sorry Riley. All of this is my fault."

She pulled back, looking up at him. "No Jake. Why would you say that? None of this is your fault."

"Yes, it is. Why did I buy that expensive car anyway? That's not even who I am." He took Riley's hand and they started walking. "And now that I think about it, the custom plates draw even more attention to it. Whoever did this, knew we were from Ontario—a long way from home, and stranded in some hick area that we're not familiar with. We were like sitting ducks. Bet that guy in the gas station had something to do with this. He probably phoned up one of his hick-ass friends to bring that old piece-of-shit tow truck to take us away."

Riley added, "Yeah, well, I should have questioned the towing company's credentials. I mean, in hindsight, would Mercedes roadside assistance really send such a disgusting old tow truck? And how did it happen to arrive way before the estimated time they'd given us? Instead of sending a Snapchat to Scotty, I should have been asking to see the guy's towing licence."

Jake stopped in his tracks. "You sent Scotty a Snapchat?" he asked eagerly. "From the tow truck?"

"Yeah. It was such a disgusting mess, I thought Scotty would get a laugh out of it."

"That's great. She knows that we must have had car trouble and she and your mom will probably be getting worried about us."

"Well, as soon as we get back to some sort of civilization, I better find a phone and let them know what happened." Riley picked up the pace, feeling more motivated. "Why on earth did this scumbag have to take us so far out, anyway? Couldn't he have just dropped us at one of the highway exits?"

Jake swatted at something near his leg, then slapped it against his calf extra forcefully, bestowing a warning to others. He wiped his hand on his shorts and continued. "I don't know. Maybe this gives them time to rip out the GPS before we report it stolen."

"Oh, yeah. I guess that's how the roadside assistance woman knew our exact location when we called in." She thought for a moment. "I bet they're racking up our credit cards as we speak."

About five miles down the dirt path, the sun disappeared and the swamp came to life. It was like someone had turned up the volume ten notches. The humming and churning of millions of insects pulsated louder and louder. Crickets chirping, bullfrogs croaking and things buzzing everywhere. Riley grabbed onto Jake's arm. "I can't see where I'm stepping anymore." She was starting to freak out. Things were plopping into the water nearby. "Jake, I can't—" A sudden screeching above—*kee-aah, kee-aah!* Riley's arm shot up over her head and she dropped to the ground.

Jake crouched beside her. "It's okay, it's just a bird. Come on, climb onto my back." This time, she gladly accepted the offer and wrapped her arms around his neck as he boosted her up onto his back. He carried her for a long time, jogging a good part of the way. He didn't stop until they were back on the single-lane dirt road.

He lowered her down for a minute. "I think we're nearly out of here. We must be getting near the access road. It can't be much farther now."

"Look! I think we're in luck. I see some headlights."

CHAPTER FOUR

Michelle was getting worried. They hadn't heard from her eldest daughter, Riley, since Wednesday afternoon when she'd sent a funny Snapchat to Scotty from a tow truck. They'd both tried calling her that evening to see what had happened, but Riley hadn't answered and didn't return their calls. Now it was Friday, and there was still no word from either one of them.

The last time Michelle had actually spoken to Riley was on Tuesday. She'd said they'd be home Thursday evening and that she'd stop by to pick up Mr. Bingley. She'd promised to keep in touch and said she'd call if they were running late. There'd been no call.

Michelle didn't know what to think. Considering they'd had car trouble, it made sense that they'd be delayed, but why hadn't Riley or Jake responded to their texts or phone messages? This wasn't like Riley at all. She never let a day go by without texting or phoning. Michelle couldn't understand it. Even if they'd both somehow managed to lose their phones, surely whatever hotel they'd ended up at had a phone or internet. Something was wrong and she was getting more concerned as each hour rolled by.

She called Jake's parents in Florida to see if they'd heard anything. They hadn't, and they were worried too. Wendy said she'd gotten up early on Wednesday morning and made sandwiches for Riley and Jake to take on the road, then said goodbye when they left at 7:00 a.m. That was the last time she'd spoken to them.

Michelle couldn't just sit around worrying. She had to do something. "Scotty, can I see that screen shot you took again? What exactly did the text say?"

Scotty came closer, holding her phone out in front of her. Together they looked at the picture on the screen. Scotty read out the text. "*S.C. Posh Tow Truck, LOL*". She looked at her. "Riley was just being funny, Mom. I laughed when I saw it."

Michelle knew that, but, joke or not, this was the last communication they'd had from her. Maybe it contained a clue. "If they left Sanibel Island at seven a.m., where would they have been when she sent this Snapchat?"

Scotty appeared to be thinking about it. "Well, I figured the 'S.C.' meant South Carolina, but where exactly, I don't know. Maybe if we look up the travel distances and times, we can figure it out."

"Alright. What time did you say you received the Snapchat message from Riley?"

"Around four o'clock—just before my Environmental Sustainability class. I opened her Snap and it was super funny, so I took a screen shot. Then, after class I replied, but she still hasn't opened it." Scotty showed the screen to her. "See? Unread."

"Okay, so we know they were in a tow truck in South Carolina at four o'clock on Wednesday." Michelle walked through her calculation out loud. "We also know they left Sanibel at seven a.m. That leaves nine hours of travel time. Of course, we'd have to deduct any time that they might have stopped for gas or washroom breaks."

Scotty looked skeptical. "But Mom, we don't even know how long they might have waited for a tow truck or if there were any traffic delays along their route."

Michelle didn't appreciate her negativity. "True enough, but just humour me, will you? Let's say there was no traffic—how far might they have travelled in eight or nine hours? We know for sure they didn't travel for more than nine hours—that's something to work with."

Scotty looked back at her phone screen. "Okay, let me check the driving time from Sanibel Island to some cities along their route on Interstate 95 North." Her thumbs were moving like rapid fire on the phone's keypad. "Okay, it's seven and a half hours to Savannah, and that's right at the border of Georgia and South Carolina. It's eight hours and forty-five minutes to get to the junction of I95 and Interstate 26, where they'd head northwest."

Michelle was looking at Google Maps on her iPad, zooming in on that stretch of I95 between Savannah, Georgia and the junction of I95 and I26. "So, they were most likely somewhere in this area." She angled her iPad so Scotty could see.

"Right, but Mom, I'm just thinking: wouldn't Jake's car need to be serviced by a Mercedes Dealer? I mean, it's fairly new, so wouldn't he have a warranty or something?" The sudden excitement in her voice disappeared. "Unless they were in an accident and it was being towed to a body shop."

"I don't think they were in an accident—at least not at that point. If they were, Riley wouldn't have been joking around, sending a funny Snap." Michelle leaned back on the couch and stared off into space. *How could Riley leave us worrying like this.* In her heart, she knew she wouldn't, and that was what made it all so scary.

She brought her mind back to what Scotty had just said about Jake's car. "Scotty, you're brilliant—do you know that? How many Mercedes dealers can there possibly be in South Carolina?" She keyed in a search and looked at the list that popped up. "Actually, quite a few."

Scotty leaned in closer. "Well, we can narrow it down to the ones near I95 between Savannah and the junction at I26. How many are there in that area?" She reached across to the iPad and expanded that section. "Hilton Head or Mount Pleasant, but Hilton Head is the closest to I95."

Michelle phoned them both, but neither one had any record of servicing Jake's car. She had them search under Jake's name and Riley's name; there was nothing. She even called back and had them search under Jake's business name, Niagara Ice Wines, just in case the car was leased by his company. If they'd serviced it, surely they would have remembered the personalized plates—ICE WINE, with Jake's company logo in the middle.

Scotty's eyes started to well up. "Mom, where are they?"

Michelle put her arms around her youngest daughter. She felt choked up, too. "I wish I knew. God, I wish I knew. I keep thinking we'll hear from them any minute and there'll be some logical explanation for all of this."

As though he could sense their distress, Mr. Bingley sprang up on the couch and pressed his head against Scotty's arm. She lifted him onto her lap and stroked the thick, ginger fur behind his ears. They sat quietly for a moment, Michelle and Scotty deep in thought, Mr. Bingley purring.

Scotty broke the silence. "Do you think we should try to call dad again?"

Michelle had already made a decision. "Right now, I'm going to call the police and figure out how to report them missing." She looked at Scotty head on. "I'm not waiting any longer. And then, yes, I think we need to get in touch with your dad."

Michelle looked up the number for the Niagara Police Department and wrote it down on a note pad. Scotty and Mr. Bingley stayed right beside her, watching as she keyed in another search on the internet: *How to report a missing Canadian in the United States.* Michelle selected the top site that came up, a Government of Canada website for Missing Persons. It said, "You should immediately report the person's disappearance to the police (local and foreign, when possible)."

The site provided a long list of information to gather about the missing persons. Most of the personal details Michelle could provide, but some things they'd have to look up. "Do we have Riley's passport number, or Jake's for that matter?" Scotty asked.

"I've probably got a copy of Riley's. She renewed her passport shortly before they got married. It's good for one more year. Your dad always takes photo copies of these things and keeps them in a file folder in the den. It's in the bottom drawer of the desk." Scotty moved Mr. Bingley to the side and hurried to the den. Mr. Bingley shot off after her. Michelle shouted, "I'm sending this list to the printer too. Can you bring it back with you?"

Michelle started scrolling through her recent photos on her iPad, moving several pictures of Riley and Jake into a new album. She made sure she chose good-quality, current head shots and full body shots of both Riley and Jake. She wanted to have a good assortment ready.

Scotty was back in a flash with the copy of Riley's passport and the printed-out list of information to bring when reporting a missing person. They filled out the pages together—one for Riley and one for Jake—then drove to the Niagara police station to file the reports.

•••

It was late afternoon by the time they got home. They were both emotionally drained. Michelle went straight to the answering machine. There were no new messages. She plugged in her cell phone and slumped onto the corner of the couch. "Scotty, I feel like I'm in some alternate universe—like all of this is happening and I'm going through the motions, but not fully convinced that it's real."

"I know, I keep thinking this can't possibly be true. Then, there's moments like this where…" She couldn't finish.

Michelle got up and gave her a hug. "Scotty, we'll get through this." Scotty held her tight and Michelle could feel her body trembling. "Ah, Scotty, I know, I'm so sorry. I know this is hard. We're going to find them."

"I know, mom." She held on for just a moment longer then got each of them a tissue to blow their noses. "I'll make us some tea."

Scotty flicked the kettle on. "Well, on a positive note, at least Detective Jorden seemed nice. I think he's doing everything he can for us. I mean, he assured us he'd be looking after everything immediately." She pulled two mugs down from the cupboard. "By now, I bet he's forwarded the reports to every police department in South Carolina."

"I know, but I worry whether the police in South Carolina will be as invested as he is in finding two missing Canadians." Michelle knew Detective Jorden cared because the Marshalls were fairly well known in Niagara. Maybe the police in South Carolina would have other priorities. She'd have to be there to oversee things.

"Have you heard anything back from Dad?"

"Not yet, but I'm sure he'll call us tonight. Meanwhile, let's do whatever we can to get organized."

Michelle made a list of everything she'd need to do. Next, she started a log, recording everything she had done—who she'd spoken to, along with dates and times. She wrote down the missing persons case number and the name and contact information for the Niagara lead detective, Ben Jorden. Recording everything made her feel like she was accomplishing something.

An incoming text message dinged on her phone. Michelle closed her eyes. *Please, let it be Riley. Let her be okay.* She looked at the text. It was from Nick.

Got your voicemail message and your text. Have you heard from them yet? Are you available now for a phone call?

Michelle dialed his number; he picked up on the first ring. "Michelle, any word from Riley yet?"

Just hearing Nick's voice brought her to tears—the reality of it all sinking in again, the heavy weight on her shoulders. She held the phone tight against her ear and tried to reel in her emotions. "No, nothing at all." She took a breath. "Scotty and I reported them missing to the police this afternoon."

There was silence on Nick's end. Michelle felt so detached—literally. Nick was out in the north Atlantic, somewhere off the coast of Labrador. When he was asked to go along on this patrol, Michelle had been totally against it, but knowing how important it was to his research, she eventually gave in. "Michelle, I'm so sorry I'm not there with you." Then another pause. "What did the police say?"

"They're notifying all the authorities in South Carolina. They'll be checking hospital admissions, and if there's still no word by tomorrow, they suggested issuing a press release to the local media, appealing for help from the public." Michelle leaned forward on the couch with her head hovering above her knees, waiting again for him to respond. "Nick, are you there?"

"Yes, yes, I'm just trying to take this all in. When they say 'local media,' they must mean down there? In South Carolina?"

"Yes. I'm going to book a flight for first thing tomorrow morning. I don't know whether we'll fly into Savannah or Hilton Head. I'll have to see what's available."

"Scotty's going with you?"

"We need you there too, Nick."

Scotty came and stood next to her. "Can I talk to dad too?"

"Listen, Nick. Scotty wants to talk to you. I've got a million things to do." As the words came out, she knew it would make him feel guilty for not being there—and maybe he should. A million things to do—without him. She still didn't understand why he'd needed to go on this patrol. "FISHPATS," they were called. They patrolled and monitored fishing vessels, making sure the nets didn't exceed regulations. Nick was out on a 440-foot vessel, a Halifax-class frigate. His software firm had been contracted by the Department of National Defence. As part of a team developing a new system to record data, he'd been invited to go on a patrol so he could see first-hand the type of work they do. In Michelle's opinion, it really wasn't necessary that he be there.

"Wait, Michelle. Keep in touch and let me know where you're staying down there. I'll make arrangements to get there as soon as I can."

"I will. I'll let you know the minute we hear anything."

"Michelle," he added. "I love you."

"I love you too."

She handed the phone to Scotty, then as a matter of course took herself into the kitchen. She opened the fridge, keeping one hand pressed against her forehead as she stared into it, wondering what they could throw together for supper. Everything she did made her think about Riley. *What was Riley having for supper? Was she getting any food, or was she lying in a hospital bed somewhere on an IV drip?* Another round of tears started to leak out. She was coming apart at the seams. She gave her head a quick shake, hoping to clear away the unbearable thoughts circulating in her mind. If she didn't pull herself together, she'd be of no use at all and would make the whole situation even harder for Scotty.

CHAPTER FIVE

Riley waved her hands wildly, hoping the driver of the approaching vehicle would see them. She and Jake started running towards the car. Jake was in the lead, his hand stretched out like he was hailing a cab. The vehicle came to a stop about twenty feet away. Riley slowed, trying to catch her breath. She was so thankful they wouldn't have to walk the rest of the way to the highway. The passenger door opened and the interior lights came on.

"Oh, shit!" Jake yelled. "It's him again! Run, Riley!"

She was rooted to the spot, stunned by the unexpected turn of events. Jake grabbed her hand and started pulling her along. "Come on, Riley! We need to get off the path."

Weeds and twigs scratched against her legs. Mucky sludge splattered up as they ran along the edge of the swamp. She turned to look back. He was gaining on them. Jake pulled her into the swamp. There was nowhere else to go.

Riley struggled to move through the cold, slimy water. It was over her knees. The bottoms of her feet were slipping inside her sandals and the heel on the right shoe was caught in the weeds and vines.

Sounds of splashing and thumping came up from behind. Longbeard's hand latched onto the back of her hair, yanking her whole body back. "Gotcha!" he exclaimed triumphantly.

Her hand broke apart from Jake's and he stumbled forward, face first into the swamp. By the time he'd pulled himself up, Longbeard had his gun against her head. "Y'all settle down, or somebody's gonna get hurt," he said.

"What do you want from us?" Jake demanded, raising his hands in surrender.

Longbeard was breathing hard. "Shut up and move!" His knuckles pressed into Riley's head where he'd secured a clump of her hair. He shoved her along towards the car, jabbing her back with his gun and issuing warnings to Jake. "Try anything and she's dead."

A hazy bright aura surrounded the parked vehicle. The engine was idling, pumping its hot exhaust into the cool night air and defusing the light from the open trunk. A silhouette of a stalky figure loomed in front.

Riley's heart was pounding and her legs were shaking. They were getting closer to the car, and she was trying to remember every detail.

The man wore a black zip-up nylon jacket. Most of his face was hidden behind a camouflage-patterned bandana, but she could tell he was white, probably about five foot eight. His baseball hat had the same camouflage pattern. "Throw 'em in the trunk," he ordered, then turned away and got back into the driver's seat. This was the man in charge.

Now, it was just Longbeard, pushing his gun against her and ordering them into the trunk. She couldn't do it. Something came over her, and she just couldn't do it. She'd seen enough episodes of *Dateline* to know your chances of survival drop drastically once you get in the car.

Riley held her ground. "No, we're not getting in." She started flailing her arms and twisting her body, trying to break free. Longbeard overpowered her with ease and yanked her arms behind her back. "Ow! You're hurting me!" She stomped the square heel of her sandal onto his foot as hard as she could.

Longbeard nearly let her go as he fumbled for a second. "Bitch!"

Jake took a swing at him and hit the side of his head. He stumbled, pulling Riley along with him. Before Jake could swing again, she was back in a choke hold.

The stalky man in charge got out of the car and came towards her, his gun pointed straight into her face. He glared at her. "Shut up, you rich bitch!" He pushed the gun into her forehead. "One more word, and I'll be putting a bullet clean through yer skull."

Riley didn't speak. She didn't move.

He handed Longbeard a roll of duct tape and ordered Jake up against the back of the car. "Tape him up good." He kept his gun pressed against Riley's head while Longbeard taped Jake's wrists behind his back and bound his ankles together. He put a strip across his mouth, then pushed him into the trunk, shoving him in deeper with his foot.

Riley was next. When the trunk lid closed, she was hysterical. Her mouth had also been taped, and she was having trouble breathing through her nose. The more upset she got, the more her nose ran. She was shivering uncontrollably. She kept trying to scream, but the only thing that came out was a loud humming noise. "Mmmm, mmmm!".

She felt Jake's body moving—he was trying to turn over, but there was no space. She pressed her forehead against his back, trying to calm herself down. His shirt was cold and wet from the swamp. She started screaming again. "Mmmm, mmmm." On and on, until she suddenly realized the tape over her mouth was starting to loosen. She kept screaming, stretching her mouth open and closed and rubbing it against the wetness on Jake's back.

Voices were coming from inside the car. Riley stopped for a moment to listen. "We're gonna need to make the call," a woman said.

What does that mean? Were they deciding whether to kill them? Why is a woman involved with this? Who are these people?

Riley could tell they were still on the bumpy dirt path, probably headed back to where they'd come from. Another big bump, and now Jake's wet body was pressed against hers. She was still shivering, sniffling and taking rapid short breaths through her nose—in and out, in and out.

Jake wrestled next to her, wriggling his feet back and forth, trying to loosen the duct tape around his ankles.

Riley tried to do the same and continued working at the piece across her mouth. "Mmmm, mmmm."

She didn't know what they would do if they did manage to get the tape off. How could they take on two or three people with guns? *Why are they doing this to us?* She couldn't understand it; if they wanted to kill them, wouldn't they have just done that already? Or, were they taking them farther out to dump their bodies in some swampland where they'd never be found? *Oh my god. We'll never be found.*

The road got bumpier and an unusual sound came from underneath the chassis. Grass or weeds maybe, rubbing against the bottom of the car. *Where are they taking us? This is insane.*

"Mmmm!", she continued. "Mmmm!" She stopped suddenly. "Jake," she whispered. "I got the tape off my mouth."

She tried to wiggle her body down along his back to get to his wrists. She locked her feet under his legs for leverage and slid herself down. She could feel his hands just below her chin. She whispered, "Jake, move your wrists out a bit. I'll try to bite through the tape."

The flap of tape hanging from her mouth kept getting in the way. She flicked her head to the side and quickly brought her mouth back to the tape on his wrists. She bit and yanked back on it, but nothing happened. It was too thick. "I can't bite through it, Jake. I need to find where the tape ends and peel back a layer."

The car stopped and the car doors opened. She clamped her teeth along the edge of the tape and gave it one last pull.

CHAPTER SIX

As soon as Michelle had booked their morning flight, they drove over to Jake and Riley's house. She wanted to look for Jake's passport information and get his car's vehicle identification number. She'd told detective Jorden she would send the VIN to him as soon as she could.

It was freezing outside, and the crisp night air gave them a fresh burst of energy. Their boots squeaked and crunched in the snow as they hurried up the driveway and onto the porch. Michelle kicked each boot against the top step, removing whatever snow she could.

Scotty pulled the spare key out of her pocket. It was on a special keychain that Riley had given her. It was shaped like a blue whale and made of recycled plastic from the

Save Our Oceans Foundation. Scotty cupped it between her hands and closed her eyes like she was making a wish. Michelle swallowed the lump in her throat.

Once inside, Michelle led them upstairs to the spare room that Jake used as an office. Scotty turned on the light. "Mom, this feels weird being in Jake's office when they're not home. It's like we're invading their space. Do you think he'll mind that we're going through his stuff?"

"I think he'd expect nothing less under the circumstances. I'll check the file cabinet and see if anything's in there."

She started flipping through the hanging file folders, sliding each one to the front as she went along. "Remind me to compliment Jake on his organizational skills." She pulled out a folder and opened it on the desk. "Bingo. Here's the vehicle bill of sale with the make, model and VIN." She took a photo of the document and sent the image to Detective Jorden's email, asking that he confirm receipt.

They couldn't find a copy of Jake's passport or any records with passport information, but his laptop was on top of the credenza. "Scotty, can you check out his laptop and see if you can find anything in there?"

Scotty lifted the lid and turned it on. "I'd need a password to open it."

"Oh, of course," Michelle said in a defeated tone.

"Actually Mom, I think I might know it. When I stayed with them last month while you and dad were away, Jake had to reset his password and Riley was laughing her head off about it. She said he was such a clown and told me what it was—Laptop123."

"Okay, try it."

It opened, putting them directly into his email account. Scotty hesitated. "This feels wrong. I don't know if we should be looking at these." Michelle took over and scrolled through the unopened emails. One popped out. It was from Mercedes 24-hour Roadside Assistance. Subject line: 'How did we do?' The email was thanking him for using roadside assistance and asking him to rate their service.

"Of course. Scotty, why didn't we think of this? It makes perfect sense. They called roadside assistance. Maybe Detective Jorden can track down the tow truck driver and find out where they were towed to."

Michelle looked at the keyboard, then stepped aside. "Scotty please, you're so much faster than I am. Can you forward this email to me and Detective Jorden? Ask him to contact Mercedes Roadside Assistance with the VIN I just sent him." Michelle was hovering over her. "And ask him to let me know whatever he's able to find out ASAP."

Scotty included words in the email like "It would be much appreciated" and "If you wouldn't mind," just to ease the tone a bit.

"Good, Scotty. That's better." Michelle nodded. Sometimes, she could come across sounding a little abrupt, but she really didn't mean to. She just knew what needed to get done and didn't waste time about it. If a man spoke that way, no one would think twice.

After sending the email, Scotty searched in various files for Jake's passport details. Michelle pointed at the time in the top right corner of the screen. "We've gotta go. I still need to print out copies of the missing-persons flyer I made and then take Mr. Bingley across the road to Carolyn's house. She said she'd look after him for as long as we need her."

"I'll take care of that, Mom, while you get packed."

"What would I ever do without you Scotty." She took a moment and held Scotty in her arms. "I love you so much."

"I love you too, mom." Scotty started to cry. "And I love Riley so much—I don't know what I'd do without…"

Michelle could feel her pain. She knew how strong the bond was between her daughters. They were as close as two siblings could be. Even though Riley was six years older, they were best friends. Growing up, Riley had included Scotty in everything, making her feel like the most important person in her life.

Scotty had wanted to be just like her. If Riley did soccer, Scotty did soccer. If Riley did dance, Scotty did dance. In the summers, Riley would babysit, and they'd spend hours together in the kitchen. Riley would be the master chef and Scotty, her sous chef. They'd have so much fun making up lunch creations. Michelle hadn't minded buying all the extra ingredients. What they were making was so much more than lunches.

She remembered when Riley had started getting serious about Jake, how Scotty had worried that her relationship with her older sister would change, but that wasn't the case. As it turned out, Jake wasn't a threat at all. In fact, he was so thrilled to become a 'brother-in-law,' he started calling Scotty "Sis" the night he and Riley got engaged. He was a wonderful big brother to Scotty and a perfect son-in-law. Michelle found comfort in knowing Riley was with him— he'd look after her and protect her from harm.

CHAPTER SEVEN

Mack hurried across the field, crouched over, trying to stay out of sight. The rain was pelting down, stinging his face as he headed into the wind. He had to squint to see. Only about a hundred yards to go, then he'd cross the access road. His bright orange jumpsuit was soaked. He thought about taking it off to be less conspicuous, but he'd need it later; it would be cold at night. He dropped to his knees and started rubbing mud all over the suit, trying to camouflage himself. *What have I done?*

He'd been working outside on a painting detail along the left wing of the Ridgeview Correctional Facility when the violent storm had come through. By the time he'd finished putting the lids on the paint cans, everyone else had been taken inside. The wind had suddenly intensified and strong gusts whipped sheets of rain across the courtyard. He'd grabbed a few paint cans and headed to the nearest door, by the supply entrance. Normally, there would be a guard at that door and another one fifty feet out at the supply entrance gate. He couldn't see either one of them.

The lock-down signal was blaring. Mack pulled on the supply entrance door. It was locked. Everyone had taken shelter and he'd been left out in the yard. He ran over to the booth at the supply entrance gate in search of the guard. He wasn't there, and the gate had been left partially open.

Mack hadn't planned on escaping—there hadn't been time to think about it. It was just a fortuitous opportunity that had presented itself, but now he wondered if he'd made the best choice. Had he been in the right place at the right time and simply seized the opportunity, or had he just made things a thousand times worse?

What would his family think? At least in Ridgeview, he could have visitors and his parents and sister came to see him regularly. Now, he'd be on the run and might never see them again—a hefty price for his freedom.

Freedom. He thought about his family and the generations before him. Those who had truly fought for freedom. Perhaps it was an omen that he shared the name of his enslaved ancestor, Mack—sold in Charleston, South Carolina at the age of seven. There had been six generations of freedom since slavery was abolished. How many more generations would it take to have equal rights or access to the same opportunities?

Mack had been the first in his family to graduate from college. His parents had been so proud. His dream was to be an educator. He wanted to teach students critical thinking skills so they could question and challenge the biases in the information they received. Today, more than ever, students needed to know how to evaluate material from different sources—how to determine fact from fiction. They needed to learn how to think objectively, preferably at a young age. That dream had been destroyed years ago.

He pounded his fist into the ground, splattering more mud over himself. He'd made a mistake—he shouldn't have run. He gritted his teeth and tilted his head up, letting the rain mix with his tears. There was no turning back now. He was on the run, and he'd have to get moving fast.

Ridgeview was a low-security level-two correctional centre. Even still, he felt certain they'd have police across the state searching for him. The local Ridgeview police would take a special interest in finding him. After all, it was their lying patrol officers who put him there in the first place.

Mack crossed the access road heading east, hoping to somehow make his way across the lowlands and follow one of the rivers to the coast. They'd never expect him to go in that direction. Nobody in their right mind would. The area was full of swamplands and extremely dangerous.

Now, out of sight from the highway, he allowed himself to stand to his full height and started jogging through the rows of pine trees. The ground was soft from all the rain, and his canvas slip-on shoes squished into the ground with each step.

THE LOWLANDS

A mile or two in, he came across a pathway. The ground was a little higher along the path and not as soggy. He started to run faster, focusing on his breathing and the rhythm of his steps. He'd been on the cross-country track team in college and led them to victory in his final year. Now, five years later, all of that seemed like a lifetime ago. He lengthened his stride, sprinting down the path.

An hour went by and the path disappeared. He ran through weeds, farther into the swampy woodland. The rain had pretty much stopped.

Several miles later he saw an opening in the trees. He ran toward it and came to a clearing with small log cabins. Four of them.

They were old and unusually small and had no windows. At first glance, they looked like outhouses, except they had chimneys. They were spread out, about twenty feet apart. The farthest one back had been overtaken by the swamp.

He approached the first cabin. It looked solidly built, with its logs and stone chimney. At best, it was eight feet wide by maybe ten feet long. The steel latch on the door was stuck. Probably hadn't been opened in years. Mack looked for a rock and then pounded the latch from underneath until it gave way and he pulled the door open. Inside, a spider dangling on a web drifted back then hastily ascended into the logs above.

There was an old iron skillet on the floor, two wooden-framed cots and two wooden stools set in front of the fireplace. He wondered what the place had been used for. It was way too small to live in permanently. He took the frying pan out with him and then opened the other three cabins to see what else he could find. They were all the same other than a kettle in one and a half-rotted deer hide in another. That's when it occurred to him. *Hunting. These were probably for hunters back in the day.*

He took the kettle and frying pan to the second-last cabin, the one farthest back but not in the swamp. He swept out the inside with a bushy pine branch. The floor was solid with wide wood planks and even though the narrow bed frames held no mattresses, he'd be happy to sleep on the slatted wood support. He was grateful. It was a gift.

Mack pulled off the bright orange jumpsuit and rolled it up as tight as he could, then stood on it, squeezing out much of the wetness. The rain had stopped, so he hung it over a tree branch next to the cabin, hoping it would dry out by nightfall. A moment later, he changed his mind and took it inside, laying it over the bed frame instead. Maybe he was being paranoid. Nobody would see his jumpsuit. Nobody would be coming out here.

Mack rubbed his hands against his forearms. He was feeling the chill now that he'd stopped running. The temperature would probably dip into the low 50s during the night, and he contemplated starting a fire in the fireplace. He knew how to do it. He'd done it before on camping trips. But what if someone saw the smoke? He'd wait until after dark, when the smoke wouldn't be visible.

He quickly gathered small pieces of kindling as well as some larger logs and put them in a pile next to the cabin. He'd need tinder, a spindle and a fireboard. Not an easy feat when everything was wet from the rain. He spotted a standing dead tree nearby and peeled back a chunk of the bark. Inside was a layer of soft, dry stringy phloem he could use as tinder.

He took a thin branch off the dead tree and broke it into smaller pieces, keeping a nice smooth two-foot length to use as his spindle. Now just a fireboard—the base that the spindle would press into and spin back and forth, creating enough friction to start a small ember and light the tinder. He knew exactly what would work.

Mack went back in the cabin and pulled one of the quarter-inch-thick slats off the bed frame. It was perfect. It even had a knot in the wood right along the edge where he would press in with the spindle.

What else? He tried to think. What else would he need? He was thirsty. He hadn't finished his carton of milk on his lunch tray and wished he could have it now. There were plenty of puddles with rain water to pick from, or there was the swamp. He guessed the rainwater might be cleaner.

Using the frying pan as a ladle, he skimmed water from the surface of a puddle and poured it carefully into the kettle. He'd get the fireplace going during the night and boil the water in the kettle. Another gift.

Mack started organizing everything inside. It would be dark in an hour. He set the old kettle and frying pan next to the fireplace where he could easily find them in the dark, then sat down on the stool waiting for nightfall.

CHAPTER EIGHT

The lid popped open an inch and the light came on in the trunk. Now Riley could see where the tape was starting to tear between Jake's wrists. "Hold still," she whispered and bit onto the top edge. She pulled back on an angle and felt the tape ripping a little more. "I think I got it started. Maybe you'll be able to rip it the rest of the way."

She could hear Longbeard talking. "Should I get them out of the trunk?"

"Not yet," the other man said. "Best get everything ready first."

The woman's voice was the clearest; she must be sitting in the backseat. "No friggin' way! Not my good blankets! I only just bought 'em."

The man laughed. "You'll be able to buy all the new blankets you want soon enough."

Riley pushed her face into Jake's back, trying to re-stick the piece of tape across her mouth. She didn't want them to see she'd gotten it off. She'd be the first one in view when they opened the trunk and she didn't want to give anything away. She could feel Jake jerking his hands, trying to pull them apart.

The man kept talking. "Okay, Zachary, why don't ya show the Marshalls to their new suite." He was laughing. "Make sure you get a picture of 'em first."

Riley's heart was pounding. The car doors opened and closed again. The trunk lid lifted. Longbeard stood there eying her bare legs. He dragged his gun along her thigh. She pulled her legs back, disgusted. He laughed and puckered his lips at her. A new and horrible thought entered her mind. *Oh, god. What's he going to do?*

He set his gun down and pulled out his phone. He was holding it up near his face, fiddling with it, opening the camera app.

Riley carefully lifted her legs over the gun and slid it back. Longbeard hadn't noticed. "Say cheese." He smiled and held the phone over them. It clicked as he took their picture.

She felt a thump behind her. Jake had pulled his hands apart. He grabbed the gun from under her legs and ripped the tape off his mouth. He aimed the gun at Longbeard. His voice was low, and he sounded like he was talking through his teeth. "Back away, or your dead."

Longbeard stood there like a zombie. "I mean it," Jake repeated. "Back away." Longbeard took a few steps back, and Jake ripped the tape off Riley's wrists. As soon as her hands were free, she undid the tape from her ankles. Jake whispered, "Run as fast as you can, and don't stop, no matter what." He nudged her to get out of the trunk.

She started to crawl out. One leg and then the other.

Longbeard lunged at her, grabbing her arm and pulling her in front of him.

"No! Let me go!" she screamed as she tried to break free.

Jake lowered the gun. The disheartened look on his face would stay with her forever.

Then, without warning, Longbeard slammed the lid of the trunk against Jake's head. His body crumbled. Riley screamed at the top of her lungs. Longbeard slammed the lid shut.

He pulled his arm tighter around her neck. "You can scream till the cows come home—there ain't nobody for miles gonna hear ya."

The man in charge was out of the car and coming toward them. He pointed his finger at Longbeard like a parent scolding a child. "What in the Sam Hill's goin' on?"

"It's not my fault. He got my gun! They done got their tape off."

"Get them into the cabin now!" he demanded. He pushed the trunk-release button on his key fob. The lid popped open slightly, and he stepped back.

Longbeard held Riley in front of himself as a shield. "Ya better just put that gun down and don't be gettin' any more ideas," he hollered. "I got your wife right here and my gun on her." He slowly raised the lid. Jake lay there motionless.

"Jake!" Riley screamed. "No!" He looked like he was dead. The trunk lid had come down so hard on his head. "No, Jake!" She tried to pull away from Longbeard.

"What the hey-ell!" The masked man pushed her and Longbeard aside. He leaned into the trunk, sticking his gun into Jake's chest, and felt under his jaw for a pulse. "He's fine. Just knocked out is all."

Riley elbowed Longbeard repeatedly, trying to break free. She wanted to get to Jake.

The man in charge intervened, grabbing her hair. "Shut up, or I'm gonna jerk ya bald!"

Longbeard pulled Jake out of the trunk and dragged him into a small log cabin. Riley was taken in next. "There's a flashlight in the corner there and some necessities. Y'all make yourselves at home." They closed the heavy wood door. Everything was pitch-black.

A chain rattled against the door. "Gimme the lock, Zachary," the man in charge said.

"No!" she screamed. "Please, don't lock us in here. Please." She fell to her knees and crawled toward Jake. She bumped into his torso and leaned in closer to hold him. "Jake, Jake. Are you okay?" There was no response, but his chest was rising and falling. She felt her way to the corner to look for the flashlight and turned it on.

"Oh my god. Jake, please wake up." She shone the light on his head and gingerly ran her hand over it. A goosebump was already forming. She undid the tape around his ankles and removed the remaining tape from his wrists. "Jake," she whispered in a tearful voice. "Jake, please be okay." She leaned down and kissed his forehead, then raised his head slightly and slid one of the blankets underneath. She didn't know what to do. There was no ice to make an icepack with. She had no idea how to treat a concussion, and what if there was brain bleed?

The car started up. She hurried to the door, pressing her hands against the thick wood, yelling into it. "Wait! Please don't leave us locked in here. We need a doctor! Help!" The car drove away, and she fell to her knees, sobbing.

• • •

Mack was preparing to light his fire when he heard the vehicle approach. At first, he thought his mind was playing tricks on him. It was probably just the wind or distant thunder. But then car doors were opening and closing. There was no mistaking that. He threw on his jumpsuit, socks and shoes. Adrenalin coursed through his body. He was ready to run.

Ever so slightly, he opened his cabin door and peered out. *It's not the cops.* He let out a breath. It was a large four-door sedan. Maybe an older Lincoln or Oldsmobile. People were moving around the car and going back and forth into the first cabin. Two men and one woman passed in front of the headlights.

A moment later, an ear-piercing scream. His body shook. He strained to see what was happening. The trunk was open. A woman was being held by one man at gunpoint while another man dragged a body into the first cabin. The woman struggled and then was taken into the cabin too.

The couple was obviously in trouble. His first inclination was to help, but what could he possibly do? He was a fugitive in an orange prison jumpsuit. They'd likely shoot him down before he got halfway there. He stood rocking back and forth, his palms pressed against his temples. Then something made him think of his sister. What if it were her screaming for help and no one came? A surge of momentum kicked in. He was ready; he burst out of the cabin.

Three car doors opened together and Mack held himself against the cabin door, holding his breath, as the two men and one woman got inside. He stood quietly, hoping they hadn't seen him. The engine started up and the vehicle drove off.

As soon as they were out of sight, Mack hurried over to the cabin where the couple had been taken. He heard the woman sobbing and calling out the man's name. "Jake, Jake."

He leaned in closer to the door. "Ma'am. Are you okay?" He heard her gasp. He'd startled her.

"Hello, yes, hello! Who's there? We need help! Please, let us out!"

Mack pulled on the thick chain, but there was no give. "They've got the door chained up tight and a heavy-duty lock on it. I can't open it."

"Oh, please, whoever you are, please. There must be a way—my husband is hurt." She was still sobbing.

"Ma'am, I'm sorry. It won't budge. I don't have any tools to cut through this. I can't get it open."

"What about a window?" Riley asked. "Maybe there's another way out of here."

He hated to be the bearer of bad news. "I'm afraid not. No windows. The only opening to these cabins is the door."

"Who are you?" she asked. "Are you one of them?"

"My name's Mack. I was staying in one of the cabins here and heard all the commotion. I'm not one of them."

"Mack. Okay, Mack? Can you call for help? Call the police—an ambulance too. My husband's unconscious."

"Jake. Jake." Her voice had moved away, then she came back to the door. "Please, Mack. I don't know what to do."

He tried to think. She sounded desperate. How could he get help? Nobody would ever find this place unless they were brought here. He heard a man say "Riley." He listened at the door.

"Jake! Are you okay?"

"I think so."

"No. Just stay put," she said. "Don't try to get up. Just rest there for a few minutes while I talk to Mack."

"Mack? Who's Mack?"

"He's gonna help us, Jake. Please just lie still." Her voice got louder. "Mack, are you there? Did you call for help?"

"Ma'am, I'm sorry. I don't have a phone, and even if I did, there'd be no service way out here. And besides that, I don't quite know how to tell anyone how to find us. Is your husband okay?"

"I'm okay, Mack. My name is Jake Marshall and my wife's name is, Riley."

"We've been abducted," Riley said, "and I don't know when they might come back. Maybe you could go and get help?"

He didn't know what to say. How could he go and get help? Nobody would believe him, and he'd be thrown in jail faster than green grass through a goose.

"Mack, you still there?" Jake asked.

Mack squatted, holding his head in his hands, trying to think. He wanted to help them. He wanted some good to come out of all of this—something to make everything worthwhile. "I'm still here," he said, then stood up. "Jake, Riley, there's something I need to tell you."

CHAPTER NINE

After boarding the plane, Michelle and Scotty stowed their carry-on bags in the overhead compartment. Michelle kept out the file folder she'd organized. It was an expandable kraft folder with a flap and stretchy elasticized band to secure the contents. She held it in her lap and then settled in for take-off.

Flying was about her least favourite thing to do. Under normal circumstances, she'd be worrying about the take off and squeezing Nick's hand at least until they reached cruising altitude. But today was different. She didn't feel afraid of flying. Her only concern was reaching their destination and finding Riley and Jake.

Scotty finished adjusting her seat belt and plugged in her phone. "So, what's the plan when we get to Savannah, mom?"

Michelle was typing on her phone. "Hang on a sec, Scotty. I just want to finish sending this email to Detective Jorden. I don't know why he hasn't responded yet—we sent him the info about Jake's car and the roadside assistance email last night. Surely he's looked into it by now."

"Mom, it's only seven a.m. Maybe he'll get back to you soon. He might be working on more than this one case."

"Exactly, and that's why we need to keep after him. I don't want him to think he can just pass this off. Plus, if we can find out what dealership they were towed to, we'll make that our first stop." Michelle finished typing and hit the Send button. "You know what, Scotty? I should have called the roadside assistance people myself to find out where they were towed to. I probably could've gotten an answer way quicker than waiting for Ben Jorden."

Neither of them had had much sleep—three hours at best. They'd left Niagara at 3:00 a.m. to get to Toronto by 5:00 a.m. in order to check in the required two hours ahead of their international flight.

"Mom, we should try to get some sleep. It's going to be a long day." Scotty put in her earphones and closed her eyes.

Michelle patted Scotty's hand, then tucked her folder into the pouch in front of her. She let her head fall back next to Scotty's. *Please let everything be okay. Please let Riley and Jake be okay. Please let me find them safe.* She repeated it over and over in her head until she was suddenly in her car driving to the Niagara Community Soccer Park.

Riley was only six years old and didn't want to be late for her very important game. "Mommy, hurry up—we have to be on time. I told Cara I'd give her one of my orange hairbands to match our jerseys."

Nick was working late, and Michelle had Scotty with her too—she was sleeping peacefully in her car seat. Then Riley yelled, "Mommy, I forgot my socks!" She started crying, and Scotty woke up and started crying too. Michelle promised Riley everything would be okay—she'd drop her off with her team and then go back home and get the socks.

Now she was walking fast, trying to get back to the field where she'd dropped off Riley. In her right arm she was carrying Scotty and in her left, a lawn chair, a diaper bag and Riley's socks. *Thank god it's not my turn to bring the halftime snacks. Or is it?* She started stressing about the snacks but kept hurrying along. Her arms ached, and it felt like she'd been walking forever. Finally they arrived, and Scotty started squirming in her arm, pointing at a group of six-year-olds in their fluorescent orange jerseys. Michelle set up her lawn chair along the sidelines with the other parents. *That's odd.* She didn't recognize any of them. She scanned all the orange jerseys on the field for Riley but couldn't find her. Panic ensued as the realization came to her—this isn't Riley's team.

She looked over the park, searching the other pitches for another orange team. Now the referee was in front of her. Maybe he knew where Riley was. He spoke with a southern accent and told her to go to the back of the park—to the pitch behind the trees. *That's odd.* She'd never noticed those trees before. *Why would they have children playing way back there?* She started running toward them, to the back of the park. More and more trees blocked her view and she couldn't see any bright orange. She tried to move faster, but something was holding her back. Her legs were slogging against some sort of resistance. It was like trying to run while waist deep in water. She felt an overwhelming dread. *Please let me find her, please let her be okay.*

"Mom." Scotty nudged her shoulder gently. "Mom. Wake up—we're going to be landing in a few minutes."

• • •

Once they landed in Savannah, Michelle went straight to the car-rental booth while Scotty hit up Starbucks to grab sandwiches and cappuccinos with extra espresso shots. They located their rental vehicle in the outdoor lot. As they were loading their bags into the car, Michelle's phone rang. She grabbed it out of her purse and looked at the screen. It was Ben Jorden. "Detective Jorden, have you found them?"

"No, nothing solid to go on yet, Michelle, but I do have some positive news."

"Yes?" she said anxiously.

"There's no record of either one of them being admitted to any hospitals and no unidentified deaths or recent deaths matching their descriptions."

"That is good news." Michelle closed her eyes for a moment and took a breath. "What about Mercedes Roadside Assistance. Were you able to find out which dealership they were towed to?"

"Well, here's the thing. The Mercedes tow truck driver says there was no one there when he arrived. He'd been dispatched to a gas station just off I95 North near Yemassee, South Carolina, but when he got there, they were gone. The attendant at the gas station told him they'd already got a tow from someone else."

"Why would they get a tow from someone else? That doesn't make sense."

Michelle strained to hear Ben's response over the roar of a jet passing directly above them. "Apparently, they were exceptionally busy due to a storm, and the Mercedes tow truck driver arrived three hours after they'd called. Maybe they got tired of waiting and decided to call an independent towing company."

"I suppose that's possible."

"Mercedes tried doing a locate on the vehicle last night but were unsuccessful. The vehicle's GPS locator is unresponsive."

"What does that mean, Ben?"

"It means that the vehicle's hidden GPS locator was tampered with. It means that whoever took their vehicle knew how to remove or deactivate the car's locator. I'm guessing it was someone who's fairly proficient at this—not your run-of-the-mill amateur car thief."

"What about their phones? Has the mobile network provided any details yet?"

"No signals from their phones, either." The detective paused. "I should have the detailed phone activity records shortly, as well as their banking and credit card transactions too. Maybe there'll be something to go on, there."

"Okay, Ben. We're just leaving the airport in Savannah. Scotty and I will go straight to this Yemassee gas station. Have the local police gone there yet?"

"I'll call the Yemassee police to follow up. They'll be handling the case now—it's in their jurisdiction."

Michelle heard him shuffling through some papers. "Okay, listen," she said, feeling exasperated. "Could you email me the address of this gas station in Yemassee and the name of the local detective you've been talking to there? I'll need their contact information too."

"Michelle, I'm typing as we speak," Ben said. "You'll have it in a few minutes."

"Ben, there was something else I came across on the internet. It was something about a Canadian Government Emergency Watch and Response agency. I tried to call their number last night, but I didn't get through to anyone. Is that something I need to do?"

"I've looked after it, Michelle. We used the Interpol channels to request cooperation from the U.S. Police. I've also talked personally with the police department in Yemassee as well as those in the surrounding areas."

"Okay, thanks, Ben."

"You're welcome. And, Michelle, we'll keep doing everything we can from our end."

Scotty drove while Michelle updated her log, entering the time of her conversation with Detective Jorden and what they'd discussed. Next, she drafted a list of questions for the Yemassee police. She was staring out the window, repeatedly clicking the top of her pen, extending and retracting the ballpoint tip.

"Mom, please stop."

"Okay, okay. So, we need to know who the gas station attendant was who saw them leave in another tow truck. Maybe they can describe the truck and—"

"Hey, I just thought of something. Most gas stations have security cameras, don't they? Maybe they'll have video of the tow truck that picked them up. The police should check that."

"Yes, okay, good." Michelle added that to her list of items to discuss with police. "Ask about attendant who saw them leave and about video cameras at the gas station.' What else?"

Scotty glanced at her. "Well, didn't Detective Jorden say we should do a press release with the local media? Do the police arrange that, or do we?"

"Exactly. Someone needs to get on top of that right away. The sooner we get their pictures out there, the more likely someone might remember seeing them."

Michelle's phone chimed with an incoming email. "It's from Ben Jorden. I'll key in the address of the gas station." Michelle entered the address and then read the email again. "Looks like a Captain Charles Adams will be meeting us there."

CHAPTER TEN

Andy felt extremely awkward. Captain Adams had called him over, only to take a personal call on his cell. He'd raised his finger at him like he'd only be a minute and motioned for Andy to sit down. The voice on the other end of the line started coming through loud and clear. "I need the money now, Chuck," a woman yelled. "It was supposed to be in by the first of the month and you know it. I got a court order, and if it's not in my account today, I'm gonna file a complaint."

The captain's jaw tensed and his neck started getting red. He stood up and turned his back to Andy. "You've got no right to talk to me like this," he said angrily. "You'll get your allowance when I'm good and ready to pay it."

He hung up, downed the rest of his coffee and adjusted his holster as though he were reclaiming his authority. He was Captain Charles Adams, second in command of the Yemassee Police Force. Not many people would dare talk to him like that.

He smiled at Andy, shaking his head, trying to make light of the situation. "Piece of advice for ya, Andy. Don't ever get married. They'll take ya for everything you got."

Andy smiled and gave a short laugh to help the captain save face. It seemed required and would have been more awkward if he hadn't. He wished he'd never heard any of the call or his imprudent comments.

The Yemassee force was relatively small, but those in uniform were held in high regard by the townsfolk. Especially the captain. He'd kept their community safe for the past twenty years, enforcing the law and keeping the order. His reputation was impeccable, aside from his recent divorce. He commanded eight traffic officers, six patrol officers, a patrol sergeant, one canine handler and his dog, Nero, and an evidence custodian. Above him was the new chief of police. Andy hadn't met him yet.

Andy was a patrol officer, the newest one on the force. He'd taken the position just two months ago. The patrol sergeant said he was the most qualified officer they'd ever hired. He had a college degree in criminal justice and had scored exceptionally high on the physical and academic training exams at the police academy. Lately, he'd been thinking about switching over to the county sherriff's office, where he'd have a better chance for advancement, but Yemassee was his hometown and where he preferred to stay.

Charles pulled in his chair. "Andy, looks like we got ourselves a missing persons case—ya interested?"

"Yes, sir," Andy said without hesitation. He hoped he didn't appear overly excited.

"It's Charles. You can drop the 'sir'."

"Okay, Charles, then." Andy didn't like to use first names for superiors unless asked to. When he'd first started, it seemed odd to hear other officers and staff call the boss "Charles." Some called him "Captain Charles." Andy didn't know yet if the captain's informality was for show, to make him look like a real good guy, or if he really was one. It was clear, however, that even though people were on a first-name basis with him, they never forgot who they were talking to. From what Andy had seen so far, everyone respected him. Except his ex.

"It's a Canadian couple," Charles said. "Last seen here in Yemassee on Wednesday afternoon." He pushed the file folder towards Andy. "Now we've got ourselves some yahoo detective, Ben Jorden from Canada, tellin' us what to do." He pointed at the flashing light on his desk phone, then pushed the button.

"Ben, ya still there? I've got one of our best officers here with me, Andy Solterra. We've got you on speaker."

Ben briefly introduced himself to Andy, then carried on. "As I was saying, I'm hoping you can check out the service centre where Jake and Riley Marshall were last seen. They'd called Mercedes Roadside Assistance, but when the tow truck arrived, the couple was gone. According to Mercedes, the gas station attendant told their driver that some other tow truck had already come and got them.

Could you follow up on that and meet with Riley's mother and sister there? They're on their way there now."

Andy glanced up from taking notes. Charles looked irritated. "On their way? I thought you said they're from Canada."

"They are. They flew into Savannah this morning. The mother's name is Michelle. I'm sending her the address of the service station. She and her other daughter, Scotty, should be there in about an hour. I'll pass along your contact information."

"We'll see them there." Charles hung up.

The service station where the couple had last been seen was J.J.'s. Jeremy Jones had been running it for years. Everyone knew him. Each year he sponsored one of the town's little league baseball teams. Heck of a good guy. Sarah worked there too.

Andy flipped through the papers and photos in the file folder. Ben had faxed these documents hours ago. He wondered how long they'd been sitting in the fax machine.

• • •

Andy and Charles drove out to J.J.'s Service Station, where the couple had last been seen. It was north of town, just off the I95. There wasn't much else to speak of at that exit; a used-furniture store, a rundown motel and a ramp to the highway overpass leading into Yemassee. All the chain restaurants and hotels were two exits back.

They went into the back office with J.J. to review the surveillance video. They started with the camera mounted outside the entrance. It afforded a full view of all the gas pumps and everyone coming in and out the front doors.

"That's him." Andy pointed at the screen. "He's leaving right there, but I can't see where he's going."

Charles leaned in closer. "J.J., you got another camera that shows the rest of your parking lot? Something that might show him goin' to his car?"

J.J. looked at Charles. "Nope. The other camera broke down 'bout a week ago." Haven't had a chance to get it fixed." Andy noticed J.J.'s hands fidgeting while he spoke. First he had them on his hips, then in his pockets and then out again. "I remember seein 'em, though. He was a real nice fella. Wanted us to know they'd be parked there for a spell, waitin' for a tow."

Andy took it all down in his notepad. "Can we look further on the video and see if there's footage of the tow truck that picked them up?"

There was nothing. Only the one clip of Jake coming out of the service centre carrying what looked like bottles of water in one hand and something else behind his back.

"What's he hiding there?" Charles asked. "Something sure looks suspicious. What's this young fella up to?"

J.J. paused the video and Andy took a closer look. "It's a couple of those Haagen-Dazs ice cream bars. I recognize the packaging."

Charles chuckled, slapped J.J. on the back lightly and thanked him for his help. It seemed like he was wrapping up the interview. "Well," he said, dragging out the word, "If you think of anything else, J.J., you be sure to let us know. We'll be waiting outside for the missing woman's mother. She'll be here shortly."

Andy didn't want to cut in, but he'd be the one responsible for the written report and wanted to make sure it was complete. Doing a thorough job on his first big case was important. "Um, I wonder if we could just back up a bit here and see if there's any video showing Jake going into the store?" He tried to ignore the salty look from Charles.

J.J. scrolled back. There was nothing besides the view of him coming out and walking over to the side of the lot, out of camera range. J.J. shrugged. "Must have been glitching out on account of the storm. Looks like we just have that one picture of him leaving."

Andy thought that seemed strange.

Charles asked J.J. to freeze the frame showing Jake leaving the store. "Andy, get a copy of this here clip and make a note of what he's wearing. We'll need it for the missing-person description."

Andy didn't want to push—he was intimidated by Charles. At the same time, he felt like this whole process was being rushed. "Well, I'd really like to go through all of these clips more carefully." He looked at J.J. "If you don't mind, I'll take all of it for further examination."

J.J. opened his mouth but nothing came out. Charles filled in the space. "We'll get to that later, Andy. Now, J.J., my information says one of your attendants told the Mercedes Roadside Assistance tow truck driver that the young Marshall couple had already got a tow from someone else. That right?"

"That'd be Hector. He was emptying the garbage bins by the pumps and saw them get picked up. He's not in today. He works Monday to Friday, eight to four."

Andy wrote Hector's name down and asked J.J. if he could get his last name and contact information. "Maybe I can get a hold of him now and ask him what he saw."

J.J. walked over to a file cabinet and stretched out the extendable key chain clipped to his beltloop. "I keep all the employee private records in here." He pulled out Hector's file and gave Andy his address and phone number. J.J. glanced at his watch. "You might catch him at home. Otherwise, he and his buddies spend most of their time at Earl's Country Club, shootin' eight ball. The kid's a pool shark." He gave Charles a stern look and pointed his finger at him. "He's a good kid—y'all go easy on 'im, now."

There was a knock at the door and Sarah, the cashier, stuck her head in. "Excuse me, gentlemen. There's a couple of women out front askin' to see Captain Adams. They say they're Riley Marshall's mother and sister."

• • •

As they waited outside for Captain Adams, Michelle and Scotty walked around the gas pumps looking for surveillance cameras. "I only see two," Michelle said. "One over the doorway and one over there at the corner."

The bells at the top of the door jingled as two officers came out and headed toward them. The one in front hiked up his pants as he walked and took a wider than normal stride. He nodded and tipped his hat. "Afternoon, ma'am, miss. I'm Captain Charles Adams. Y'all can call me Charles, and this here is Officer Andy Solterra."

Michelle noted his southern accent. His dialect was full of long vowels, and he spoke at a slow pace. She extended her hand as she introduced herself and Scotty. Charles took her hand gently, holding only her fingers, and gently shook it. Then did the same with Scotty.

Michelle ignored the patronizing handshake and didn't waste any time on small talk. She was eager to hear the update, hoping for some good news. "Have you found out anything about my daughter, Riley and my son-in-law, Jake? Any leads on where they might be?"

"Ma'am, lem'me start by giving you an update on the progress we've made so far." He raised one foot up to the curb by the pumps. "We've determined for a fact that your daughter and son-in-law were here on Wednesday afternoon. We've also learned that they were gone before the Mercedes Roadside Assistance tow truck arrived."

"Yes, we already know that. Ben Jorden from the Niagara Police gave us an update this morning." She spoke quickly, anxious to get things moving along.

Charles continued. "Now, we've checked the surveillance tapes and found footage of your son-in-law coming out of this here store." He nodded toward it. "The young man purchased two water bottles and two ice cream bars."

Michelle interjected. "Jake. The young man—his name is Jake."

"Right. Then Jake walked over yonder there, out of camera range." Charles pointed to the side of the lot.

"What about the other camera on the corner there?" Scotty pointed at it. "Wouldn't it capture that side of the lot?"

"Unfortunately, that one isn't working."

"Oh, for heaven's sake." Michelle was frustrated. Things seemed to be moving in slow motion. She wanted answers and she wanted them now. Just being there, standing in the parking lot where her daughter was last seen, was difficult enough. She didn't pick up any sense of urgency from this Captain Adams. "What about the tow truck? Is there any video of the tow truck that took them?"

Scotty gave her a look that signalled her tone was too abrupt. Well, of course she was sounding abrupt. She was trying to find her missing daughter.

"I'm afraid not," Charles said.

"What about the attendant who works here who saw them get towed?" Michelle went on. "Can he identify the tow truck that picked them up? Has anyone talked to him?"

Charles nodded for Andy to take this one. "Unfortunately, Hector's off today," Andy said. "But we'll be trying to locate him as soon as we're done here."

"Trying to locate him?" Michelle stared at Andy. "We need to talk to him immediately and find out what he saw." She put her hands on her hips, waiting for his response.

"Yes, ma'am. We'll be going to track him down, straight from here."

"And what about a press conference of some sort?" She directed this question to the captain. "Do you have any local media we could organize? I'd like to get photos of Riley and Jake in all the local newspapers and on the television news—maybe someone out there has seen them."

She could tell from the captain's body language that he wasn't too receptive. He wasn't nodding. He wasn't showing any signs of agreement; just raising his hands a little, as if to say "Woah down, lady."

"Well now," he began slowly. "We don't normally organize that sort of thing, but that's not to say we can't. Let's see what we can pull together." He smiled and put his hand on Andy's shoulder. "First off, we're going to track down the service attendant and then Andy here can see what he can do about organizing a media release for later on this afternoon."

He talked so slowly Michelle thought she was going to lose her mind. If his investigation moved at this pace, nothing would ever get done. She wanted to clap her hands together and shout "Let's go! Get moving!"

She handed each of them a note with her name and phone number. "Please call me as soon as you find out anything. Can you give me your numbers too, please?" She got out her pen and paper, ready to write them down.

"Andy, give her the number at the station. That'd be the best place to reach us."

Andy took her pen and paper and wrote down the number. Below it, he wrote his cell number and circled it. Michelle glanced at the page. That one simple gesture meant so much. He cared.

CHAPTER ELEVEN

They sat in the rental car for a moment after Captain Adams and Officer Solterra drove off. Michelle started writing down their names and the details of what they'd discussed in her log book. Next, she'd add Andy's cell phone number to her phone contacts, to have it handy.

She shook her head in disgust. "I'm so disappointed. They're moving at a snail's pace. They've had hours to get on this. Can you believe they haven't even talked to that service attendant yet? What was his name—Hector something-or-other? I mean, my god, he's a key witness—he's the one who saw the tow truck that took them away."

Scotty was looking out the window. "Do you think they're going straight to Hector's place?" They watched the police car turn onto the overpass, crossing over the highway toward town. "Want me to follow him?"

The idea took Michelle by surprise, but she liked it. "Yes, go, Scotty—go."

Scotty pulled out and got on the ramp to the overpass. She sped up until they could see the police car about a block or so ahead. The driver was signalling left and making the turn. Scotty signalled and moved into the left turn lane. The light turned orange, and she hadn't made it to the intersection. Michelle saw Scotty's foot still on the gas and an oncoming car coming through. "Stop, Scotty!" They both hit the brakes—Scotty stepping on the real one and Michelle pressing her foot into the floor on the passenger side.

Michelle leaned forward to look past Scotty, trying to keep sight of them. "They're stopping. They're only about five or six houses down."

When the light turned green and the intersection was clear, Scotty made her left onto Evans Avenue. It was an older residential street. The police car had pulled into a driveway a few houses up. "Just pull over right here, Scotty. I don't want them to see us."

Scotty put the car in park and turned off the engine. "Okay. So, now we know where Hector lives. There's the Captain and Andy on the porch."

"And here comes Hector," Michelle announced as a young man, about seventeen or eighteen years old, stepped outside, letting the screen door bang behind him. He leaned against the railing on the porch with his hands deep inside the pockets of his oversized jeans. The captain asked him something. Hector pulled his wallet out of his pocket and held it out to them. Andy examined his I.D. and then gave it back.

Hector kept his head down. Each time he moved along the railing a bit farther, the captain stepped closer. He was just a kid, and it was obvious he felt threatened by the way the captain was interrogating him. Hector kept shaking his head, No. Then his hands came out of his pockets and he held them out to each side, again shaking his head, No.

Andy tucked his note pad in his shirt pocket and went back to the car while the captain stayed on the porch.

"Oh my God! What's he doing?"

Scotty had seen it too. "Yeah, no kidding! What's that all about?" The captain had Hector pinned up against the front of the house. "He's scaring the crap out of this poor kid." The captain slammed him against the bricks a second time. "What's he trying to do? Beat an answer out of him?"

Michelle jumped as her cell phone rang. "It's Detective Jorden." She swiped her finger across the screen to accept the call. "Hello Ben? You're on speaker." She prayed he had some good news for them.

Michelle and Scotty kept their eyes on the porch as Captain Adams finished roughing up Hector. "Michelle, we just heard back from Visa," Ben said. "They've given me a list of the most recent purchases made on Jake and Riley's credit cards. Do you have a moment now to go over them?"

Charles poked his finger into Hector's face a few more times, then turned and walked down the steps.

"Okay, Ben, go ahead." Michelle pulled open her log book and turned to a fresh page.

"Looking at Wednesday, the day they went missing, there are a number of charges. First item is for fifty dollars at a BP Station in Fort Myers."

"That makes sense. They would have gassed up before leaving. What else?"

"Looks like more gas—forty dollars at a Sunoco station in Richmond Hill, Georgia. Then, there's a credit from a hotel in Columbia, which I presume is where they had planned to stay Wednesday night?"

"Could be. They thought they'd make the trip home in two days, so that sounds about right."

"Okay, nothing unusual there. Then, there was another charge for a hotel in Hilton Head, South Carolina. It's a hotel not far from the Mercedes dealership where they were being towed. I've already followed up on that one, and the hotel says they never checked in."

Michelle pursed her lips together and momentarily closed her eyes. It hurt so much to hear those words—*they never checked in.* "Is there anything else, Ben? Anything that looks fraudulent?" She was hoping they'd get a fresh lead on something.

"There was a charge to Golfnow for a hundred and forty-nine dollars. It was a tee time reservation for a course in Hilton Head—again, not far from the dealership and hotel they'd reserved. It was booked for two players at ten a.m., Thursday. Like the hotel, they were a no-show."

Michelle's eyes were starting to fill. She pulled a tissue out of her purse.

"The last item is a small purchase at J.J.'s Service Centre in Yemassee, South Carolina for nine dollars and twenty-two cents. I don't know what it was for, but it confirms the Mercedes Roadside Assistance information; they were definitely there."

She dabbed her eyes. "It was two water bottles and two ice cream bars. The nine twenty-two; that's what they bought." Her voice broke.

"Michelle, I'm afraid their cell phone records didn't show much, either. The last activity was an outgoing call to that hotel in Columbia. Likely to cancel their stay."

"I see." She pressed her lips together tightly again. It helped her gain control.

"Did you meet Captain Adams at the service centre in Yemassee?"

"We did. They had surveillance video of Jake coming out of the store, but nothing else. Nothing showing the tow truck picking them up."

"What about the attendant?"

"They're questioning him right now, but something tells me not much is going to come of it."

Scotty whispered, "Tell him what we saw. Tell him about Captain Adams."

Michelle shook her head and mouthed "Not now." She continued talking to Ben. "I'm hoping they'll arrange some sort of press conference for later this afternoon."

"Good. Let me know if there's anything I can do at this end. Take care, Michelle."

"Will do. Thanks, Ben." She hung up just as the police car backed out of the driveway and headed their way. Scotty and Michelle ducked down.

"Mom, why didn't you tell Detective Jorden about Captain Adams? What we just saw."

"Because maybe that's how they do things in South Carolina—I don't know. Plus, police have this undying loyalty to each other. I don't want them to get their backs up against us right from the get-go. We need their help."

"Well, I wish I'd filmed it on my phone. It's not right to bully a person like that. This Captain Adams, he acts like he's some super macho cop man, but I think he's a chauvinistic creep." Scotty made a face like she'd just tasted something bad and wanted to spit it out.

"Okay, Scotty." Michelle raised her hand. "I'm not a fan either, but let's hope we hear from Andy Solterra soon and see what he has to say about their meeting with Hector. Meanwhile, we need to find a hotel room and get settled somewhere. I promised your dad I'd let him know where we're staying.

CHAPTER TWELVE

Riley checked on Jake throughout the night. She asked him his name, the year and other random questions to make sure he was cognizant. After five or six times, Jake suggested they use another method. He traced an infinity symbol on her hand. "Riley, so long as I remember us, that's all that matters." It was the symbol engraved on the inner bands of their wedding rings.

At some point Riley dozed off, awaking with a jolt to the newfound realization of their predicament. Fresh tears ran down her face and her throat got that tight feeling, like someone was choking her again. She tried to think. It was still dark, but not as pitch-black as it had been earlier. *It must be almost morning.* She tried to be hopeful. *Once it's daylight, Mack will get us out.* They had to get out of there, and he was their only hope.

Her feet were so cold. She took turns tucking her toes under her calves, trying to warm them up. She wished she had warm socks and her cozy fleece sweat pants on. She thought of her mom tearfully. She'd always tell her to dress warmly and in layers. She could almost hear her saying "You can always take off a layer if you're too hot, Riley, but you can't add one if you don't have one with you." She was always looking out for her and Scotty. She'd be worried right now, wondering why she hadn't called or texted.

Wisps of daylight started to thread through the logs of the cabin. It was still dark inside, but there was enough light to find her way without the flashlight. She'd been careful not to use the batteries unnecessarily. Reluctantly, she lifted off her blanket and went to the corner where their supplies had been left. There was a bucket with a lid, and a roll of toilet paper. She'd already used the bucket several times. She couldn't understand why she had to keep peeing. Maybe it was a physical reaction to the shock.

There was a case of water bottles, and a grocery bag sat on top. There were packages of crackers and cheese and half a dozen protein bars in the bag. *Not much to work with.* At least on *Chopped*, the chefs can go to the pantry to add to the basket ingredients. There was no pantry here.

When Riley had first enrolled in culinary school, she and her mom used to play their own version of *Chopped* at home. Her mom had called it *Chopped, Niagara Edition*. She'd secretly choose a few local ingredients and put them in a basket. Riley would have thirty minutes to create a dish using those items along with any other items from their pantry. Her mom, dad and Scotty would be the judges and eat whatever she came up with, even if it wasn't the greatest. They were all so supportive.

With a loan, co-signed by her parents, she'd opened a small catering business and not long after that, she'd met Jake. He had booked a small event through her website. He'd needed someone to cater an afternoon wine tasting where he was introducing his latest Riesling ice wine.

Riley put together charcuterie boards with strong cheeses and salty meats. She also served spicy Thai shrimp appetizers. Everything paired perfectly, and the guests raved about both the ice wine and her appetizers. Afterward, Jake came over to thank her for her hard work and tell her how impressed he was. He said he'd be put in a good word for her with her boss. When he called the next day, Riley burst out laughing and explained that she was the owner. A year later, they were engaged.

She looked back at the supplies and the water bottles. It was seeing the water bottles that triggered it. She couldn't hold off any longer—she had to pee again. She undid her shorts and squatted over the bucket. She finished, put the lid back on top and saw Jake was waking up.

He propped himself up on his elbows. "Riley," he whispered.

"Jake." She sat on the edge of the slatted bed frame beside him. "How are you feeling? How's your head?"

"I'm fine, I think. Are you okay? How's your cheek?" he said, squinting. There wasn't enough light to make out much detail.

"I think it's alright. When I pulled the duct tape off, it started bleeding again, but it seems okay now." She let her head drop onto his shoulder and started to cry. "What are we going to do?"

He held her and kissed the top of her head. "I don't know, but I've got a feeling they'll be back today. We should try to come up with a plan."

Riley sniffled and lifted her head to look at him. She wiped away the tears with the back of her hand. "It's too dangerous. I nearly got you killed last night. I'm so sorry."

"No, Riley. I choked. I should've just pulled the trigger when I had the gun in my hand. I could've shot him." He looked into her eyes. "I won't make that mistake again."

She shook her head. "Oh, Jake, this is all just so bizarre."

"Maybe it's not so bizarre. Do you remember your bestie, Longbeard, taking our picture in the trunk?"

"How could I forget? By the way, his name is Zachary. I heard the guy in charge call him that."

"Okay, so why do you think Zachary took our picture?"

"I know Jake—I know what that means." She felt annoyed. This was because of his family's money.

Jake spelled it out anyway. "They probably found out my family has money and they're going to hold us for ransom." He sat up and put his hands on her shoulders. "The good news is, they'll want to keep us alive for a while."

"But we've seen Zachary's face. We could identify him." She contemplated that. "Even if they do keep us alive for a while, they'll have to kill us at some point. Won't they?"

He didn't answer.

"Jake, we need to get out of here. Now that it's daylight, maybe Mack can get us out or go and get help."

He shook his head. "Riley, I think we need to accept the fact that Mack probably isn't here anymore. He's a felon—you heard him. He's not going to stay here and risk his life to help us."

"No, you're wrong." She started shouting, "Mack! Mack!"

"Everything okay in there?" Mack's deep voice came from outside their cabin door less than ten seconds later.

Riley looked at Jake. "Told you so," she mouthed. There'd been no doubt in her mind. Mack had been truthful, and she trusted him completely. He wouldn't abandon them.

"I can't tell you how good it is to hear your voice," Jake said.

"How's your head, Jake? You doing okay?"

"So far, so good. So, what does it look like out there? Do you see any way to get us out?"

"No, not a way out," Mack said, "but I might have figured out a way to pass things in and out. Can you open the flu on your fireplace?"

"That's great," Riley said. "We've got water bottles and protein bars in here."

"I boiled a kettle full of rain water in my fireplace last night, but I sure could use one of those protein bars."

Jake squatted in front of the chimney while Riley held the flashlight. "Okay, I found the lever." He pushed it up, opening the flu, then lay down on his back to look up the chimney. He took the flashlight from her and shone it up inside. "Mack," he called. "Yeah, it's way too narrow to fit through, and even if I could, there's a steel cage on the top, likely to prevent animals from getting in."

• • •

Mack lifted the long branch he'd been working on since dawn. He raised it so the tip was positioned on the top of the chimney. He started rotating the branch in his hands, unravelling the ten-foot length of vine he'd wound around the end. A small rock was tied to the end of the vine, big enough to give it enough weight to reach the bottom but small enough to pass through the steel grate up top.

He kept turning the branch until he heard Jake yell "I got it!" A moment later, Jake shouted out, "Okay, Mack, reel it up!"

Mack twisted the branch around and around, winding the vine back up, then raised the branch up and away from the chimney. "I got it!" he yelled. "Easiest catch I've ever reeled in."

When he was a teenager, Mack's dad would take him fishing. Sometimes on weekends they'd go to the lake and rent a row boat. Mack would do the rowing. He liked to see how fast and how far he could take them. For him, that was more fun than the actual fishing. He felt a real sense of pride watching the dock disappear. His dad would nod at him. "How about that, Mack. You see how hard work will take you a long way." *If only life were that simple.*

He had worked hard. He'd studied hard, graduated with honours and was ready to start a career in teaching. Then, everything he'd worked for was taken from him. His whole life had been turned upside down. Just like Riley and Jake's. They may have come from completely different worlds, but right now they were all in the same boat, and Mack was determined to help them.

CHAPTER THIRTEEN

Michelle and Scotty stood off to the side at J.J.'s Service Centre while Captain Adams made the missing-persons announcement to the news outlets. Michelle felt like she was on a movie set. It was surreal.

Charles started with a description of the young couple as Andy lifted the freshly printed posterboard up onto an easel. The local office supply store had enlarged Michelle's flyer with the pictures of Riley and Jake and Jake's car, showing the Ontario licence plate ICE WINE. The cameras zoomed in on the poster.

Charles then released the information they had so far. He started by identifying Jake and Riley Marshall of Niagara Falls, Ontario, pointing to their pictures. He explained that they were on their way home from Florida and had experienced car trouble. "On Wednesday afternoon at approximately three forty-five p.m., Jake and Riley Marshall's silver sports car was loaded onto a flatbed tow truck right over there." He pointed to where they had been parked. "They were supposed to be towed to a dealership in Hilton Head, but they never arrived."

He continued with a plea for help from the public. "We need to work together as a community and help locate this missing couple."

He placed his hand on the edge of the posterboard. "Now, if anyone has seen these two or has any information regarding their whereabouts, we ask you to come forward and share it with us."

He motioned for the cameras to follow along with him over to Michelle. He put his arm around her shoulders, a comforting gesture, and asked if she would like to say a few words.

She hadn't put much thought into what she might say. She started by thanking everyone for being there and then tried to give a more personalized description of Riley and Jake. She was only one or two sentences in when she got choked up. "I'm sorry." She tried to compose herself and carry on. "Riley and Jake, we love you very much." She barely got the words out and paused for a second to take a breath. "Please, if anyone out there might know where they are, please help us bring them home safely."

Afterward, some of the reporters came over for one-on-one interviews with Michelle and Scotty. Michelle emphasized the importance of finding the flatbed tow truck. "If you know anyone with a tow truck that might have picked them up on Wednesday afternoon, please let us know. Or if anyone might have seen a tow truck carrying a silver Mercedes sports car with custom Ontario licence plates, ICE WINE."

Privately, a newspaper reporter from the *Yemassee Review* asked Michelle if the family was offering a reward. It caught her off guard. She hadn't even thought about that. Discussing it with Jake's parents was certainly something to consider. She made a mental note to call Wendy after they were done. She wanted to give the Marshalls an update anyway.

"I wonder if, for now, you could not mention anything one way or the other regarding a reward," Michelle said. "I'm hoping anyone out there with pertinent information will come forward with it right away."

The young woman didn't hesitate. "Oh, of course, I understand." She handed Michelle her business card. "If you think of anything else, let me know. I hope your daughter and son-in-law are found real soon, safe and sound."

Michelle glanced at the card. "Thank you, Cindy." The woman walked away as Michelle put the card in her purse.

That seemed to be the end of it. The television networks had left, reporters scurrying back to their newsrooms to make their deadlines for the six o'clock news.

Scotty linked arms with her and leaned her head on her shoulder. "You did well, Mom."

"Did I?"

Scotty faced her. "You're doing everything you possible can, and I definitely got the feeling that everyone here genuinely wants to help. I'm pretty sure all of the reporters took some of your flyers, plus Andy gave each of them the online link to access the other photos. Even Captain Adams did a decent job."

"I suppose he did," she agreed reluctantly. "For someone who didn't seem too interested in a media release initially, he sure did put on a show for the cameras. It was the most engaged I've seen him since we've been here."

Andy Solterra headed toward them. "How are you holding up, ladies?" His tone and expression confirmed his sincerity. "Listen, I'm sorry I didn't get a moment to speak to you before the press arrived."

"We're hanging in there, Andy—really hoping for some good news, though." Michelle put her arm around Scotty's shoulder.

"I want you to know, I've been working on this case all afternoon. We spoke to Hector, the attendant who works here, and he says he didn't notice much about the tow truck that picked up Jake and Riley. Said it was just a regular old flatbed, nothing special about it that he could recall. He said he didn't see Jake or Riley and didn't remember much of anything about the tow truck driver either, other than it was a man. Apparently, when Hector looked over that way, the driver had his back to him, so he never saw his face."

"So, what's the next step?" Michelle asked.

Andy tried to sound hopeful. "Well, I went through the video surveillance footage from the service centre, and when I focussed in on the clips around the time when Hector was outside emptying the garbage, I noticed that two other vehicles had been at the pumps filling up."

Michelle understood where he was going with this. "Of course. Maybe someone else saw the tow truck."

"Now, I don't want you getting too excited just yet. One of the vehicles had Wisconsin plates, an older gent, and he was facing the other direction. The second vehicle was a local—a woman in her fifties, I'd guess. I showed the clip to Sarah, the cashier inside, and she knows her—says she gasses up here all the time."

Michelle saw a new strand of hope dangling before them. "Have you been able to contact her yet? What's her name?"

"I've already called her. Her husband said she'd phone me back just as soon as she gets home. She went to visit her sister this afternoon, but he expects her home for supper."

"Will you talk with her right away, as soon as she gets home?" Michelle asked.

"I will. We're also hoping to get some fresh leads from this press conference. Believe me, we're doing everything we can."

Michelle and Scotty both nodded and thanked him. "Please call me as soon as you talk with her," Michelle said. "What did you say her name was again?"

Andy let out a deep breath. "It's Miranda Galloway, and I shouldn't be telling you that. Listen, Michelle, I know it's hard, but you have to trust us to do our job."

"Thank you, Andy. I'm keeping notes on the investigation. We truly appreciate everything you're doing."

He walked them to their car and opened the passenger door for Michelle. Scotty hopped in the driver's seat and started up the engine. Pretty much everyone had left. Andy was the only one there, waiting in the police cruiser for Charles, who was still in the store talking with J.J.

Scotty pulled out onto the road and Michelle got out her journal to add the new information to her notes. The pen slipped through her fingers and fell between the seat and the console. "Oh, I dropped my pen." She felt around the bottom of her seat, but she couldn't quite reach it. "Hold up, Scotty. Can you pull in across the way for a minute? I don't want to unbuckle while you're driving, and if I don't get these notes down right away, I'm going to forget something."

"Sure." Scotty signalled and turned into the used-furniture store parking lot across from the service centre and slowed down to park.

•••

Back at J.J.'s, Andy was still waiting for Charles to finish talking with J.J. He wanted to let him know he was going over to Miranda Galloway's house. He pulled forward, toward the store entrance, passing between the first row of pumps and the store. He held his gaze on Charles and J.J. Something wasn't right. Charles looked angry. He was saying something with a stern look on his face, and then he passed J.J. a rolled-up wad of cash. *What on earth?*

Andy quickly turned his head away and drove past. He didn't know what to think. *Had he seen that right? Why would Charles hand a roll of cash to J.J.?* He stopped the car just on the other side of the store entrance and put it in park.

His mind was racing. Should he go inside and confront them? He decided against that. If he'd seen what he thought he'd seen, they'd probably deny it and Charles would take him off the case. None of this made any sense. Maybe if it was the other way around and he saw J.J. paying Charles, but why would Charles be paying J.J.?

Andy thought about how earlier in the day Charles had seemed lackadaisical about examining the surveillance videos at J.J.'s. Something about that didn't seem right, either. If Andy hadn't insisted on taking all of the videos, he never would have found out Miranda Galloway was a possible witness.

Another thing seemed odd, too. Charles was way over the top when they were interrogating Hector. It seemed like he was intent on making Hector out to be some kind of a delinquent. All of these things added up to something peculiar, but for now, Andy didn't want to let on.

• • •

Scotty pulled into a parking spot at the used-furniture store across from J.J.'s Service Centre.

Michelle raised her hand. "Oh my god—Scotty, take a look. Right there, above the door." She pointed to the security camera. "It's facing out toward the service centre." Scotty yanked the keys out of the ignition and they hurried into the store.

Michelle led the way, weaving them around the used dining room suites and trying to ignore the musty smell. An older woman got up from the counter at the back of the store and approached them. "Y'all need some help with something?"

"Yes, hello," Michelle started. "My name is Michelle Barton and this is my daughter, Scotty."

The woman smiled and touched her index finger to her name badge. "Sylvie".

"We're here from Canada trying to find my older daughter, Riley Marshall, and her husband, Jake. They were last seen at the service centre across the road on Wednesday afternoon."

Sylvie looked as though she'd had a revelation. "Is that what all that fuss is goin' on over there? I seen all the TV cameras earlier."

"That's right. We're hoping somebody might have seen the tow truck that picked up their car and took them away."

"Wednesday afternoon, ya say?" Sylvie stared off into space, then declared with certainty, "No, no, I was busy moppin' up—all that rain we had done put two inches a water out back here. Everything got soaked to the bone. I said, I ain't never seen a storm come on like that." She shook her head, still in disbelief about the storm, then got herself back on topic. "So, yer lookin' for your daughter. Y'all seem like real nice folk—I sure hope ya find 'er."

"Thank you." Michelle nodded to her. "We noticed you have a security camera out front and thought maybe it might have captured a picture of the tow truck that picked them up."

"Oh, I'd have to ask Bobby to take a look. He'd be the one who'd know about that."

"Is Bobby here?" Michelle asked eagerly.

"Well, I was fixin' to call him. Y'all hold on now."

Instead of getting out her cell phone, as Scotty and Michelle had expected, Sylvie walked to the back wall of the store and opened up a door. A power sander whirred and buzzed. She hollered, "Bobby! We need some help out here!" and walked back over to them. "He'll be out in two shakes of a lamb's tail. Y'all wanna sit a spell?"

CHAPTER FOURTEEN

Caleb sat on the end of the bed, watching while she rummaged through the suitcases. She was enjoying trying on Riley Marshall's clothes. "Whataya thank a this one?" She twirled around in a coral-coloured blouse. "Fits real nice, don't ya thank?"

"Hot dayum, Beth-Anne." He looked her up and down.

She waved off his compliment and was about to pull out another blouse when something else caught her eye. She lifted out a soft velvety pouch and loosened the drawstrings at the top. "Oh—my—Lord. Caleb, would ya take a look at these—aren't they just the prettiest friggin' pearls you ever done seen?" She dropped the blouse back into the suitcase and handed him the strand to fasten on.

His fingers fumbled at the back of her neck as he did up the clasp. "Beth-Anne, you need to quit rootin' through their stuff for half a minute and let's figure out what we're gonna do about Zachary."

She wished Caleb had never let Zachary in on this. She didn't trust him. "Well, there ain't no choice in the matter. I don't know what ya gotta thank about." She put her hands squarely on her hips. "You know as well as I, they can identify him—they seen him—they seen him twice." She went back to the suitcase and picked up the blouse. She held it up to herself at the mirror. "Not only that, someone else might a seen him too or recognized his tow truck. If Zachary gets caught, he'll bring it all back on us."

Caleb nodded. There was no denying it. "We'll do it today, then?"

"You, not we. You're the one who brought him into this, so, you'll be the one to take him out. And the sooner the better." She was still eying the contents of the suitcase. "Tell Zachary we'll pick him up to go check on the Marshalls. You can do it out there."

Caleb grabbed her from behind and spun her around. "How'd you get to be so cute? I swear, Beth-Anne, you talk like that and I can't help myself." He slid his hands down from her waist and squeezed her ass.

She shoved him away. "And when we get there, make sure Zachary empties out their piss pot before ya take care of him. Ain't no friggin' way I'm doin' that." She bent down to the luggage again. "Know what? I might just wear one a these here dresses." She lifted out a floral sundress and held it up.

"Well hurry up, then," Caleb said. "I wanna go down to Ridgeview first and get a couple more a them pay-as-you-go phones. They got no record a who's usin' 'em. We're gonna need them when we call Jake Marshall's daddy."

"Well, you better get the damn number today or you won't be callin' nobody." She stepped into the dress and turned her back to him. "Zip me up while yer just standin' there."

CHAPTER FIFTEEN

Zachary sat in the backseat of the car, feeling like an unwanted extra. Beth-Anne was up front. She kept leaning over to Caleb—close as cat's breath. She was all gussied up and flirting with him, acting like Zachary wasn't even there. *She never did pay me no never mind. Treats me like dirt, always bossing me around.*

Caleb pulled the car alongside the front of the cabin and he and Beth-Anne started putting on their bandanas. Beth-Anne flipped down her visor to see how she looked in the vanity mirror. She caught his eye. "Whatcha lookin' at, Zachary?" she snarled. She twisted in her seat to look at him directly. "You ought to be the one to go in; they've already seen you."

He didn't want to take instructions from her, but he didn't have much choice. Caleb was sweet on her and whatever Beth-Anne wanted, Beth-Anne got. She had Caleb whipped. "And take them those extra water bottles and foodstuff," she demanded. There was a case of water bottles and a bag in the backseat. "And Zachary, yer gonna need to empty out their piss pot first, then you can take in their supplies." Zachary was thinking he'd like to dump their piss pot right over her head.

He pulled out his gun and started to open his car door. Beth-Anne raised her voice. "I ain't done talkin', Zachary." He stopped and waited while she opened the glove box and pulled out a pack of gum. She unwrapped a stick, lifted her bandana, folded the piece into her mouth and tossed the wrapper out the window. Next, she took out her Glock 43 nine-millimeter and set it on her lap. "All right, I'm ready. Now y'all can go."

Caleb took position behind the rear end of the driver's side, stretching his arms out across the trunk. He was ready with his gun aimed at the cabin door, giving Zachary cover. He nodded at him, to go ahead.

Zachary felt good knowing Caleb had his back. That's how it always used to be, before Beth-Anne came on the scene. One time, he and Caleb were getting skunk-drunk down at the old dock. Zachary hadn't seen the gator coming up behind him, but Caleb did and shot it clean through the head. If it weren't for Caleb, he'd a been done like dinner.

Zachary walked up to the cabin door and unlocked the chain around the latch. "Y'all stand back now," he shouted.

"Back away from the door!" He unwrapped the chain, lifted the latch and slowly opened the door. Jake was lying there on the floor, right where they'd left him the night before. His wife was backed up against the wall. She was holding one hand over her eyes, shielding them from the daylight coming through the doorway.

"What's he lying there for?" Zachary didn't want any trouble this time around. Caleb would take a duck fit.

"He's still unconscious. Please, we need a doctor," Riley begged.

Zachary pointed his gun at her. "Now, just stay put. I'm gonna get yer supplies brought in, and then I'll take a look at him." He took their bucket to the doorway, dumped it around the side of the door, then brought it back in.

"Now, don't get any ideas while I get your things." He kept the gun on Riley. "We got two other guns out there, pointed right at this doorway. Try to get out and yer dead."

• • •

Riley's heart was racing. She clenched the jagged rock behind her back, ready to attack. If Zachary bent down to check on Jake, that would be her opportunity. Jake had a rock too. They were ready.

Zachary was coming back in with their supplies. A decision had to be made, now. Riley was hesitant. They'd have the advantage of a surprise attack, but what about Mack? If there were two of them out there with guns, he wouldn't have a chance. They'd need to call it off and wait for a better opportunity.

Jake must have realized the same thing. He shook his head at her, indicating a no-go.

Riley screamed out their signal as loud as she could. "Stop!"

Zachary looked incredulous. "What are ya yellin'—"

A loud bang went off and Zachary's head jerked forward. His eyes locked on hers. His baffled expression seemed to evaporate and his bulky physique thumped onto the floorboards. Blood started spurting from the back of his head.

Jake yanked his foot out from under him and scrambled to his feet. Riley stood frozen, her hands trembling in front of her mouth.

"Mack must have got one of their guns." Jake stepped toward the doorway.

But it wasn't Mack. It was the other man, the man in charge. He had his gun pointed at Jake. "Back up!" He shouted. The woman was right behind him, pointing her gun at them too. Jake backed up to stand in front of Riley, protecting her.

The man picked up Zackary's gun and started dragging out his body while the woman stood guard. He was tugging him by his feet, jerking him along, a few inches at a time. Zachary's long beard worked like a mop, swabbing up the blood trailing him out. Once he was past the door, the man closed it and chained it up.

It was very dark again. Riley was shaking in Jake's arms. She whispered, her words sounding choppy. "When you were in the doorway, could you see Mack? Do you think he's okay?"

"I couldn't see Mack. It was just those two."

Everything stayed quiet for a long time. The car hadn't started up, so they knew they were still out there somewhere. "They're probably dragging his body into the bush or the swamp," Jake said softly.

She wouldn't let go of his arm. She was haunted by the look on Zachary's face, the blood and the whole chain of events. Something else was bothering her too. There was something oddly familiar about the woman. It was so weird. She'd been standing out there with a gun, wearing a floral sundress.

My dress!

"Jake, she was wearing my dress."

That wasn't all. The woman had looked like none of it was a big deal. A dead man was being dragged out right in front of her and she was standing there cool as a cucumber. "I think they planned on killing him. These people are cold-blooded killers."

Jake put his finger to her lips. "Shhhh. They're coming back." Muffled voices were just outside the cabin door.

The man who killed Zachary spoke. "Jakey, it's time to get down to it. I'm gonna need a number to call yer daddy, maybe text him that nice photo of you two."

Riley spoke up. "Just tell him, Jake. The sooner they get their money, the sooner we'll get out of here."

"That's right. The little lady's gettin' the idea." he chuckled.

"The sooner they get their money, the sooner we'll be dead," he whispered to Riley. "I don't know their phone number," he shouted out. "They're not home right now—they're in Florida on vacation. I had their number in my contacts on my phone, but your goon tossed our phones in the swamp."

"Don't be givin' me anymore a yer friggin' shit," the woman said. "They must have a cell. What's their goddamned cell number?"

"They don't use their Canadian cell numbers when they're in Florida. They got a new number through AT&T. I don't know what it is. I swear."

• • •

Beth-Anne was done talking at them. She spat her gum out. The wad splatted against the cabin door and dropped into the weeds. "Fine then," she said. "Y'all can just enjoy yer friggin' stay here." She stomped to the car, got in and slammed her door shut.

What the hell.

Caleb was still at the cabin door. He was getting out the key, as though he were going to open it again.

"Come on!" She whipped her hand across, motioning for him to get in the car, and opened her window. "What the hell are ya doing?"

He walked over, smirking. "I thought I'd motivate them a little." He showed her his knife. "Maybe cut off one of their fingers. Then, they'll start talkin'."

Beth-Anne was bowled over. This was a side of Caleb she hadn't seen before. He'd just shot and killed Zachary and had hardly flinched. Mind you, it hadn't bothered her either. But, now, he was talking about cutting off fingers? *Maybe that would work.*

CHAPTER SIXTEEN

Miranda Galloway pulled into her driveway just after six. Andy noted the concern on her face when she saw a police car there. He got out quickly and approached her. "Is everything all right, officer?" she asked.

"Everything's fine ma'am." He introduced himself. "Just hoping to talk to you for a few minutes. Are you Miranda Galloway?"

"Yes, I'm Miranda. Would you like to come inside, officer?"

"Thank you kindly, ma'am." He followed her up to the porch and waited as she unlocked the front door.

"Stuart, I'm home!" she shouted as they walked in.

"Mandy, a police officer called. You need to get back to him." Stuart came around the corner into the front hall. "Oh, I see you've caught up with her, officer."

"Stuart, this is Officer Andy Solterra," she said.

Andy reached to shake Stuart's hand. "Hello, Stuart. We spoke earlier on the phone." He got out his notepad and pen. "I'm real sorry to bother you, folks. I just have a few urgent questions for Miranda."

"Oh, I can't imagine what this might be about. Come in, come in." She led him into the front room. "Now, how can I help you."

"Thank you, ma'am. It has to do with a young missing couple from Canada. They were last seen at J.J.'s Service Centre on Wednesday afternoon."

"Oh, dear." She was starting to understand. "I was there filling up at J.J.'s on Wednesday afternoon."

"We think you might have seen the couple. They had car trouble and were parked at the side of the lot." Andy took out one of the flyers from inside his breast pocket and showed it to her.

Miranda looked at the flyer and back to Andy. "Yes, I do remember seeing that fancy car and the young woman. She was climbing up into the cab of the tow truck. I felt real sorry for her. Pretty as a peach, she was—and having to git up into that old tow truck and all."

"Did you see the driver of the tow truck?" He had his pen ready to jot down anything she might have noticed.

"Well, now, he didn't look any better off than the old truck. He was a rough lookin' fella with a long beard—middle aged, I'd say. I wasn't really paying much attention, so I don't recall more than that."

Andy made a few notes. "This is very helpful. Can you tell me anything more about the tow truck? Any special markings or logos?"

She stared right past him, looking at the wall. "Now, come to think of it, it didn't have any writing on it. Usually, they all have their company names on the sides, but this one didn't have anything—just plain white, I think. It looked old and a bit rusty and real dirty—like you could write your name in the dirt."

Andy nodded. "Did you happen to see the licence plates? Were they South Carolina plates or something different?"

Miranda shook her head. "No, I can't say. I only saw it from the side—never did see the front or the back. It was the kind that you drive the car up onto. What do you call them?" She looked at her husband for help.

"A flatbed tow truck," he said.

"That's it."

Andy wrote that down, then glanced back up at her. "Mrs. Galloway, you've been very helpful. I wonder, do you think you would recognize the man if you were to see him again?"

"I believe I would. I'd recognize that long beard, I think."

"Would you be willing to work with our sketch artist to do a composite sketch?"

"Of course. I could try."

"I'll set that up for first thing tomorrow morning." Andy gave her his card. "In the meantime, if you think of anything else, please give me a call directly."

"Wait," she said, her finger in the air. "When I came out from paying and was walking back to my car, I saw them driving over the ramp getting on the I95 South."

Andy thanked them both for their time. "Well, I best let the two of you get to your supper."

Andy hurried back out to his car. Finally, he had something to go on.

CHAPTER SEVENTEEN

While they waited for Bobby to appear, Michelle and Scotty sat at one of the used dining sets. Michelle took out her phone to check her messages. She hadn't heard back from Nick since texting him with their hotel information. "Oh, dear, I've missed a call from Wendy. I promised her I'd keep her up to date and planned on calling her right after the press conference."

"Go ahead and call her now while we're waiting, Mom. If Bobby comes out before you're done, I'll ask him to start checking their camera videos for Wednesday afternoon."

Michelle hesitated, but Scotty insisted. "You know better than anyone what it's like to be left waiting when you're worrying. Please, just go outside and give her a quick call."

"You're right. Okay, I'll be in the car, where I've got all my notes to refer to." Michelle tried to gather her thoughts. She'd have to ask Wendy about the possibility of offering a reward, and they'd need to decide on an amount. She called the cell number she'd used the day before. Wendy told her it was the best number to reach her at, but it went to voicemail. "Wendy, it's Michelle returning your call. Scotty and I are here in Yemassee, South Carolina where the kids were last seen. Just wanted to touch base. There's no word on them yet, I'm afraid. The police here may have a witness who saw the tow truck that picked them up. We'll know more about that this evening. Call me back when you have a moment."

Michelle went back to the store. Sylvie was busy helping a woman try out a Lazy Boy chair. Scotty was at the back of the store talking to a man, presumably Bobby. They were focused on the desktop computer monitor as Michelle approached. "Find anything?" she asked.

Scotty pulled her head back from the screen. "You can see the tow truck and the driver, but it's too distant to really make out any detail." She turned to the man. "Bobby, this is my mom, Michelle."

"Thank you for looking at this for us. We really appreciate your help." Michelle extended her hand, but Bobby declined the gesture.

"My hands are still smellin' a turpentine and furniture stain. I better not." He raised them in the air to show her how dirty they were. Sawdust fell from his sleeve as he returned his hands to the keyboard. "Right here is the first clip showing them arriving and the young man checking on his tire."

Michelle leaned in, trying to see. Bobby used a pen to point at where they were on the monitor screen. "You're right. It's hard to make out much detail." She wanted Andy to take a look at this too. "Bobby, would you be able to show this to the police as well? I think Officer Solterra will want to go over all of these videos. Maybe they can work with it and try to zoom in on sections."

"It'd be my pleasure." He looked back to the monitor. "Now hang on, there's one more here. Shows them pullin' out onto the road. It's a little closer to the camera. Might even be able to see a part of the licence plate. Right there. D'ya see that?"

Scotty took a photo of the screen with her phone, then zoomed in on the plate. "It's mostly unreadable. It's so dirty."

"It's a Ford," Bobby said. "I recognize the logo on the grill—older model, I'd reckon."

Michelle called Andy's cell phone. He answered right away. "Andy, it's Michelle. Scotty and I are across the road from J.J.'s in the used-furniture store. They've got a surveillance camera and they've got video of the tow truck that took away Riley and Jake."

"I'm on my way. Should be there in about five minutes." He hung up.

Finally, they were getting somewhere. "If only we had this information before the press conference. We could have shown pictures of the tow truck. Somebody must know who owns this thing, especially when we know it's a late-model Ford. If we can get a clearer magnification on that partial plate, that would really help."

Scotty's eyes lit up. "Mom, we can phone that reporter from the newspaper and see if she can add it into her story. We're going to need Andy to arrange another press conference for tomorrow. He might have more information to add as well, if he spoke with that other witness."

Bobby was rummaging in the cabinet below the counter. "Where did that thang-a-majigger go? Gotcha." He straightened up. "This might help." He opened a small container, pulled out two USB sticks and set them down beside the computer. "I'll just copy all the videos onto these USBs so you and the police can each have copies."

"Oh, that would be perfect," Scotty said. "Thank you so much for all of your help."

Michelle reached over and touched the top of his hand. "Bobby, I can't tell you how much we appreciate this. Thank you very much."

CHAPTER EIGHTEEN

"Here they come," Rob announced.

Wendy glanced up at the squadron of brown pelicans soaring fifty feet above them and then at Rob's captivated expression. It never ceased to amaze him when they dove straight down and crashed into the water. His face would light up as he watched them.

A wave brushed over her ankles and rolled back out, revealing a small, glossy seashell. She bent from the waist down to pick it up—her pose known as the 'Sanibel Stoop.' She clutched the cell phone with one hand in her pocket while she examined the seashell with the other. It was a Lightning Whelk with pink and brown stripes.

Rob came over to take a look. She forced a smile. "It's not as big as the ones Jake and Riley collected, but it's a pretty one."

She couldn't get her mind off the fact that they were missing. She'd been sitting with her phone beside her all morning until Rob had finally forced her to come for a short walk along the beach. She knew he was worrying too. Jake and Riley were supposed to have been back in Niagara on Thursday night, and this was Saturday. Something was seriously wrong.

Rob linked his arm through hers. "Wendy, I looked up flights to Hilton Head, and I think maybe we should leave early tomorrow morning. We can't just sit here waiting to hear something—it's making me crazy. We need to be there helping."

Wendy couldn't have agreed more. Now she had a mission. "Let's go home and get packed, and I'll give Michelle a call to let her know we'll be coming tomorrow."

They made their way back from the beach, crossing their decked ramp over the dunes and grasses and headed up their walkway. Their landline phone was ringing inside the lanai as they approached the house. Rob ran ahead and dashed in the door. "Hello," he said, a little out of breath.

Wendy hoped it was Jake and Riley. Rob's back was to her, but he sounded very serious. "Who is this?" he said briskly.

Her heart sank. Maybe it was bad news. There was a pause and then Rob said, "What do you want? Who is this?"

Wendy didn't know if it was an annoying telemarketer or if there was a problem with the phone and Rob couldn't hear whoever it was.

He turned toward her. He was ghostly pale and beads of sweat were forming on his forehead. He fell to his knees, dropped the phone and began clenching his chest.

"Oh my god! Rob! What's happening?" He was on the floor. "Oh my god. Is it your heart?" She quickly pressed the disconnect button on the phone and dialed 911.

• • •

"He friggin' hung up on me. Here I'm trying to tell 'im we got their son, and he friggin' hangs up on me." Beth-Anne whipped the burner phone halfway across the room onto the couch, narrowly missing Caleb. "Here we go to the trouble a gettin' their number, and he friggin' hangs up?"

To be fair, it hadn't been much trouble at all. *Didn't take but a few minutes to get the number.* She wondered if Caleb would have gone through with it, cutting off Jake's finger and all, had she let him. 'Course, none of that was necessary. She'd told him not to pay them no never mind; she'd get the number without resorting to violence.

She prided herself on being so resourceful. She had simply searched for Niagara Ice Wine on the computer, then called the toll-free number listed right there on the website.

After explaining to the receptionist that her call was of an urgent matter regarding Jake Marshall, she was put straight through to his assistant, Sharon. Beth-Anne identified herself as an agent with the South Carolina Search and Rescue team, then asked Sharon for Jake's parents' phone number in Florida.

At first she had been a bit hesitant, so Beth-Anne poured it on a little thicker. "Ma'am, we're gonna need their number right now. I can't go into detail, but the situation here is urgent." That's was all it took. Sharon gave her Rob and Wendy's number.

If there was one thing Beth-Anne was good at, it was playing people. It came to her naturally, like a gift. Back when she worked retail, she was by far the best at upselling. Some of the other sales clerks were too pushy. Beth-Anne knew how to reel them in slowly. Just the right flattery here and there and they'd have to have the more expensive dress. She understood vanity and how looking good meant feeling a whole lot better.

The dumpy-assed manager knew nothing about women's needs. When he looked at women's clothing, he thought about what he wanted to see them in, not what they could see themselves wearing. She could have run that store a whole lot better than him, but she never did get the chance. Even after she got him terminated for inappropriate behaviour, they hired another man to take over. Right then and there, she realized her opportunities were limited.

• • •

The ambulance had raced across the Sanibel Causeway, sirens blaring, headed for HealthPark Medical Centre in Fort Myers. Luckily, it was an early Saturday afternoon and traffic was light. Wendy had sat up front with the driver, where she could be buckled in.

When they'd arrived at the emergency entrance, Rob had been whisked away before she could even see how he was doing. Now, she sat alone in a crowded emergency room waiting area. Across from her, a young boy, about five or six years old, played with a wooden bead maze game, sliding the wooden cubes and spheres up, down and around the twisted, colourful wire tracks.

He reminded her so much of Jake at that age. Jake—she wished she could call him to let him know his father was in the hospital. She lowered her head into her hands and started to cry. All of these horrible things were happening, and she had no control over any of them.

The little boy stopped playing. He pulled out a tissue from the box on the magazine table and brought it to her. "It's okay," he said. "Everything's gonna be okay."

Wendy took the tissue and thanked him. "Yes, you're right. Everything's going to be okay." She looked up and smiled at the boy's mother.

CHAPTER NINETEEN

Michelle and Scotty carried their take-out food into the lobby. Michelle stopped in front the gift shop and convenience store. She handed Scotty her bag and their room card. "I'll grab us a few drinks and meet you up in our room."

She chose an assortment of drinks and snacks and headed over to the cashier. A display rack of socks stood beside the cash desk. A bright orange pair caught her eye, and she immediately thought of her dream on the plane—Riley needed her socks. She picked up a few pairs of the fluffiest ones and put everything down on the counter to pay.

When she came up to their room, she emptied the bag and saw that Scotty had cleared the hotel brochures off the table and set out their food. Michelle grabbed their drinks and came over to join her.

"What's with all the socks you've got there?" Scotty asked.

"They were right there in front of me at the checkout and reminded me of my dream on the plane. I had to buy them; it was one of those things." That was what they called it—"one of those things"—when one of them felt compelled to do something that wasn't exactly rational. Like athletes who perform a specific ritual before a game or people who carry a lucky penny. It was just one of those things.

Once they finished eating, Michelle tried texting Nick again. She hoped the reason he hadn't responded was because he was on a flight, making his way to them. She had no idea how long it might take for him to arrive. First, he'd have to travel from the ship, somewhere out on the north Atlantic, back to the mainland. The Halifax-class frigate had its own helicopter landing pad. Michelle presumed, in an emergency like this, they would fly him on the helicopter to Labrador, or, if they weren't too far north, maybe to St. Johns, Newfoundland. Of course, that would all be weather permitting. If he made it to St. Johns, he could get a flight to Toronto and from Toronto to Savannah.

"Maybe you should try calling Wendy again." Scotty reminded her.

"Yes, I'll do that right now."

This time Wendy answered. She sounded desperate. "Michelle, please give me some good news."

"I wish I could, Wendy."

"Have they found anything yet? Any leads at all?"

"Well, so far we have a lead on the tow truck that picked them up, and there's a witness who saw the driver. The police are updating the media this evening with a description of the driver, the make of the truck and a partial plate number. Then, we hope there will be another full press conference again tomorrow."

"Let's hope—" Wendy's voice cracked. "Something comes of it." She cleared her throat. "Rob and I were planning to come tomorrow. We wanted to be there to help, but I'm afraid that's not going to be possible now."

Michelle didn't understand what Wendy meant. Why wouldn't it be possible? She was certain that Wendy was crying. "Is everything okay, Wendy?"

Wendy's voice cracked again. "No, I'm afraid not. Rob had a heart attack early this afternoon and we're at a hospital in Fort Myers."

"Oh my god, Wendy." Michelle stood up, shocked. "I'm so sorry to hear that. Is he okay?"

"He's stable at the moment; they have him in their coronary care unit and he's being scheduled for emergency bypass surgery." She was crying now. "I haven't been able to speak to him."

Michelle couldn't believe it. She tried to think of something to say. It was beyond words. "Oh, Wendy, is there anything we can do?"

"No, no. I'm just glad you and Scotty are there and doing everything you can to find Jake and Riley. I'm so sorry we can't be there with you to help."

"Oh, please don't worry about us. You need to be with Rob right now. I'm just so sorry to hear this news."

"Thank you. And thank you for everything you and Scotty are doing."

Michelle took a breath and switched the phone to her other hand. She felt a little uneasy about bringing up the subject of a reward. "Wendy, there's something else I wanted to ask you about, and I'm afraid it can't wait. One of the reporters today asked me if we were offering a reward."

Before Michelle could say another word, Wendy blurted, "Yes, Michelle. Whatever you think. We'll look after that—whatever amount you see fit."

"Nick and I will share the cost. I'll talk to the police about it tomorrow and see what they think. I'd like to get some advice on this first."

Michelle was still blown away by the news about Rob. "And Wendy, please give our love to Rob and let us know how he's doing."

"Of course, and you must keep me posted on everything that's happening there. We're worrying every second of every day. I'm sure you know what I mean. Goodbye for now."

Michelle set her phone on the table and sat on the edge of her bed. "Good God! Could things possibly get any worse?"

"What, mom? What did she say? Is something wrong with Mr. Marshall?"

"He's had a heart attack and needs bypass surgery." Michelle's eyes started to fill.

"That's so awful." Scotty gave her a hug. "Jake would be flipping out right now if he knew this was happening."

"I just hope they can get through this." Michelle pulled out a tissue and blew her nose. "My god, it couldn't have happened at a worse time. Imagine, that kind of stress on top of all of this." She shook her head.

"What did she say about offering a reward? Did she think it was a good idea?"

"She told me to go ahead. I don't think she put any thought into it, though. I think she's relying on our judgement." She looked at Scotty. "What do you think? Would that just bring out all the crazies looking for a windfall, or would it give extra encouragement for someone who might know something to come forward?"

"I wish we could talk to dad about it. Has he messaged you back yet?"

"Not yet; he must be on his way." Michelle held Scotty's arm as they sat together on the edge of Michelle's bed. "Scotty, how are we supposed to know what to do? We have no experience in dealing with missing-persons cases, and, as nice as Andy seems, I don't think he's had that much experience either."

"I know. And the captain, who might have more experience, is just sitting back having Andy do everything."

Scotty suddenly stood up. "Mom, we could hire a private investigator—like one of those retired FBI guys that people hire on *Unsolved Mysteries*."

Michelle was intrigued by the idea, but uncertain as to how that would be possible. "I don't know, Scotty. It's definitely something to think about, but how would we go about finding someone like that?"

"I'll see what I can find on the internet." Scotty propped up the pillows on her bed and sat with her legs stretched out on the comforter. She opened her laptop. "Oh, wow. This is good, I guess."

"What?" Michelle asked.

"I started following some of the local news outlets on Twitter and Instagram. They've got all kinds of stuff about Riley and Jake online." She tilted her laptop toward Michelle. "Look."

"Well, that is good. The more exposure the better."

Scotty looked back at the screen. A concerned expression came over her face. "Looks like there's an even bigger story trending. Someone has escaped from a correctional institute near here. They're saying he could be armed and dangerous and not to approach him."

Michelle felt sick. "Oh, no. That's not good. The police will focus on catching him and not on finding Riley and Jake."

Scotty kept reading. "It's the Ridgeview Police that are heading that search. You know what? I remember driving through Ridgeview just before arriving in Yemassee. It really is close by."

Scotty went on to another article. "Oh great. Here's a picture of Captain Charles Adams alongside the Ridgeview police captain. They were together at a press conference yesterday."

"Well, I'm going to call Charles first thing in the morning and make sure his priority is on finding Jake and Riley and not the search for this escaped prisoner."

CHAPTER TWENTY

It had been two days since Zachary had been killed. Riley was a wreck, desperate to get out of there. In the night, something had crawled on her arm and she'd totally flipped out. Jake shone their flashlight all around and couldn't see anything. He shook out her blanket and stayed awake with her for hours. They both listened to the hoot of an owl. Over and over it sang out *Who-cooks-for-you? Who-cooks-for-you?* At least that's what it sounded like.

She had probably cried more in the last few days than she had her entire life. She didn't mean to be such a crybaby. One minute she'd be having a conversation with Jake, the next she'd be fighting back tears. The least little thing would set her off. She needed to get a hold of herself. Today, she thought, she would try to be more resilient.

She got up and stepped over Zachary's dried-up blood stain to check on their supplies. "Jake, we're down to our last few protein bars, and there's only one more package of crackers and cheese." She stared at the packaging, holding it up to a strand of light coming in between the logs. She mumbled, "I doubt it."

"What?" Jake asked.

"It says, 'Made with real cheese.' I don't know about that. Do you think it's real cheese?" She tore open one end of the package. "I'll eat one and see what I think."

Jake stood up. "Riley, don't you think we should ration them? How many crackers are in that package?" He looked at her intently.

"Are you serious right now? Are you actually trying to lay a guilt trip on me for wanting to eat a cracker?" She pulled one out before handing over the package for safekeeping. "Here, take them, Mr. Cracker Police. There were six crackers in this package, and now there are five."

"Okay, fine. That leaves two each for Mack and I, and one more for you to have later. We'll keep the nutrition bars for tomorrow."

They were both losing it. Jake kept pressing his hand against his head. She knew he'd been getting headaches, and yesterday he'd complained of feeling dizzy and nauseous. They didn't know if these were symptoms of a concussion or maybe that combined with a lack of food and sleep.

Riley sat on the edge of the bedframe and looked up at him. "Jake, I'm sorry. Are you okay?"

"Just another headache. I'm okay." He sat next to her. "Riley, I'm sorry too. Do you want another cracker?" He offered her the package and put his other arm around her.

"No, no, thank you. I was only going to have one." She was still hurt that he thought she would have eaten more than her share. "Jake, I'm so scared we're going to die out here. What if they don't come back?"

He squeezed her shoulder and pulled her in close. "They'll be back. And this time, it'll be just the two of them. Mack will do a surprise attack on whichever one stays outside, and you and I will take down whoever comes in." He sounded very confident their plan would work. "We've got this, Riley."

"I know we've got a plan for when they come back, but what if they never come back?"

"Don't worry. They'll be back. They're going to need to know how to get in touch with my parents."

Riley wasn't convinced. "For all we know, maybe they already have. Maybe they found them on Facebook or got their email somehow. Come to think of it, maybe they got their phone number from someone else. Who else knows their number?"

"Just their closest friends and your parents, of course." He hesitated. "Oh, and I guess while we were staying with them, I gave their number to Sharon at the office." Now there was uncertainty in his expression. "Okay, well, it's possible they got their number from someone else," he admitted. "Either way, they'll want to keep us alive at least until they secure the ransom."

Riley tilted her head to one side. "And then what?"

"Riley, don't move a muscle," Jake said firmly. His eyes were fixed on something behind her head.

"Oh, my god. What is it?" She was immediately rattled but tried her best to hold still.

Jake opened his hands and moved slowly around her. He smacked them together in a big clap. "Got it!" he said.

"Jake! What was it?" She turned to try to see.

"Just one of those annoying mosquitos. That's probably what was on your arm last night." He said nonchalantly.

Riley grabbed the flashlight and shone it on the floor. She caught a glimpse of it before his foot covered it. "Oh my god! That wasn't a mosquito. It was a spider!"

Even the squished remains were a substantial size. She jerked her shoulders up to her neck and shook her body vigorously. She started brushing off her clothes and patting down her hair in case there was another one on her.

"It's okay, Riley. There's nothing there. You're okay." He was trying his best to calm her down. She wondered if it might have been venomous—not that it really mattered. Either way, she was totally freaked out.

Mack knocked on their door. "Jake, Riley? Everything okay in there?"

"It was just a spider," Jake answered.

"We're okay. Jake killed it." Riley finally let out a sigh of relief but continued to wiggle her shoulders sporadically.

"We're all good." Jake changed the subject. "Hey, did you hear the owl last night? Riley and I both thought it sounded like it was saying 'Who-cooks-for-you?' over and over. Maybe that's just because we're hungry, eh?"

Mack laughed. "No, you heard it correctly. It's a Barrer Owl. They're well known for saying that. Speaking of wildlife, I checked down near the edge of the marsh where they dumped Zachary's body."

"Yeah?" Jake and Riley waited.

"It's gone. His body isn't there anymore."

"What do you mean?" Riley asked. "He was dead—he couldn't have walked away."

"That's just it. He was probably dragged off by animals or maybe a gator. I don't know."

Jake looked concerned. "That means the police might never find his body."

"I guess not," Mack said. "I was thinking I'd take his clothes, but I'm too late."

"That would have been a good idea," Jake said. "Listen, I've been trying to lift out a floor board using one of the jagged rocks you dropped down. I've been shoving it between the boards, trying to pry it loose. It's stuck down pretty good, though. Wish I had a crowbar or something better to work with."

Mack laughed, then Jake realized what he'd just said. "Yeah, yeah, I know. If only we had a crowbar, we'd just break open the chain on the door."

"Well, Jake, there's not much point in lifting the floorboards. There's a concrete foundation under these cabins. I sure would like a crowbar, though." Mack had tried to pry open the chain using various sticks, but it was no use. The links on the chain were thick. "Maybe tonight I'll try to find my way out of here and see about getting some tools."

"What are you talking about?" Riley asked.

"I'm thinking maybe we've been waiting too long." Mack sounded very serious. "After dark I could try to get help or find a house somewhere and 'borrow' some tools. Maybe I could actually find a crow bar."

Jake went to the door and leaned his hands against it. "No, Mack. We already considered all of the options, and we can't chance that. You're an escaped prisoner—a Black man, wearing an orange jumpsuit. Let's face it—if anybody sees you, they'll shoot first and ask questions later. It's too dangerous. We're better off with you staying here, for all of our sakes."

•••

Over the last few days, they'd become close. Sometimes the three of them would talk for hours at a time, telling each other about their families and what they hoped for in life. Riley loved Mack's deep voice. It had a smoothness and sincerity that seemed to relax her.

One time, he was telling them about his sister and how she participates in all the climate crisis demonstrations, just like Scotty. "Ohhh, Riley," he laughed, "If our sisters ever get together, those oil companies won't know what hit them."

Riley and Jake laughed too. "Then, when they're done there," Riley added, "they'll be signing up together to go out on the *Sea Shepherd* and stop all the whale hunters."

"I'm so proud of them, Riley."

"I know. I am too." Her throat tightened as if she might cry. She missed Scotty so much.

Mack was quiet now too. He was probably hurting as much as she was. Riley wished things hadn't turned out this way for him. He deserved his life back.

She could picture him as a teacher. He'd be amazing and the kids would love him. He was thoughtful and kind—one of those people who genuinely wanted to help others. She was so glad he was there with them. She knew she and Jake would do everything possible to help him if they ever got out of there.

It had been heartbreaking when Mack told them his story—about how he'd ended up in prison. It had all happened after he finished college. He'd moved back home for a short while until he could find a teaching job and get his career started. That was when he met Nancy online. The two had been messaging each other for just over a month. She was a white girl from Ridgeview.

On their first date, Mack borrowed his dad's car and drove from Allendale to meet her in Ridgeview. They met up at a shopping plaza. For some reason, Nancy didn't want him to pick her up at her house. They grabbed a bite to eat at the diner in the plaza and then took his car to the movie theatre.

When they came out from the theatre, a group of white guys started following and harassing them, shouting racist slurs at him. Nancy's brother was one of them. They hurried to Mack's car, keeping quiet, trying not to provoke them. Two of the guys started kicking his dad's car, denting the door. That was when things escalated.

When Mack tried to stop them, they started kicking him. He tried to defend himself and punched one of them in the face, pretty hard. That guy fell to the ground moaning, but the others had him outnumbered. Two grabbed his arms and held him back while the other two began savagely beating him.

When the Ridgeview Police showed up, Mack was initially relieved. All the guys took off except for the one he'd punched, who was still lying on the ground. The officers immediately drew their guns, yelled at Mack to get his hands up, then shoved him against the car. He tried to explain he was the one who had been assaulted, but it didn't look that way with one white guy on the ground. As it turned out, that guy was Nancy's brother.

He accused Mack of starting the fight and of assaulting him. Nancy knelt on the ground next to her brother and backed up his story. Mack couldn't believe it. The officers pulled his hands behind his back and cuffed him. Nancy helped her brother to his feet and stood silently by as he insisted on pressing charges.

From there, things got worse. The cops searched his dad's car and found drugs and an unregistered gun in the console—neither of which had been there before the search. Mack's family couldn't afford a good lawyer, and everything came down to his word against two of Ridgeview's finest, Nancy's brother and Nancy herself.

In court, she broke down crying when Mack's lawyer questioned her, and for a brief moment Mack thought she would tell the truth. Instead, she dried her tears; the whole thing had been such a traumatic event for her. When all was said and done, he was sentenced to ten years at Ridgeview Correctional Centre for possession of drugs, assault with a deadly weapon and assault of a police officer. He'd served five years so far.

Mack now faced an additional ten years for escaping—that is, if they didn't shoot him first.

CHAPTER TWENTY-ONE

It was long past midnight when Andy got home. He went to bed, only to toss and turn, unable to sleep. He couldn't decide what to do about Charles. Should he confront him about the wad of cash he'd seen him pass to J.J., or should he go directly to the new chief and report Charles's unusual behaviour?

The problem was, he had no proof, and he couldn't swear with one-hundred-percent certainty that it was a roll of cash. He'd likely end up looking like a traitor for ratting out another officer—the captain, no less.

Some of the other patrol officers were already giving him the cold shoulder. They were ticked he'd been given this opportunity when he was the newest one there. He could only imagine what they'd say if he accused the captain of some sort of wrongdoing.

Andy kept thinking about it while he showered and dressed. He couldn't wrap his head around what he'd seen. Charles paying off J.J. just didn't make sense.

Andy knew one thing for sure: he didn't want to be taken off this case. He needed to get the lowdown on J.J. somehow and find out what he might be mixed up in. He'd have to keep it under the captain's radar.

His cell phone rang. "Hello." He glanced at his watch. It was already after 7:00 a.m. and he had Miranda Galloway coming in at eight to do the sketch.

"Andy. Charles here." His tone was abrupt. "Michelle's been phoning the station since six and she won't let up." Andy glanced again at his cell phone; he had several missed calls.

"She thinks she's the one running this investigation," Charles said. The line crackled.

"You still there, Charles?"

"Hang on, Andy, I'm just pulling over. I'm down the street from Hector's place, keeping an eye on him. This kid's gonna slip up and do something stupid, I know it. I want you to order a surveillance detail to start immediately."

Why the heck was Charles so intent on making Hector out to be the bad guy. "Okay. I'm headed to the station now."

"When you get there, you need to set up another press conference to give out all the updates. Michelle says we need to include pictures of the tow truck and a description of the driver." Andy heard the irritation in his voice. "Guess she thinks she can do our jobs better than we can." He scoffed.

"I'm on it, captain. I'll call Michelle right now." Andy had already figured on doing a press conference at noon. He'd have the composite sketch of the driver by then and, he hoped, a clearer picture of the tow truck. He'd already called in a tech guy, who was working on enhancing the video clips. If things went really well, they might even have the registration on the tow truck soon.

• • •

After talking on the phone with Charles and then Andy, Michelle and Scotty went down to the lobby to grab some breakfast at the hotel buffet. They planned on meeting Andy at eleven at the police station prior to the noon-hour press conference. Michelle wanted to talk to him ahead of time about offering a cash reward.

Scotty stood at the waffle station waiting for the beep. Michelle sat at a table, staring into space, deep in thought. Earlier, she'd gone through the yellow page directory up in their room. She'd called every tow-truck company on the list, asking each and every one if they had a white, older-model, Ford flatbed. None of them did. Michelle had figured as much. Anybody driving a filthy old tow truck like that probably wouldn't be spending money on a yellow page ad. This guy had to be some sort of independent tow.

"Michelle."

She turned toward the voice and immediately stood up. Tears came out of nowhere as she fell into Nick's arms.

"Dad!" Scotty shouted. She came barreling over to join in the hug.

Michelle wiped away her tears. "Thank god you're here, Nick. Why didn't you call or message me back?"

Scotty cut in. "Dad, I'm so glad you're here."

"My phone died somewhere between St. Johns and Toronto. I didn't pack the charging cord and—"

"Oh, never mind." Michelle hugged him again. "We have so much to tell you."

Nick held them both tight for a moment longer, then asked, "Any word on Riley and Jake?"

"No, nothing, but we've got a lead on the tow truck and the driver who picked them up." She pulled a chair out for him. He looked worn out. He hadn't shaved in days and his eyes were red; bags sat under them. He pushed his duffle bag under the table and they sat down together. Nick took Michelle's hand and held it as she started to fill him in.

Scotty went to retrieve her breakfast and returned with a waffle and three coffees. "Dad, did she tell you about Mr. Marshall?"

Nick looked puzzled.

Scotty enlightened him. "He had a heart attack yesterday and they had to do emergency bypass surgery last night."

"What?" Nick looked shocked. "That's awful."

"Mom, have you heard back from Mrs. Marshall?"

Michelle looked at her watch. "No, I haven't. If she was up all night, perhaps she's resting now. I don't want to disturb her. I'm really hoping no news is good news."

Michelle and Scotty took turns filling Nick in on everything that had happened, then they went back up to their room to let him shower before the press conference.

CHAPTER TWENTY-TWO

Beth-Anne was fed up with the situation. It was taking a month of Sundays. *Why, in the name of the Father, Son and Holy Spirit, weren't the Marshalls answering their damn phone?*

Caleb turned on the television for the local noon-hour newscast. He stood in front of the set. "Look, it's the top story, Beth-Anne."

"How am I supposed to look when you're standing right in front of it?"

He slowly stepped out of her line of sight.

"Just take yer own sweet time." She exhaled forcefully.

The police were holding another press conference. This time the news cameras were set up in front of the police station. A *Breaking News* banner scrolled across the bottom of the screen.

The police started by showing video footage they'd obtained from the used-furniture store across from J.J.'s Service Centre. They repeatedly showed a clip of the tow truck pulling out. They had highlighted the truck with a circle drawn around it. After that, they showed close-ups of the tow truck. They were grainy, but Captain Adams added a verbal description stating the make, model and colour. The news network put up a clear stock photo of an older-model white Ford flatbed tow truck.

Next, they introduced a composite sketch of the driver. "Holy she-it!" Beth-Anne said. "That done looks just like Zachary." She stepped closer, staring at the screen.

"Don't matter none." Caleb was quick to point out. "They won't be finding him anytime soon."

"Shush!" Beth-Anne barked. She turned up the volume as Captain Adams gave the family a moment to speak. Their names scrolled across the bottom of the screen. "Nick and Michelle Barton."

This time, both Riley's parents were there, pleading for help locating their daughter and son-in-law. Then Nick dropped a bombshell: they were offering a fifty-thousand-dollar reward for information that might lead to their recovery. Caleb looked at Beth-Anne, his jaw hanging open.

"Well, that's hardly spit," Beth-Anne declared. "They'll be payin' us a heck-tonne more than that." She raised a finger. "Ya know what, Caleb? Maybe we ought to contact Riley's parents instead of the Marshalls. They're right here in town, and it sounds like they want their daughter back real bad. There ain't no point in us keepin' on callin' Florida. Let Riley's parents sort it all out."

"It don't make no never mind to me, Beth-Anne. In either case, we're gonna need to drop off more food and water if we want to keep them alive. It's been three days."

"What do ya mean, *if?*" *And why was Caleb grinning like that? He had that weird look on his face again, like after he'd shot Zachary. He was enjoying it. Having the power to decide on whether someone should live or die.*

CHAPTER TWENTY-THREE

After the press conference, Andy drove out to J.J.'s Service Centre. He was hoping J.J. wouldn't be working on a Sunday and maybe he could talk with Sarah, the cashier, in private. He pulled up to the pumps, filled the tank and went inside to pay.

There was only one other customer in the store; she'd walked in just ahead of him. Andy waited patiently while the woman wrestled with a decision on a chocolate bar. At first, she picked up a Butterfinger bar, then reluctantly put it back. She stepped forward to the cash desk, then suddenly stepped back. This time, she selected a Snickers. For a full twenty seconds, she held it lovingly in her hand before returning it to the shelf. Finally, she chose the dark-chocolate KitKat.

Andy chuckled as he approached the cash desk next. Sarah smiled at him. "Which one would you have picked, Andy?"

"Oh, I would have taken the Butterfinger." He was still smiling. "And you?"

"Definitely the Butterfinger."

Andy thought she had such a nice smile. He'd liked Sarah from the first time they'd met. That was in high school, nearly a decade ago. He'd never gotten the nerve to ask her out. Now, so much time had gone by, it would probably seem weird. Andy set a Butterfinger bar on the counter. "Sold."

"Well, I hope you're planning to break off a small piece for me," she said jokingly. She scanned the barcode. "Listen, Andy, on a more serious note, have you had any luck finding the missing couple yet? Was Mrs. Galloway able to help?"

"Mrs. Galloway was very helpful, and we sure hope to find them soon." He got out his wallet to pay. "Thank you again, Sarah, for your help identifying her."

"Oh, sure, no problem." She punched something into her screen. "With the chocolate bar, that comes to $41.89."

Andy tapped his credit card on the machine. "Listen, Sarah, I was wondering if I could ask you a few more questions?"

"Well, all right, I suppose. Don't know that I'd be of any help, though."

"I'm hoping we can keep this conversation just between you and me. Is that okay?"

She looked puzzled. "I guess so."

"Well, I was wondering what you might know about Charles. I mean Captain Adams."

"You're asking me? I don't know much about him at all, other than the rumours about him and his ex-wife. Apparently, she has to chase him down each month for the alimony payments."

"How do you know that?" Andy asked.

"Well, kinda through the grape vine." She shrugged her shoulders. "D'ya know Ava at the hair salon? I heard it from her."

Andy was aware of the financial battle between Charles and his ex. He'd heard it firsthand from Charles, who often complained about having to pay her. It was really no surprise he was making her chase him down for money. "What about Charles and J.J.? Would you describe them as friends?"

"Mmmm. Not really sure if I'd say friends." Sarah seemed hesitant. "I don't know if it's right, that I should be saying anything about J.J., or his relationship with Charles."

She was obviously starting to feel uncomfortable. "Sarah, I don't mean to put you on the spot."

She looked around as if she were checking to be sure no one could hear them. She lowered her voice. "Charles comes in a few times a week, and he and J.J. have meetings in the back office. I don't get the impression that they're friends though—sometimes J.J. seems pretty prickly after they're done."

"Meetings?" Andy was surprised. "Do you know what kind of meetings?"

"Business, I figure. They go to J.J.'s office and talk there. Same as when other businessmen come and meet with J.J."

"So, you don't know any specifics?"

"If I had to guess, I'd say something to do with the local chamber of commerce. Sometimes the director of the chamber comes in, too."

Andy thought this sounded unusual. "Do you recall if there were any meetings on Wednesday?"

Sarah bit her lip while she thought back. "Just the Captain. He was here until after the storm passed through." She looked out the window. A car had pulled up to the pumps outside. Sarah tapped the activation button on her screen.

Andy tried to hide his astonishment. "So, the Captain was here with J.J. when the Marshalls were waiting for their tow truck?"

"I suppose he was, but he left long before they got picked up."

Charles hadn't mentioned anything about being there the day the Marshalls went missing.

He decided not to press Sarah for anything more. She looked like she might regret having said anything. "Well, I'd best let you get back to work."

"Andy, hold on a sec. I want you to know that J.J. is a really nice man. If you think he might be involved somehow with the missing couple, you're barking up the wrong tree."

"No, Sarah. I'm not suggesting that at all. Just asking some questions, that's all, trying to get things straight in my head. You've been very helpful, and let's keep this visit between us. I wouldn't want to hurt anyone's feelings if they thought I was asking questions about them." He smiled at her and she nodded in agreement. "Thanks again, Sarah. Have a good day."

She called after him. "Wait, Andy. You forgot your Butterfinger bar."

"It's for you." He smiled at her again as he went out the door.

• • •

By the time Andy got back to the station, Charles had already organized a warrant and backup officers. Two different people had called in to identify the man in the sketch. Both identified him as Zachary Duncan, and they both wanted the fifty-thousand-dollar reward.

Gravel spun out from Charles's wheels as he peeled out of the parking lot. Andy followed in his car, and two other officers followed him in a cruiser. They sped to the far end of town, lights flashing, across the rural back roads leading to Zachary's house.

As they approached, Andy noted the flatbed tow truck parked right there, next to the house. A rush of adrenaline pulsed through his body. His muscles were tensing up, and he felt jittery, like he might jump out of his skin. If Riley and Jake were inside, he was ready to break down doors to save them.

Two officers covered the front as Andy and Charles went around back. Andy busted in through the back door. "Police!" He and Charles moved through each room with their guns drawn. Nobody was there, and there was no sign of a struggle.

Once the other officers came in, Andy stepped outside for a few minutes to unwind and get some air. He walked over to the tow truck. Being sure not to touch anything, he looked in through the side window before pulling out his phone and opening the screenshot Scotty had sent him. It was the picture she'd saved from Riley's Snapchat message showing the inside of the truck. This was it, all right. The same Hula dancer bobblehead on the filthy dash. The same overflowing ashtray hanging out on an angle.

The two other officers came out and started taping off the area. "Where's Charles?" he asked one of them. The officer pointed back at the house.

The idea that Charles was in the house alone bothered Andy. He hurried back in through the front door. There was a noise coming from the bedroom. Andy went down the hallway quietly and stood at the edge of the doorway. Charles's back was to him. He was in front of the dresser with the top drawer pulled open, lifting out cash and setting it on top of the dresser. "What's going on here captain?"

Charles didn't flinch. "Looks like some of this cash is Canadian. I'm gonna go out on a limb and say it probably belonged to Jake and Riley Marshall. Grab me one of those evidence bags there, will ya." He picked up the cash in his gloved hand and tucked it inside the bag that Andy held open.

Andy wondered what would have happened to that cash if he hadn't walked in just then. Would Charles have pocketed the money? Even worse, what if there were other evidence Charles had already eliminated? Andy couldn't stand it anymore. This case was too important. Lives were at risk. His mind was made up—he'd talk to the new chief of police as soon as he got back to the station.

CHAPTER TWENTY-FOUR

The situation was surreal. Wendy stood beside Rob's ICU hospital bed, holding his hand. Tubes and hoses everywhere—so many that she couldn't bring herself to look at what they were connected to.

She tried to focus on Rob's face. His beautiful hazel eyes were closed. The thin crinkles at the corners of his eyes looked subdued. She pictured him smiling. When Rob smiled, those creases would deepen and smile with him. He looked peaceful, she thought, despite the visual chaos and noise coming from the monitors and various pieces of equipment. A long strip of tape on the bridge of his nose secured a transparent tube going in his nostril. A larger tube-like contraption covered his mouth, branching out into two extendable hoses. He was breathing through a mechanical ventilator. Karen, the ICU nurse, had prepared Wendy ahead of time by telling her about the ventilator, but it was difficult to see nonetheless. She cupped her free hand over her mouth. She tried to hold back her tears and pull herself together.

Karen was coming back into the room. Her white rubbery shoes made little squeaking noises as the soles gripped and released the resin flooring. Wendy watched her closely as she checked on Rob's monitors and made notes on a clipboard. Her expression didn't offer any clues as to his condition.

She looked at Wendy. "Would you like me to pull over a chair for you, Mrs. Marshall?"

"Yes, thank you so much. I'm about ready to drop." Wendy had been awake most of the night and desperately needed some rest. "I wish there was something I could do for him. I feel so useless."

"There you go, Mrs. Marshall." Karen set the chair next to the bed.

"You're so kind. Thank you." Wendy eased herself down onto the chair and once again held Rob's hand.

The nurse seemed like a very nice person. Wendy had liked her straight off and, more importantly, she trusted her.

"You must be exhausted," Karen said. "Why don't you go home for a little while and get some rest, then come back this afternoon. My shift runs until three p.m., and I promise I'll watch him closely. If there's any change at all, I'll call you."

Wendy pondered the idea. She was no good to him right now anyways. Perhaps it would be best if she went home for a few hours. Even so, she hated to leave him alone and could hardly bring herself to let go of his hand. Finally, she leaned over and kissed his forehead gently. "I'll be back in a few hours," she said quietly. "I love you so much." She thanked the nurse again and went down to the main doors to get a cab.

Leaving the hospital in a cab reminded her of when Jake had been in the hospital as a boy. He'd had appendicitis. She and Rob had stayed up all night with him. The morning after his surgery, Wendy took a cab home to get some sleep. Rob stayed with Jake; a few hours later, they traded off and Rob went home to rest.

They were a close family. 'The three amigos,' Jake used to call them. If only he could be here now. Wendy kept praying for him and Riley, then praying for Rob, back and forth, back and forth. *Sometimes in life, that's all you can do.*

At home, she set her alarm for 2:00 p.m. That would give her a few hours to sleep. She set her tea beside her on the coffee table and curled up on the couch, drifting off before the tea had cooled.

• • •

It was just before 1:55 p.m. when Wendy's phone rang. *Oh, god.* She was almost afraid to answer it. Was Rob okay? *I should have stayed at the hospital with him.* She pressed the button to accept the call.

"Mrs. Marshall?" a woman asked.

"Yes, yes, this is Wendy Marshall."

"It's Karen from the ICU at HealthPark Medical

Centre." Before Wendy could get a word out, Karen gave her the good news. "Rob's doing very well. The doctor says they'll likely remove the ventilator in a few hours."

"Oh, thank God. I'll be there as soon as I can. Thank you for calling, Karen."

CHAPTER TWENTY-FIVE

After the press conference wrapped up, they got into Michelle's rental car. Nick sat in the passenger seat. "I think the press conference went well," he said.

"Now what?" Scotty asked from the back.

"Now we wait and see if the police get any leads," Nick said optimistically.

Michelle glanced at Scotty in the rear-view mirror. Her daughter was on the verge of tears. "Scotty, we're going to find them—we're not leaving until we do."

Her reassuring words didn't help. Scotty's big blue eyes filled and droplets fell to her lap as she lowered her head. Nick handed her a tissue from the box up front. Michelle was tearing up too and pulled the car off to the side of the road. "I just need a minute."

"I'm sorry, Mom, if I got you started again."

"It's not your fault, Scotty. I've been holding this in for hours. These press conferences have a way of maxing out my emotions." Nick handed her a tissue too. She sighed and dabbed it gently under her eyes. "Part of me wants to run away and drown in my sorrows—another part is determined not to give up hope and spend every waking minute searching for them."

"Let's try to stick with the determined part," Nick said. "We all need to try and stay hopeful."

Michelle finished drying her tears and blew her nose. "You're right. It's just so hard not knowing where they are or what's happening to them."

Nick leaned over and caressed her cheek. His hand felt warm and comforting. He brushed away a remaining tear with his thumb and gave her a sympathetic smile. "We have to believe they're okay and that we're going to find them."

Michelle nodded. "I know." She took a deep breath. "Okay, are we all ready to go?"

Nick pointed to a drive-through up ahead. "How about we grab a bite to eat? Then I'd like to go and take a look around at J.J.'s Service Centre, where they were last seen."

"Sure, it's not too far from here. Okay with you, Scotty?"

"Sounds good to me."

• • •

They arrived at J.J.'s shortly after Andy had left. Michelle parked at the side next to the air pump. "Dad, this is right where Jake and Riley were parked while they were waiting for the tow."

Nick's jaw tensed and his eye brows furrowed. Michelle remembered how distressed she'd felt when she and Scotty had first arrived here. It was difficult knowing this was the last place they had been seen. Now she was parked right in the same spot where Riley and Jake were taken.

Michelle and Scotty stayed in the car while Nick got out to look around. He walked near the gas pumps and checked out the security cameras. He came back to Michelle's open window. "So, it's just the two security cameras there?" He pointed at them.

"The one facing this way wasn't working. They only have video from the camera above the door, facing the pumps."

"And that's how they found Miranda Galloway—the woman who helped with the police sketch of the tow-truck driver?"

"Right," Michelle said. "Andy re-examined the footage, focussing on the time when Hector was emptying the garbage. That was when the tow truck had arrived."

Scotty took over. "Hector said he didn't see the driver, but Andy realized two other cars had pulled in around that same time. One was from out of state and the other was—"

"Miranda Galloway," Nick filled in. "Scotty, is that the video you have a copy of?"

"No, Andy has that. I've got a copy of the video from that used-furniture store over there." She pointed across the road. "I can show it to you on my laptop back at the hotel if you want."

"Sure." He bent down a little lower to the open window, resting his hand against it. "I'm just trying to think… how many people would have known they were sitting here waiting for a tow? Did Andy look at all the video prior to the tow truck arriving?"

"What are you thinking, Nick?" Michelle asked.

"I'm thinking someone was here who knew they were stranded and waiting for a tow. Next thing you know, this other tow truck shows up and takes them away. I'm thinking that someone who was here must have been involved in this."

"Dad, that could be anyone. Or it could have been somebody driving by and saw they had a flat. Or someone staying at that crap-hole motel around the bend."

"True, but I think the police should thoroughly check out everybody that was here."

"I'm sure Andy's done that. We know for certain they questioned Hector. As a matter of fact, I'd say they questioned him a little too harshly."

"That's for sure." Scotty rolled her eyes. "It was more like bullying than questioning."

"Then, there's Sarah, the cashier. I can't believe she would be involved," Michelle said. "She's been helping us. Plus, she's the one who identified Miranda Galloway. I doubt she'd be helping if she had anything to do with it."

Scotty leaned forward between the front seats. "So, that only leaves J.J., and he was so kind to us the day we arrived. He was legitimately concerned for their well-being. He even offered us free drinks from the store. Dad, he totally wants to help any way he can."

"Offering free drinks hardly means he's innocent." Nick took his hand off the car and straightened up. He let out a loud sigh.

"Nick, I think Scotty's right about J.J.," Michelle added. "Plus, I'm pretty sure the captain and Andy had talked to him before we even arrived. Andy told us that J.J. fully cooperated and let them go through all the surveillance videos."

Nick shrugged. "And conveniently, the one camera wasn't working. I have to wonder if that's true. I don't mean to be sceptical, but did Andy and Charles check that out for themselves? Did they actually look and see? Or did they just take J.J.'s word for it?"

"Well, let's make a list of questions for Andy and see what he says." Michelle took out her note pad and pen and started to write.

CHAPTER TWENTY-SIX

It was getting on to three o'clock by the time they pulled into the hotel. As they walked toward the entrance, Michelle checked her phone. "Still no word from Wendy. I'm really worried about Rob."

"Mom, how about, while I show dad the videos, you give Wendy a call."

Nick strode a few steps ahead and opened the door. As they entered the lobby, the young girl at the front desk waved Michelle over. "Ma'am, there's a package that's been left here for you."

"Oh?" Michelle lifted the parcel. It was a brown kraft envelope. One of the thick ones, lined with bubble wrap. Michelle squeezed it in her hands, wondering what it could be.

"Who's it from?" Nick asked.

"I don't know. There's no return address." She gave the package a puzzled look.

Scotty held the elevator door open and they all got in. The elevator started its ascent. Michelle ripped open the top of the envelope and looked inside. "What on earth?" She pulled out a cell phone. It had a note wrapped up with it. "Oh, my god!"

She held it up for Nick and Scotty to see.

NO POLICE! WILL CALL AT 5:00 P.M. WITH INSTRUCTIONS. LOOK AT PHOTO ON PHONE.

"What?!" Scotty exclaimed. The elevator door opened at their floor.

Nick grabbed the envelope. "I'm going back to the lobby to try to find out who delivered this." He jabbed at the 'L' button on the elevator panel. "I'll meet you back in the room in a few minutes."

Michelle and Scotty walked down the hallway to their room. Michelle's hand was shaking so badly, she couldn't hold the key-card up to the scanner. Scotty got the door and they went inside.

Michelle used both hands to hold the phone steady, then pressed her thumb down on the photo icon to open the picture gallery. "No, no, no." She fell to her knees.

"Mom? Oh, Mom, please, let me see. What is it?"

Michelle turned the screen toward her. Scotty's jaw went slack and her red, watery eyes brimmed over. "Oh, Riley."

Michelle reached for her purse on the floor and pulled out her phone. "I better call Andy right away."

"No, mom!" Scotty knelt down beside her. "It said no police. Let's wait and see what Dad thinks."

A minute later Nick opened the door. He nearly tripped over them as he came barreling in. Michelle handed the phone to him. "Nick, what are we going to do?"

He stared at the screen. His face went hollow. Michelle didn't recognize that expression. He set the phone down, sat down and put his face into his hands.

Michelle stood and gave Scotty a hand up. They sat on either side of him. "Are you okay?" Michelle asked, putting her arm around him.

He cleared his throat and straightened up. "Yeah. Yeah, I'm okay. You?"

"We're okay. What did they say downstairs? Did anyone see who dropped this off?"

"No." He got up. "Apparently it was just left there on the counter. Nobody saw who dropped it off, and they don't have any security cameras."

"What are we going to do, Dad? Should we phone the police? The note says no police."

Michelle's phone started ringing. She looked at the screen. "It's Andy."

Nick shook his head. "Don't say anything about this yet."

She put Andy on speaker. "Hello."

"Michelle, it's Andy. I've got an update." She held her breath. "We've identified the tow-truck driver. His name is Zachary Duncan. We searched his house this afternoon; I'm just leaving there now."

"What about Riley and Jake?" she asked desperately.

"No sign of them or this Zachary fella—nobody was home. His tow truck was left in plain sight, parked right on his property. No sign of Jake's car."

Nick leaned toward the phone. "Andy, this is Nick. Michelle has you on speaker. You think this Zachary Duncan took them somewhere else in another vehicle?"

"Possibly, or he may have dropped them somewhere else first. The only other vehicle registered in Zachary's name is a Nissan Rogue, and that was left on his property too."

"So, what happens now?" Michelle asked.

"We find out everything we can about Zachary—who his friends are, where he goes, where he works—and follow up with the two people who called in to identify him. Maybe someone knows something more. We're on top of this, Michelle. I just wanted to keep you apprised of the situation."

Michelle looked at Nick and pointed to the burner phone and note lying on the bed. She mouthed, "Should I tell him?"

Nick shook his head. "Okay, Andy," she said. "Thank you for calling. Please let us know the second you find out anything else."

CHAPTER TWENTY-SEVEN

"Caleb, get yer ass in here! It's after five," she shouted. Beth-Anne had everything set up at the kitchen table, ready for Caleb to make the call. *I swear, if I left things up to him, nothing would ever get done.*

He ambled in and dragged his chair back from the table. It scraped along the tile like nails on a chalkboard. The back legs were missing the little felt pads on the bottom. Seemingly unaware, he scraped it some more as he got settled in. "I'm ready when you are, Beth-Anne." He pushed up his sleeves. "Ya got the number?"

"Course I got the friggn' number. Whataya thank?" She turned the paper toward him. "Can ya follow this?" Sometimes she wondered what she'd ever seen in him.

He looked it over. "Thought we decided on five million. This here says ten."

"Well, now it's gonna be five more. That's the price they pay for not taking our call the first time." She flung her hair back over her shoulders. "They can afford it."

Caleb started keying in the number. He had a serious look about him. Beth-Anne was excited. It felt more lifelike than when they'd called the Marshalls. She guessed seeing Riley's family on the news accounted for that. She could almost picture them. Riley's mama would have that pathetic look on her face.

Caleb hit the connect button, and her heart nearly skipped a beat. Someone picked up on the first ring.

"Hello." Nick's voice cut through. "Where's my daughter?"

Caleb stuck to the script. "No police!" he instructed. "If you tell the police, your daughter's dead. Got it?"

"We didn't tell the police." he said. "Please, where are Riley and Jake? We need to know if they're okay."

Beth-Anne thought he was being truthful about not calling the police, but it was hard to be sure. He sounded so pitifully desperate, she might have misconstrued.

"Not so fast," Caleb said. "Not until we get the money. Five million in unmarked bills—cash—tomorrow."

Beth-Anne kicked him under the table and jammed her finger onto the page where she'd changed it to ten. He ignored her.

Nick started talking again. "How do I get five million by tomorrow? We don't have that kind of money."

The wife's voice suddenly came over the line. She sounded distraught. "We'll get the money somehow! Please don't hurt them."

"That's more like it." Caleb's mouth turned up at the corners. He was loving the power he had over them.

"How do we know they're still alive?" Nick demanded.

"You'll have to trust me now, won't ya." He winked at Beth-Anne. "You go on and get the money together and have it ready by three o'clock tomorrow. I'll call then with instructions." Caleb hung up.

"What the hell, Caleb! What are you all smirkin' about? I said ten million."

He stuck his finger in her face. "Don't be gettin' yer feathers ruffled. They'll be lucky to gather up five by tomorrow afternoon—the banks 'round here ain't got that kind a cash on hand. These folks are gonna need to go to Savannah or Hilton Head to muster up that much."

Beth-Anne swatted his finger away. She hated it when he tried to get the upper hand on things. "Fine, then."

Caleb was still smirking. "When we get the money, are we gonna tell them where they're at?" He seemed to be leaving that aspect of it entirely up to her.

"Maybe in a few days, once we're established elsewhere. Guess we ought to take them more food and water and such."

Caleb picked her up and swung her around. "Better get your bikini packed. We'll be sittin' on a beach in the Florida Keys real soon." He was grinning like a possum eating a sweet potato.

"Don't be actin' all enthusiastic just yet, Caleb. We've still got some figuring to do, sorting out the logistics of it and all. Like, where are they gonna drop off the money?"

She needed to do some figuring of her own, too. Getting her hands on that much money—she could be living life however she chose. She sure wouldn't need Caleb anymore.

• • •

"Did you get it all Scotty?" Nick asked, getting up from their table.

"Yeah." She played it back for him. She'd recorded the call with her phone's voice memo app.

"Good job. Now, if we decide to tell the police, we can at least give them audio of the call." He started pacing back and forth in front of the dresser.

Michelle stood up. "What are we going to do, Nick? We need help. I think we should have told Andy. Or maybe we should hire a professional investigator, like Scotty suggested earlier."

"No," he said. "Right now, we need to keep our options open."

He was talking like *he* knew best, Michelle thought.

"We should be ready to go ahead with their instructions and get the ransom money arranged. Michelle, we really don't have any other choice right now."

She didn't appreciate the way he was talking to her. It seemed as though he was making this decision by himself. *Suddenly, now, he's going to call the shots?*

Michelle had raised both daughters without much help from him. While he was out of town or working late, she'd made all the decisions. "Well, this isn't entirely up to you, Nick."

He was taken aback. "So, you're willing to risk their lives?" he snapped.

"No!" She turned away. "That's not fair."

"Stop it!" Scotty shouted. Tears ran down her face.

"Oh, Scotty, I'm so sorry," Michelle said contritely.

Nick held his arms open to both of them. "I'm sorry too," he said softly as Scotty leaned into his arms. "You're right, Michelle. We should think this through together. I'm sorry."

His face looked tired and haggard. She joined in the hug and apologized again. "Arguing is the last thing we should be doing right now."

"It's okay." Scotty gave them a reprieve. "Dad, you haven't slept since I don't know when and Mom, you've been looking after everything. We're all under enormous stress."

Michelle sat on the bed. "Well, I don't know what the answer is, and we don't have five million dollars anyways."

"The Marshall's do and obviously that's why Jake and Riley were taken."

"That's true, Scotty," Michelle said, "But what if turning over the ransom note and phone to the police could help them find the kidnappers? There might be clues here."

Scotty picked up the phone. "Yeah, I bet for sure they'd check this for finger prints, and the note too."

"Probably the only prints, are ours," Nick said. "The kidnappers wouldn't be that stupid."

"Dad, what if the police could look at the photo of them in the trunk and try to determine the make of the vehicle?"

"Let me take another look." He spread his fingers apart on the screen, expanding the photo. "I don't see anything here that might offer a clue as to what type of vehicle it is."

His face suddenly crumpled and he dropped the phone on the bed. "God! I want to kill these fucking bastards!" He walked over to the window.

"Nick?" Michelle picked up the phone and went to him.

"I'm sorry," he whispered, shaking his head. "I just feel so goddamned helpless."

Michelle looked at the photo. Enlarged like this, she could see the expression on Riley's face—the fear in her eyes. Her insides felt like they were being twisted in knots.

"Hey, what if the police can find out where the phone was purchased; that might offer a clue," Scotty suggested. "Maybe they can figure out who bought it."

"I don't know," Nick said, "but I'm thinking if we tell the police we've had a ransom call, they might bring in the FBI."

Michelle was confused. "Are you saying we should tell the police, now?"

"No, I'm thinking that if a bunch of FBI agents were suddenly brought in, it would be pretty obvious that we told police about the ransom." He rubbed his fingertips against his forehead. "Michelle, what if these bastards follow through on their threat?"

"So, we're right back where we started." Michelle had nothing more to say. They were talking in circles.

"Can both of you please just stop for a minute? It's not just Riley we're talking about—Jake's life is at stake too. You need to tell the Marshalls about this. It's their decision as well."

"You're right, Scotty. We need to let them know what's happening and make a decision together."

"I'll phone Wendy," Nick said. "She'll need to get us the money right away if we decide to pay the ransom. What's her number?"

CHAPTER TWENTY-EIGHT

Andy was waiting outside the chief's office. His palms were sweating and he was starting to second-guess his decision. The door opened, and the new chief of police asked him to come in.

The room looked a lot different from how it did before. It resembled a regular office now. The large, intimidating portrait from behind the desk had been removed. General Wade Hampton III had finally left the building. This was a good sign.

"Chief O'Brien. I'm sorry to bother you, sir."

"No bother at all, Andy. It's a pleasure to meet you. What can I do for you?" He reached out to shake Andy's hand. If he noticed it was clammy, he didn't let on. "Why don't you have a seat there, Andy." He motioned to the two chairs in front of his desk.

"Thank you, sir." Andy sat down across from him, feeling as though he couldn't catch his breath.

"How's the case coming along? I hear things were moving quickly this afternoon with leads coming in." He folded his hands on top of his desk. "Captain Adams tells me you're working very hard."

A compliment from Charles to the Chief? Andy was thrown off for a second but forced himself to get to the point. "I'm actually here about Captain Adams. There's a matter I'd like to discuss with you. I'm concerned about something I saw, and I don't quite know what the protocol is." Andy rubbed his palms against his pants.

"Well, Andy, why don't you tell me about it, and then we'll decide on the protocol."

This was it. The moment had come. There was no turning back. "I saw Charles handing a large roll of cash to J.J., the owner of J.J.'s Service Centre. It happened yesterday, right after the press conference."

Chief O'Brien didn't respond. He kept his face neutral, and there was no body language to interpret. He sat perfectly still, looking at Andy, who suddenly had major regrets. Had he made the wrong decision to come forward?

"And you think this might be somehow related to the Marshall case?"

"I can't help but suspect that, yes sir."

"Did you speak with Captain Adams directly about this?"

"No, sir. I didn't know what to do."

"Is there anything else, Andy?"

Andy didn't know how to read him. It felt like the chief was shutting him down. He'd asked if there was anything else, but Andy took it as "We're done." He should have just asked Charles about it. "No, sir. Nothing else."

"Well, it sounds to me like you're making a very serious allegation against the captain of our police force. Do you realize that?"

Andy couldn't hold eye contact. He looked down. "Yes, sir. I hope I've done the right thing."

The chief stood up. The meeting was over. "Thank you for bringing this to my attention, Andy. I know it must have been a difficult thing to do."

"Yes, extremely difficult."

"Rest assured Andy, I take this sort of thing very seriously. Leave it with me."

Chief O'Brien walked to the door and held it open for him.

Andy was dismayed. He walked down the hall back to his desk. *Leave it with him? What does that mean? Is the chief going to tell Charles what I said?* Everything was suddenly a big mess, and he wished he hadn't reported anything. Things could get awkward if Charles found out about it. He could probably kiss his job goodbye.

"Andy." Jan waved him over. She held up a pink message slip. "Detective Ben Jorden called from the Niagara Falls Police Department. They have a lead regarding the Marshall couple. He asked for Charles, but he's out— he's gone back to question the two fellas who identified Zachery Duncan to see what else they might know."

Andy took the slip and hurried back to his desk to make the call. Ben picked up right away.

"As you can guess, Andy, the case has been all over the news here too. It's of particular interest, since the Marshalls are fairly well known in Niagara."

Andy listened intently as Ben got straight to the point. "We got a lead from a family in Hamilton, a city not far from Niagara. This family, the Taylors, were driving home from Florida and passed through South Carolina the day Riley and Jake went missing. They remembered seeing a tow truck carrying a sports car with Ontario custom plates. Anyway, they heard on the news that the Marshalls went missing in South Carolina and saw the video clip with Jake's car up on the flatbed. They swear it was the same one."

"Wow, okay. Where and when did they see it?" Andy pulled up a road map on his computer screen.

"Just after four p.m. on Wednesday, February twenty-third. The Taylors said they'd accidentally gotten off the I95 at Coosawatchie, made a couple of wrong turns and ended up on some access road. That's where they saw the flatbed tow truck carrying Jake's car. It was turning southeast onto some back road. They pinpointed the location for us on Google Maps. I'm emailing it to you now."

With Ben still on the line, Andy opened the map. The location was in a remote area. Not much of anything there, and it was nowhere near Zachary's house. "Did they see if the Marshalls were in the tow truck, or just the driver?"

"Unfortunately, they only noticed the silver sports car on the flat bed and the Ontario custom plates."

"Thanks so much for passing along the tip. We'll keep in touch."

He thought about the timing. It made sense. The tow truck picked them up at J.J.'s at approximately 3:45 p.m. and they were seen by the Taylor family at this location just after four. Timing wise that was about right. Plus, Miranda Galloway had said they got on the southbound ramp to the I95.

He looked at the map again, then printed out four copies, taking one over to Jan's desk. "Jan, I'm wondering if you can do a property search?" He laid the map out in front of them. "I'm looking at this area." He drew a large circle around the spot where the tow truck had been seen. "See if you can find out the land registrations for this entire sector."

"That's a big region, Andy, and the registry office is closed. I'll need to pull a few strings. It might take a while, but I'm on it."

"Thanks, Jan." He looked at his watch. There was only an hour of daylight left. It would be useless to start searching out there at night. The more he thought about it, the more he doubted they'd be in that area. On the satellite map, he couldn't see any houses or buildings. In fact, there was virtually nothing to be seen; just miles and miles of forested wetlands. The tow truck could have been headed anywhere when the Taylor family spotted it. Either way, he'd get the volunteers to coordinate a search of the area first thing in the morning.

CHAPTER TWENTY-NINE

Riley wrapped the blanket around her feet and pulled the rest up over her legs. It was chilly in the evenings, and soon the cabin would be pitch-black. Jake sat across from her on the opposite bedframe.

"Riley, I've been thinking a lot about our families and how worried they must be."

"Me, too. I keep thinking about what they must be going through. They're probably wondering if we're even alive." She couldn't see his outline anymore. "Jake?"

He got up and sat beside her. "I'm here."

She held on to him. "Nighttime is the worst. It's so dark."

"Do you want me to turn on the flashlight for a bit?"

She pulled him back as he started to get up. "No, we'd better save the batteries for when we really need it. Just stay here beside me?"

"There's nowhere else I'd rather be than next to you." He smiled at her. "I know it sounds cheesy, but I mean it, Riley. I'd rather be here with you, than with anyone else anywhere."

"I love you, too." Riley leaned into him. "When we get out of here, I'm never going to be in the dark again. I'm going to buy nightlights for every room in our house."

"While you're doing that, I'm going to stretch out in our soft, cozy bed and maybe never get out." They both laughed.

"Well, maybe to eat." She added. "I'll make us your favourite pasta and we'll have wine—"

"Oh, that crab alfredo thing with the white wine sauce! You're killing me. I'm practically drooling. What's for dessert?"

"How about tiramisu, and after that we'll eat another meal."

"And the whole family will be there. My mom and dad, your mom and dad, Scotty, your grandparents—all of us together." Jake leaned his head against hers. "Riley, that's all that matters to me."

"I know." Over the last few days, she'd been thinking a lot about family. She was starting to rethink her priorities in life. Maybe opening another catering location wasn't top of the list. The way she felt now, starting a family seemed more important, but they hadn't talked about it in years. Not since that awful argument four years ago.

They'd only been married a matter of weeks. "I'm hoping our first child will be a girl," Jake had said one morning. "A sweet little rambunctious one, just like you."

"What?" She recalled how stunned she'd been in that moment. She wasn't ready to start a family, and his casual comment had taken her completely by surprise. "Jake, my business is just taking off, and, down the road, I want to expand and start up more locations."

"I know, but we really don't need your income," he'd said.

She'd nearly lost her mind. "You're suggesting that we put my career on hold because we don't need my income?" Before he could get another word out, she'd cut him off. "If that's what you think, you don't know me at all."

He'd tried to explain. "That's not what I meant. I just know how much you love children, and I thought—"

It was too late. She was furious that he'd discounted her career over his. Becoming a chef had never been about an income source. It was part of her identity. She stormed out of the room before he could tell her she was overreacting. Later, after she'd calmed down and Jake had apologized for his stupid comment, they'd dropped the subject and hadn't discussed it since.

Right now, family was what she longed for. Without that, nothing else had much meaning. She thought about Mack and his family. "What about Mack? There's got to be a way to get him back with his family, too."

"We won't give up until he is," Jake said.

Riley knew he meant that, and so did she. As a matter of fact, she wanted more than just getting Mack released.

She wanted the lying, corrupt cops to pay for what they'd done. She wanted them fired, criminally charged and sued for damages. And ditto for that mendacious little Nancy bitch and her racist brother. Her stomach started growling.

"Was that yours or mine?" Jake asked.

"Mine. It thinks if it growls loudly enough, I'll feed it." She rubbed her hand across her abdomen. "Jake, in all seriousness, I don't know how long we can all survive out here. It's been three days since they were last here. We're out of food, and there's only enough water for another day or two."

"I know, but I feel certain that they'll be back soon. After all, they didn't know we'd be sharing the food with another person. They'll probably come tomorrow. We have to be ready and stick to our plan."

"Well, if they don't come at some point soon, we may have to take a chance on Mack going to try to get help or find tools to get us out of here."

• • •

Mack had walked over to say goodnight and overheard the last part of their conversation. Riley was saying they were out of food. He felt awful; they'd been sharing it with him and now they had nothing left. Earlier that morning, when he'd suggested going for help, Jake had said no, but maybe Jake was wrong. Maybe the best thing would be to get them out of there *before* the kidnappers came back. And, for all he knew, maybe the kidnappers were never coming back. It was anyone's guess.

He could go tonight. He could make it there and back in roughly six hours. He'd break into somebody's shed or the trunk of a car and get a crowbar. No one would see him. The big issue would be navigating the terrain at night and avoiding the natural predators. Alligators and venomous snakes could be anywhere along the route, and they'd be difficult to see at night. In some areas, the swampy sections were right next to the path.

He thought back to Wednesday, when he'd been on the run and come across this place. The first few miles had been a dirt path, but the trail had gradually fizzled out. The last several miles were a mix of weeds and grasses nearly up to his knees.

He'd have to go at a much slower pace. He did some calculations. If he could average five miles an hour and left at midnight, he'd be in the outskirts of Ridgeview around three in the morning. Then, say an hour at the most to break in somewhere for tools, then three hours to get back. If he could move a little quicker, he'd be back before dawn. Potentially, he could have Riley and Jake out of there first thing in the morning. He thought about how surprised and happy they'd be.

CHAPTER THIRTY

Wendy had no idea how to go about transferring five million dollars. She certainly couldn't do it right now—not on a Sunday evening. She'd have to arrange it first thing in the morning and have the funds sent through to Nick and Michelle.

The money would have to come from their main bank branch in Niagara Falls, that much she knew. She wished Rob could look after this, then quickly took it back. She'd been doing a lot of wishing lately. Maybe it was enough right now to count her blessings and be thankful he was improving.

She took her pocket-sized address book from her purse and flipped to the page for CIBC, The Canadian Imperial

Bank of Commerce. She placed her finger on the name written down. *Of course.* Walter Stevens, Private Banking, Investment Manager. His cell phone number was there too.

• • •

Scotty pulled up a chair at the table next to her dad. "I'm so glad Mr. Marshall came through his surgery okay."

"Hopefully, he'll be on the road to recovery now," Nick said optimistically.

Michelle sat on the bed. She was still feeling uncertain about their decision not to tell the police about the ransom. "I'm just astounded Wendy came to that determination so quickly."

"Like she said, Mom. The money means nothing—she'd gladly give it all away if it offered some hope of getting Jake and Riley back."

"I understand all of that, but she had no quarrel whatsoever when your dad told her about the instructions not to tell the police."

"Maybe she thought it would be best to follow their instructions."

Nick twisted in his chair to look at her. "Listen, it's not like the police aren't involved. They're searching for Riley and Jake as we speak. They know Zachary Duncan is the one who drove off with them, and they're searching for him. Listen, we've got until three p.m. tomorrow, when the kidnappers said they'd call back. Let's wait and see where we're at in the morning."

"Okay, Nick." Michelle was coming around to the idea. "It's a gamble no matter what we do."

Nick swung back around and picked up the USB sitting on the table. "Scotty, how about showing me this surveillance video you mentioned."

"Sure." Scotty inserted the USB that Bobby had given her. She went to the best clip first. "This clip shows the tow truck leaving J.J.'s, after Jake's car was put up on the flatbed." She tried to zoom in a little, but the picture got fuzzy. "You can see the grill of the tow truck, and that's how they knew it was an older-model Ford."

"Right. That's the same clip the police have been using to show the tow truck on the news. Let's take it from the beginning, though, Scotty. I just want to see all the clips in order."

"Okay, sure." Scotty scrolled back up to the top. "So, this first one is when the tow truck arrives. You can't make out a lot of detail, but you can see the driver getting out of the cab of his truck and Jake getting out of his car." She tried to zoom in again, but it was too blurry.

Michelle came closer and leaned on the back of Nick's chair. "We've looked at these quite a few times. Unfortunately, there's not much that can be done about the resolution."

"Can you play it again?" Nick asked. "This time, don't zoom in. Let's just see the whole picture."

"You got it." Scotty clicked on the little triangle to replay the clip at full screen.

Michelle pointed at the two cars at the pumps. "That woman pumping gas into her car must be Miranda

Galloway." She leaned in closer to the screen between Scotty and Nick. "And that person right there, that must be Hector?"

"Must be. It looks like he's standing by the garbage bin." Scotty said.

"Yes, but what's he doing?" She narrowed her eyes, trying to focus. "Why is his arm up like that?"

"It does look like his arm is up, but this is too far back to really see." Scotty tried to zoom in on Hector. "Wow, it really does look like his arm is up—like he's raising his hand to ask a question."

"Or, he's giving a wave to someone," Michelle suggested.

"Holy. Shit," Nick whispered as he connected the dots. "Michelle, do you think he's waving at the tow-truck driver? Do you think Hector knows this Zachary guy?"

"Well, he doesn't know Jake, so if he's waving at someone, it's gotta be Zachary."

"Mom, what about the video from J.J.'s? Wouldn't the police have seen this more clearly in that video? Should we call Andy and ask him to take a look?"

Her mind was racing. "I don't know. Nick, what do you think? Should we call Andy?"

At first, he appeared to be on side with that, then he suddenly jumped up. "Hold on a sec. Didn't you two tell me this morning that you followed Charles and Andy when they went to talk with Hector?"

Michelle knew exactly what Nick was proposing. "You're thinking we should go over to Hector's house and ask him ourselves?"

"Yes, that's exactly what I'm thinking. This little punk

might know something more that he's not telling the cops. If he does know Zachary, the odds are pretty good he's the one who called him."

"But Dad, the captain was really quite forceful. He slammed Hector into the wall and roughed him up, and he didn't get anything out of him. Mom and I both saw it."

"And here we were feeling sorry for Hector, thinking the captain had been too rough." Michelle was rethinking it now. "Maybe Charles was on the right track after all."

She glanced at Nick. She knew that look—he'd already made up his mind. "I think I'll know if he's lying," he said. "I just want to ask him for myself and see his reaction. I need to see his face."

"Nick, I don't want you getting into a fight with him. I mean, are we even legally allowed to go and question someone? And how do we get him to come out of his house? He's not going to just come out and have a chat with you."

"I can go to the door," Scotty piped in. "I'll make up something and get him outside."

"That could work," Nick said.

Michelle didn't like it. "Scotty, I don't want you getting involved. We don't know how dangerous this guy might be."

Nick gave her a look that said she was being ridiculous.

"Nick, don't. How do you know he won't hurt her? Plus, he'd probably recognize her—we've all been on the news."

"Not if I put my hair up in a messy bun and load on some makeup. Mom, I can do this. I'll get Hector outside, and dad can talk to him."

• • •

Scotty stood on the porch waiting for someone to come to the door. She was just about to knock again when she heard the bolt unlock and the door opened. A middle-aged woman was eyeballing her. "If yer looking for Hector, he ain't home."

Scotty presumed this was Hector's mom and made up something on the fly. "He's out?" She acted surprised. "Guess he musta forgot. He said he was gonna take me out tonight." She tried to put a bit of a southern twang in her words.

The woman looked her up and down. "I'm real sorry, honey." She sounded sympathetic. "Why don't you give Hector a call and remind him?"

"I don't know. Maybe I could go and meet up with him. Do you know where he went?"

"He's where he always is." She rolled her eyes. "Shootin' pool over at Earl's." She started to close the door.

"Wait. Ma'am? Do you know where Earl lives?"

The woman laughed. "Girl, you must be new in town. You don't know Earl's Club? It's the only pool hall and diner in town." She closed the door.

Scotty hurried down the sidewalk and got in the car. "No luck?" Nick asked.

"He's in town at someplace called Earl's. It's a pool hall and diner." She pulled out her phone to look it up. "Here it is—Earl's Country Club. It's Karaoke night."

"Well, let's see if I can get Hector to do some singing." Nick drove off as Scotty called out directions from her phone's GPS.

CHAPTER THIRTY-ONE

The once-gas-station-turned-restaurant was bustling. They searched for a parking spot and found one around the side. Had they been there under different circumstances, Michelle might have laughed. "Earl's Country Club. Seriously?"

"I'm impressed with that big sign for live bait and tackle," Scotty said jokingly.

"I think it's just part of the overall ambiance." Michelle said.

Nick started to get out. "You two wait here and I'll go inside and see if I can find him."

"Not a chance, Nick." Michelle was firm. "We're going to stick together." A group of men loitered next to the pickup truck across from them. "Look at these clowns. They've got hunting rifles hooked onto their back window and Confederate flag decals all over the bumper."

Nick pulled the keys from the ignition. "Okay then, let's go." The three of them got out and headed around to the front.

A gush of loud voices and music poured out as Nick opened the door. "I'll try to get us a table." He began making his way through the crowd. Michelle tried to keep her eyes on him. He turned sideways, letting a group past him on their way out.

The restaurant atmosphere was chaotic. The walls were crammed with hundreds of framed pictures, all of various sizes. The shelves below were cluttered with knick-knacks and trinkets. Oil cans and auto supplies were randomly interspersed, keeping with the gas station motif. Brightly patterned plastic table cloths festooned the packed-in tables.

Nick raised his arm, pointed to a vacant table in the corner by the window and motioned for them to follow. Scotty squeezed through ahead of Michelle and was jostled by someone carrying a full mug of beer. A few ounces splattered on the floor in front of her.

Their table was perfect. It offered a good vantage point of the restaurant and bar. The server approached before they could even pull in their chairs. "Can I get all y'all some drinks? Lime-a-ritas are on special tonight." She pulled a pen from behind her ear and pressed it against her pad. "Ma'am?"

"Just an iced tea for me, please."

"Will that be sweetened or unsweetened?"

"Sweetened, please."

"I'll have a Coke, please," Scotty said. "Mom, can I order something to eat as well? We haven't had anything since lunch."

"Go ahead," Michelle said. "Maybe we'll get something too—might as well eat while we're here."

The server pointed her pen at the plastic-coated specials card on the table. "The She-Crab Soup and Shrimp-and-Grits are on special," she said. "They're a favourite."

Scotty looked at the card. "I'll have the number four, the chicken strip basket, please."

"Hun, ya want that with fries or hushpuppies?"

"Fries, please."

Nick ordered a beer and a specialty combo basket that Michelle had pointed to on the card. Once the waitress left, Scotty slid her chair back. "I'm going to go scope things out for Dad—check out where the pool tables are and see if Hector's back there."

Michelle got up with her. "I think I'll try to find the restroom."

Scotty led the way, shuffling through the crowd along the stretch at the bar. A few steps down were the washrooms, a small souvenir shop and a side exit. Just past the exit was a room with pool tables. Scotty stopped and turned around. "Mom, I'll go check it out while you use the washroom."

"Okay, just a quick look, Scotty, and then back to the table. I'll meet you back there."

The washroom floor was wet and the grout between the tiles had blackened. The latch hung off the first stall, and the second one had a puddle around the toilet. If she were going to do a restaurant review, this would seal the deal on a zero-star rating.

When she stepped out, their target was practically in front of her. Hector was talking to a man outside the men's room. The man handed Hector a twenty from his wallet, telling him to rack up the balls for another game, then went into the washroom.

She quickly turned away and slipped into the souvenir shop. Her face was burning with anger. She wanted to grab Hector by the scruff of his neck and ask him where her daughter was. To think that she'd previously felt sorry for him. She certainly had no sympathy for him now. He was quite possibly the reason her daughter was missing.

"Can I help you with something?" the clerk asked.

As she picked up an Earl's Country Club baseball cap, she saw Hector return to the pool room.

Back at their table, Michelle set down the cap for Nick. "Scotty, did you see Hector?"

"Yup, he's in there all right. He was playing pool at the first table."

"What's this hat for?" Nick asked.

"It's to make you less recognizable. If he remembers you from the news, he might take off." She didn't bother mentioning that Hector had nearly seen her.

Scotty nodded in agreement. "Yeah, clever thinking, Mom. I saw some people looking over at us when we first came in. I bet we're the talk of the town."

Nick reluctantly put the cap on. "What ever happened to the days when men took their hats off at the dinner table?" He pulled the brim down lower. "How's that? Are you both happy now?"

"Perfect. You blend in nicely." Michelle guessed that at least half of the men in this place were wearing hats—many of them red MAGA ones.

The waitress returned with their drinks. "Y'all enjoy. I'll be back with yer meals real soon." The beverages were served in reuseable plastic cups that looked like they'd been run through the dishwasher one too many times. The Earls Country Club logos had nearly worn off.

Scotty briefed Nick on the intel she'd gathered: where the side exit was, the washrooms, the pool tables, and of course Hector. "He's wearing a green T-shirt and baggy jeans. I'd say he's medium height—shorter than you—and super scrawny. Oh, and he's got light-brown hair."

A loud screech came through the speaker system. Karaoke was about to begin. The rowdies who'd been drinking all evening started cheering and clapping for the young woman on stage. She was a Carrie Underwood wannabe singing "Jesus Take the Wheel."

"Oh, please, kill me now," Scotty said.

Nick poured his beer into the plastic mug. He took a long drink, then leaned across the table so they could hear him over the music. "Okay, I'm going down to the pool room. I don't want him leaving before I get a chance to talk to him."

"Be careful, Nick. Please." She knew how she felt when she saw Hector, and she guessed Nick would feel the same way.

"Don't worry, I'm just going to talk to him," he assured her. "You guys go ahead and eat if I'm not back when the food comes." He tipped his hat at them.

"Good luck," Scotty said.

Michelle was trembling inside. She had no idea what Nick might do to this weasely kid, and she wasn't about to stop him. She'd never felt so desperate in her whole life. *Please let him lead us to Riley and Jake. Please.* They were all committed to do whatever was necessary.

• • •

Only about a half a dozen people were still in the pool room. Most had meandered up to the crowded bar to watch the Karaoke. Nick spotted Hector right away. He was at the first table, bent over, lining up his shot. He slid the cue back and forth between his bridged fingers, then banked the ball easily into the side pocket. Just the right amount of backspin and the cue ball rolled back, perfectly aligned for the next shot—an easy kiss into the corner. Hector strutted around the table to line up his final shot, then drilled the eight ball into the side pocket. *What a show-off,* Nick thought.

Hector approached his opponent with his hand out, a wide grin on his face. "That's another twenty. Wanna go again?" The man shook his head, paid up and headed to the bar.

Hector moved around the table pulling the balls out of the pockets, ready to rack them up again. He noticed Nick standing there. "You wanna play?"

Nick picked up a cue and stood face to face with him. "I have a different game in mind."

Hector backed up. "Whataya want, man?" His grin faded. "There's nothing wrong here—I win fair and square."

"How about I ask the questions and you answer them?" Nick stepped closer until Hector was up against the wall. "How do you know Zachary Duncan?"

"What? I don't know any Zachary Duncan." His eyes darted back and forth.

"I think you do." Nick wasn't going to take any crap from this kid. "Next question. Where is he?" He leaned his pool cue under Hector's chin.

Hector pushed Nick back and scrambled away, heading for the exit. Nick grabbed the back of his shirt collar and went out with him. "Not happening, Hector." He dropped his pool cue and slammed Hector against the brick wall. "Where's Zachary, and where's my daughter?" Nick clenched his fist in front of his face.

"I don't know, man. I don't know what you're talking about." Hector suddenly pulled out a pocket knife and swiped it across at him.

"You little shit!" Nick let his fists fly and landed a couple of solid blows to Hector's face, then grabbed his wrist and banged it against the bricks until he dropped the knife, gouging his own arm in the process. He could feel blood running down inside his shirt sleeve. He threw Hector to the ground, pinning his knees against the kid's arms. "Where's Zachary and where's my daughter?"

"Told you—I don't know. Let me go!" He was kicking his legs, trying to break free.

Nick grabbed the pool cue he'd dropped on the ground and held it across Hector's throat. "Last chance, kiddo. Where's my daughter?" He pressed the pool cue down more firmly.

"Okay, okay," Hector choked out. Nick let up slightly so Hector could speak. "I called Zachary and told him there was an expensive car needing a tow, but I haven't seen him since. Honest. I thought he'd just steel the car and give me a finder's fee."

Nick was enraged. Hector had just admitted it—he was responsible for this. Nick squeezed the pool cue harder between his hands, trying to control his anger. "Where? Where would Zachary have taken them?"

"I don't know."

"You must know something. What does Zachary do with the stolen cars?"

"There's a guy that Zachary knows. He sells stolen cars and has some sort of deal with the Ridgeview Police. That's why I can't tell the cops—I don't know who's in on it."

"This guy—what's his name?" Nick pressed the cue stick down a little harder.

Hector tried to turn his head and gasped for air. "Please! I don't know his name."

Nick released the cue slightly. "You must know something about this guy. Tell me what you know."

"I seen him and his lady friend once at Zachary's place, but I don't know his name. He drives a black older-model Lincoln sedan."

"That's enough! Get off him now!" Somebody grabbed Nick from behind and pulled him off. He dropped the pool cue as Hector scuttled out from under him and ran off. It was Captain Adams. He was in plain clothes, his unmarked car a few feet back with the driver's door hanging open. "Trying to take things into your own hands, Nick? Not a good idea, unless you wanna wind up in jail."

Nick tried to explain, "Listen, Hector's the one who called Zachary to come and tow them away! He set this up! They were trying to steal Jake's car. He just admitted it!"

"Whoa down, Nick. I'm way ahead of you on this. I've had Hector under surveillance the last two days. Our off-duty officers and I have been takin' turns keepin' an eye on him, hoping he might lead us to Zachary. He sure as hell ain't gonna do that now."

Charles let him go, then stared at the blood seeping through his sleeve. "Looks like you need to get that cleaned up."

Nick pressed his hand against his upper arm. "Listen, Charles. Hector said Zachary works with some guy who sells stolen cars. Whoever this guy is, he's got some sort of deal with the Ridgeview police. You need to go and arrest Hector for his involvement in this and find out who this other guy is."

"I'll have Andy pick him up. Now, how about you let us do our jobs," Charles said sternly. He strode back to his car, stretched his arm out and pointed down the street. "There's a twenty-four-hour walk-in clinic a block over."

Nick didn't want to go back inside with blood dripping down his arm. He walked up to the window at the corner of the building and knocked on it to get Michelle and Scotty's attention.

CHAPTER THIRTY-TWO

The full moon had risen more than halfway up the sky on the eastern horizon. Mack figured it must be close to ten o'clock. It would be midnight when the moon reached the highest point. He stared up at it, thankful for the light it provided.

The February full moon is referred to as the "Snow Moon" or sometimes the "Hunger Moon" by many Indigenous tribes. The Cherokee in North and South Carolina call it the "Bone Moon," signifying a time for fasting. Mack thought how uncanny that was, that he would remember this now—how little tidbits of information stick with you and then resurface at the oddest times. He'd taken an Indigenous traditional-story-telling course for his undergrad, and now he was suddenly remembering the names of the full moons. In many of the stories, the moon was a protector. He hoped that might be true tonight; certainly, the hunger and fasting parts were bang on.

When the moon neared its highest point, he set off with his walking stick. The dense, five-foot branch was about three inches in diameter—sturdy enough to support his weight, and the spear-like tip made him feel like he was carrying a weapon. If a wild hog were to attack him, he'd be able to protect himself.

For now, he used his stick to poke through the weeds ahead of him, clearing the way. Every now and again, he'd swear he'd heard something twisting in the grasses below. All at once, something gripped his lower leg and squeezed hard. He nearly buckled over. The disabling pain seized his calf muscle with an overwhelming tightness. He knew exactly what it was—a muscle spasm. A severe cramp—probably from a lack of food and proper hydration. Mack tried to shake it off, then rubbed the back of his calf with his hand, trying to loosen up the tension. He breathed in and out deeply and slowly; waiting for it to pass.

After he stretched both legs, he continued on, making his way through the worst of the weedy section. He was several miles out now and moving along at a good pace. He'd found the narrow strips where the weeds had been flattened by the kidnappers' car. He sprinted along the track, starting to feel good, thinking about the end goal—freeing Riley and Jake—one step at a time.

A flash of light jumped through the trees ahead. Had he blinked, he might have missed it. A second later, it flickered again; distant beams of white light shooting through the forest. Mack stopped dead in his tracks and watched as the lights grew larger and brighter. "Shit!"

He started running back as fast as he could. No more thoughts of what might be lurking in the weeds. For several minutes he charged ahead, glancing behind every few seconds. It was closing in and he was out of breath. *No! This can't be happening!* He wasn't going to be able to make it back. Riley and Jake would be on their own. The heavy weight of impending doom crushed down upon him. His throat felt like it had been swallowed into the depths of his chest.

The headlights got closer. Mack moved off to the side and dropped into the weeds as the vehicle drove past. It was them. The kidnappers were headed to the cabin, and he had no way to warn Riley and Jake. He pictured them going ahead with their plan, not realizing they had no backup. If Riley and Jake were killed, this would all be on him.

He got up and started running again, trying to focus on his rhythm, lengthening his stride, moving his legs faster and faster. The small red tail lights faded out of sight.

• • •

"What are ya parking like this for?" she snapped at him. "I won't be able to see nothin'. Move it so the headlights shine into the cabin. We need to see as to what we're doin'." Beth-Anne pulled up her bandana.

Caleb angled the car, doing as she'd said, put it in park and left the engine running. He smirked at her. "Wanna take a turn to empty their piss pot?"

She glared at him from under her brow.

"Guess that means I'll be the one going in?" He tied on his bandana.

"Never mind 'bout their damn piss pot," she said. "Just make it quick, Caleb. Toss in the supplies and let's get the hell outta here."

Caleb got out of the car and went around to the trunk. He set the case of water and the food bag next to the cabin. "I'm all set," he said, getting the key out of his pocket. "You ready?"

She took position behind her open door and stretched her arms out, pointing her gun through the gap between the car and the door. "I'm ready."

Caleb undid the padlock and removed the chain. "Y'all back up against the wall in there!" He lifted the latch. "I'm comin' in. My gun's loaded and, as y'all know, I don't mind using it."

・・・

Jake whispered, "I love you, Riley. We've got this." They took their positions.

Her heart was pounding. She hoped their plan would work. She hoped she could hold up her end of it. She just needed to distract him for a second or two so Jake could pound him with the rock. They'd talked about a few different ideas for the distraction. She could fall to his feet and cling to his pantleg, begging to be set free. He'd have no choice but to look down to shake her off. Or she could shine the flashlight in his eyes. Or just act frantic, yelling "Don't shoot, don't shoot!" and move to the other side.

The cabin door opened and the light from the car's high beams flooded inside. Riley squinted, trying to see the male figure coming in. Something else glistening in the light below caught her eye. It was moving at his feet, slithering into the cabin with him. Riley screamed. "Snake!" She yelled and pointed. "Snake!"

Caleb looked down and Jake bashed the rock into the side of his head. He pulled it back and bashed him again. Caleb went down.

"Get it out!" Riley screamed. "Where did it go!" She jumped onto the bedframe and shone her flashlight across the floor and into the corners.

"What the hell's going on?" a woman by the car yelled. "Caleb! What's going on?"

CHAPTER THIRTY-THREE

Mason grabbed two bungie cords off the shelf in the garage and stretched them out between his hands. He seemed satisfied they'd do the job. It was his turn to bring the beer. He loaded the case on the back of his ATV and secured it with the bungie cords. He pulled on it a few times, just for good measure, checking that it would hold steady.

The mud on his ATV was getting pretty thick. He kicked off a couple of chunks wedged behind the wheels. His mom would be pissed about that. She was always squawking at him to tidy up the garage. *So senseless. I wish she'd quit sticking her nose in my business.*

His helmet was hanging by the chin strap on a hook on the wall. *Not tonight.* Carter was right—it was so much

THE LOWLANDS

better to let the wind blow through your hair. Quietly, Mason pulled open the big garage door, careful not to wake his parents. He pushed the ATV out and closed the door, all but an inch or so, behind him. He rolled the four-wheeler down the driveway and onto the street, coasting past a few houses before starting up the engine.

At the end of the street, he took a shortcut across the old lady's lawn, just to teach her a lesson. *That old bitch is always calling the cops on me.* He stopped right in the middle and spun the tires, ripping up grass and shooting mud against her car. He laughed. Carter and Logan would be proud. He thought about going back and doing it again—maybe taking a video with his phone. *Nah, no time for that.* Carter and Logan were meeting him at midnight. This was going to be the best night ever.

Mason slowed down. He was nearing the secret entryway to their trails. He and Logan had cut down some wire fencing a few months back, and nobody had ever bothered to fix it. They'd forged their own trails behind the access road, and they were super legit, probably the best ATV track around. In the lowlands, it was important to ride on established trails if you didn't want to worry about sinking into the marshes.

Mason turned in and then stood up to get the full effect. The ATV bounced down the rugged slope. It was full of deep ruts from all of their previous rides. When the mud was soft, their wheels would sink in and create deep grooves. When the ground dried out, the mud would harden, making it a bumpy ride. It was a thrill.

Carter and Logan were already there. They had a fire burning in the pit with their ATVs parked around it. This would be sweet.

CHAPTER THIRTY-FOUR

Andy picked up Hector outside his house and brought him down to the station. They'd been going at it for the better part of an hour. Andy figured it was hopeless—Hector wasn't talking. Charles took a turn too, but the kid denied knowing anything, denied calling Zachary and he claimed he knew nothing about Zachary stealing the Marshalls' car.

Hector's cheek and the tissue around his left eye were swelling up pretty good where Nick had punched him. He touched the wound. "I need some ice. Somebody needs to get me some ice for this or my whole eye is gonna close up."

"Why don't you tell me about your phone call to Zachary, and I'll get you some ice," Charles said.

"I keep tellin' y'all, I just made that up. The guy was gonna kill me. I had to tell him something, so I made it up."

Charles pressed him harder. "You won't be walkin' away from this, Hector. Participating in grand larceny—you'll be looking at up to ten years."

"I didn't do nothing wrong. I wanna go home. If you're not lettin' me go home, I want a lawyer."

Andy left the interrogation room and headed back to his desk. He was tired and discouraged. Hector was acting tough, but Andy could tell he was scared. And who could blame him? If, what he told Nick was actually true, the kid ought to be scared. Andy didn't know what to think. It all sounded pretty far-fetched; Ridgeview cops involved in a car-theft operation? If that was true, Hector might suspect some Yemassee cops are dirty too.

The button on his desk phone lit up as the ringer buzzed. "Andy Solterra."

"Andy. Ben Jorden again from Niagara."

"Hey, Ben. We're still working on the lead you gave us earlier. We're checking all the property registrations in that area and organizing a crew to do a search in the morning."

"Well, I got word on something else that you're gonna need to know."

"I'm listening." Andy grabbed a pen and paper.

"We had a call from a Walter Stevens. He's an investment officer at CIBC here in Niagara. Apparently, Jake Marshall's mom, Wendy Marshall, called him on his cell phone this evening from Florida. She asked for his help to transfer five million dollars to Nick Barton first thing in the morning."

Andy's mind was racing. "Oh my god. It's ransom money."

"Certainly sounds like it. She asked for the funds to be split between a dozen different banks in Hilton Head that would have large amounts of cash on hand."

Andy was flabbergasted. This case was blowing up all around him. What was the protocol for this? "Thanks for the heads up, Ben. I'll talk to Captain Adams right now." Andy hung up the phone. He didn't really want to talk to Charles about it. He wasn't even sure if he should trust Charles. He looked at his watch. It was too late to call the chief at home. He'd have to tell the captain.

Andy headed to the interrogation room and almost bumped into him as he was coming out. "Anything?" Andy asked.

"No. He's not talking." Charles stepped around him.

"Hang on, Charles. Something big has come up. I'm not sure what the protocol is—whether we should call in the FBI"

"What is it, Andy? Just spit it out," he snapped. "I don't have time for your 'follow the rules' mentality right now."

He knows, Andy thought. *The chief must have told Charles about our conversation.* He tried not to let Charles's behaviour intimidate him. "Ben Jorden just called." Andy filled him in on what Ben had said.

Charles looked like he was going to slam his fist into something before he cupped it into his other hand. "Wendy Marshall wants to transfer money to Nick Barton? Nick seems to be running his own show here." He turned and started to head down the hall.

"So, should I call the FBI?" Andy asked.

Charles turned to him. "No. Call the Barton family and tell them we're coming over, now!"

"Well, if this is a ransom case, aren't we supposed to call the FBI? Isn't that the protocol?"

Charles looked up at the ceiling, shaking his head, then walked back toward him. "Andy, you want protocol? I'll give you protocol." He came uncomfortably close. "I'm the captain, and you take your orders from me. Ya got that?"

"Got it."

"Good. Look, all we know right now is that Wendy Marshall made an inquiry about transferring money tomorrow morning. It hasn't been done yet. It hasn't been reported yet." Andy started to respond, but Charles held up his finger, warning him not to interrupt. "First we're gonna go and talk to Nick and Michelle right now and find out exactly what's happening."

"It's almost midnight," Andy reminded him.

"Now, Andy! Phone them up and tell them we're on our way." He shook his head. "These dumb Canadians are gonna get their daughter killed."

As they headed out, Jan stopped them. "Andy, can you hold on a second? I've done the property search for all the land titles in the area you asked for." She held a folder full of printouts. "There's something here you need to see."

Charles kept going. "I'll catch up in a minute," Andy shouted after him.

· · ·

Andy and Jan went to her desk. She opened up the folder and started flipping through papers. "Here it is. There's a small piece of land, way back in there, owned by one Grayson Alexander Duncan."

"Duncan?"

"Yup. It was the last name that caught my eye too. Don't know if it might be a relative of Zachary Duncan." She handed him the printout.

"Can you show me where exactly this land is, on a map?"

Jan opened up her topographical map and laid it out on the desk. She already had it marked off. "This particular area is all wetlands now. Decades ago, it was solid ground, but there's nothing there anymore."

"Oh, I see," Andy said, disappointed.

"Well, hang on now, Andy. There's more. Not far from Grayson Duncan's plot was the old Hawk's Tooth Hunting Lodge. The lodge itself burned down more than twenty years ago. Probably nothing much left of it." She pointed to the area on the map.

Andy looked at it closely, wondering how a search party might access the area. The map showed sections with patterned blue dots. Those were the marshes. "How do you even get in there? Looks like a whole lot of wetlands."

"If you start a bit south and come in from this area here, near Ridgeview, it might work. You'd have to be familiar with the area. Maybe we can find someone who is."

Andy nodded. "Yeah, like Zachary Duncan. I bet he knows his way around in there." He tapped his pen against the desk as he thought about what to do. "Okay, Jan. I know you're tired and you've already worked a double shift, but, before you head out, can you see if you can find us a guide? We'll need someone to lead us in at first light."

"No problem, Andy. I'll stay until I have everything organized for the morning. They'll be ready to go in at sunrise."

"You're the best, Jan."

Andy hurried off, hoping to catch up with Charles, but he'd already left. *Shit!* He'd totally forgotten to phone Michelle to say they were coming over.

CHAPTER THIRTY-FIVE

Riley was still standing on the bedframe, petrified, trying to keep track of the snake.

"Stay put!" the woman yelled and fired a warning shot. "Ya hear me?" She was just a few feet from the cabin door with her gun pointed at Jake. He backed up, straddling the man's body. "Caleb, get up!" she hollered, but he wasn't moving.

Riley could hardly contain herself. She felt like her legs might run out from under her. *There it is!* It was winding its way farther into the cabin; its scaly head raised up a few inches, leading the rest of its slithery length into the corner. *I have to get out of here, right now!* She jumped off the bedframe and tried to push her way past Jake.

He held his ground, blocking her way, trying to keep her from being shot. "Let me out!" she screamed. "Let me out!"

"Riley!" he yelled. "Stop it!"

Where the heck was Mack? "Mack!" she called out. Now she'd lost sight of the snake. In a panic, she pushed forward again, this time knocking Jake to the side. The woman fired again.

Riley stumbled backward; the jolt had taken her off her feet. Her head whacked against the bedframe as she went down.

•••

"Friggin' hell!" Beth-Anne yelled. She'd had no choice in the matter; it was self-defence. The dumb bitch had been coming right at her.

Everything was going straight to shit. Caleb lay there, done. Now she had to sort out this mess he'd made. Jake was bent over trying to help his wife. Beth-Anne needed to lock down this situation, now.

She pushed the door shut and grabbed for the chain, trying to pull it over the latch. The door heaved against her, pushed from behind. Jake was forcing his body weight against it. She tried to hold her ground, pushing back with all her might, but the door was gaping open and his shoulder was squeezing through.

Beth-Anne stepped back and fired a shot. Missed. Everything was happening so fast. He was coming at her, grabbing her arms, wrestling with her, trying to take her gun. She pulled the trigger again—the shot fired into the air. He was overpowering her. She kicked hard at his shins, but he didn't let up. He rammed her up against the cabin and bent her wrist back. She was losing the gun.

She thrust her knee between his legs, driving it up as hard and fast as she could. For a split second there was nothing. Then he crumpled to the ground as if the air had been sucked right out of him. He lay there paralyzed, curled up in a ball.

She pointed her gun at him. "Now, get back in the cabin if you want to stay alive."

He wasn't moving. He was barely breathing.

"Fine, then! I ain't got time for this." She kicked the cabin door shut and pulled the chain back over the latch. "You done brought this all on yourselves." She squeezed the padlock shut. She looked down at him. He was still incapacitated, heaving a little. She wiped down the lock with her sleeve, making sure to get all her prints off.

"Time's up," She pointed the gun at his head. "Yer done."

CHAPTER THIRTY-SIX

"Stop!" Mack hollered from a distance. "Hold it right there!" He saw her in the headlights, standing above Jake.

Startled, she raised her gun in the direction of his voice, scanning the area where he might be. Jake struggled to get up. Mack had to buy some time. *Come on, Jake.*

"Drop your weapon or I'll shoot!" Mack shouted, trying to keep her attention on him.

"I ain't droppin' nothin'!" She started backing up, out of the headlights, into the darkness. Mack could still see her behind the car's driver-side door. He kept shouting while Jake rolled to the other side of the vehicle. He was on his hands and knees now. *Come on, Jake. You can do it.*

He got up, his body hunched over, and hurried towards him. Mack grabbed hold of him. "Jake, I'm sorry. I went to get help. I was a few miles out when I saw their car coming in. I got back as fast as I could. Where's Riley?"

Jake leaned on him, still unable to stand up straight, as he tried to catch his breath. "Riley's been—shot. I don't know—how bad. She's locked—in the cabin."

"No!" Mack grabbed his head as though he were in pain. "I'm so sorry. This is all my fault." He was so angry at himself for leaving. He stomped his foot into the ground. "Damn it!"

"Mack, she's going to need help," Jake said. "We need that car." He straightened up, taking his weight back onto his own two feet.

"I don't see that woman. Is she still behind it?" Mack was ready to make a run for the vehicle.

The interior lights came on and the woman climbed in. "Not anymore." Jake grabbed his shoulders. "We have to stop her somehow."

The taillights turned white as the car backed out from the cabin. Jake hurried to the other side of the path to try and stop her as she came by. The car pulled forward, its high beams coming at them fast. She was firing random shots out the window. Both Jake and Mack lunged at the car as it came by. Jake's legs caught the front bumper and he was hurled up onto the hood. Mack clung to the passenger door handle as he ran alongside. Jake's head thumped against the windshield and he tumbled off.

Mack tried to hang on as the car sped up, his feet dragging beside the car. Suddenly she hit the brakes, and he was thrown forward into the weeds.

211

The rear wheels started spinning in the dirt. Mack got up, ready to try again. The tires gained traction—the car was coming right at him. He jumped out of the way.

• • •

Beth-Anne stepped down harder on the gas. She was trying to think. *Who the hell was that and where'd he come from?* The car bounced along through the thick weeds. *He wasn't the police. Maybe it was someone who lives nearby and heard all the gun shots. Stupid Zachary.* Why on earth did they ever believe him when he said "There ain't nobody out here for miles." She slammed her fist against the console. "Frigg!"

There'd be no way to get the ransom money now. She reckoned the police would be swarming the area faster than a hot knife through butter. *All that planning—down the friggn' drain.*

Caleb must be dead, she thought. *He was just lyin' there; his body all strewn out on the cabin floor.* A branch scraped under the car. She jerked her foot off the gas, swerved and then straightened the car back onto the path. *There weren't no way to get him out—nothing I coulda done.* As soon as she'd put the lock back on the chain, she realized the key was inside with Caleb. *Maybe he shoulda given me a spare. No matter.*

Beth-Anne tried to think logically, reviewing everything in her mind. Maybe the situation wasn't as bad as she thought.

It was Caleb and Zachary who stole the car. It was Caleb who decided to kidnap the Marshalls. It was Caleb who shot Zachary. It was Caleb who made the ransom phone call. She hadn't done any of it. She'd had her bandana on the whole time, so the couple had never got a good look at her. The more she thought about it, the more she was certain the police would have absolutely nothing on her.

She'd act as though she knew nothing about this—she'd be shocked. She'd question the authorities, so surprised. "A woman was involved in all a this?" She'd get all choked up. "So, it was true—he was having an affair with another woman. I suspected he was seein' someone else but didn't want to believe it." She'd weep and cry, "How could Caleb do this to me?" Cry some more. "Be with another woman and all. And how could they do something so heinous?"

She started a to-do list in her head. She'd have to get rid of the car, wipe off her prints and dump it somewhere. The Marshalls' luggage—she'd have to get rid of that too. If she was going to act like she knew nothing, she couldn't very well leave their luggage lying around the house. *Where am I gonna dump that?* She was on the dirt road, approaching the access road.

Bang! A rock hit the side window of the car. "What the hey-ell!" She hit the brakes. An ATV came flying across the path, right in front of her, slinging mud and stones out from behind it. Another ATV came buzzing through, nearly hitting her square on. The driver spun toward her, then revved the engine and shot forward off the path.

Little shitheads. She drove off. She was nearly out of there. They hadn't seen her. She pulled onto the access road and continued making mental notes of all the things she'd need to do. She looked at the speedometer and eased off the gas. *Aint takin' no unnecessary risks.*

She reviewed it all again. Go home and get the Marshalls' luggage. Wipe it all down for prints. Get the extra burner cell phones from Caleb's desk drawer. Wipe them down for prints. Put the luggage and the cell phones in the car. Then ditch the car somewhere, being sure to wipe it down first—the steering wheel, the door handles, and everything she'd touched. There'd be no physical evidence of her involvement. Nothing to speak of.

My gun! She'd nearly forgotten about her gun. She'd need to get rid of it. *That there's the reason criminals get caught; they forget something.* Now, she'd thought of everything. It was all sorted. Maybe she'd even get to keep Caleb's house. She'd been living common-law with him for over a year. *That must count for something.*

By the time she pulled into the driveway, she'd even figured out an alibi. That would seal the deal.

CHAPTER THIRTY-SEVEN

Mack scrambled to his feet and ran back to where Jake's body lay crumpled in the weeds. "Jake, are you okay?"

Jake's arm came up at him and latched onto his jumpsuit. Mack helped him sit up. He sputtered, "Riley...help... please...help her." He slumped back down.

Mack couldn't help Riley. He had no key, no tools. Nothing had changed. He had to go and get help. But what about Jake. He seemed pretty woozy. Mack didn't know if he'd be able to make it. He'd be quicker without him, but he couldn't just leave him there lying in the weeds. He could be dragged off into the swamp, just as Zachary had. "Come on, Jake. Let's get you up."

Jake seemed dazed and slurred his words. He couldn't walk straight on his own. Mack supported him, as though he were walking a friend out of the bar after a few too many drinks. Jake leaned against him as they started down the path.

They seemed to be finding a rhythm. Every now and again, Jake called out their steps. "Lef, right, lef, right." They'd gone a little more than a mile when Jake slowed down and then flat-out stopped. He bent over and started puking up bile. "Uhh, so bad. I'm slor slorry man," he said, then went off on another long spiel about Riley. "I love her so much. You saved her—Riley. The plan—it worked right? She's okay?" Jake sat down and then slumped sideways into the weeds. His words drifted off. "Slo tired, man…" He was out.

"No, no, Jake. We can't stop now, buddy. Come on." Mack lifted him up again.

Jake shielded his eyes. "So bright, eh?" The moon was above them to the west, guiding them out. Mack got him up and moving again, but, throughout the next stretch, he was holding up most of Jake's weight.

"You still with me, Jake? We're doin' good—almost out of the weeds. It's gonna get easier up ahead." He could tell, Jake had nothing left in him. He was literally dragging his feet as Mack moved him along. There had to be a better way.

"Okay, Jake. Let's stop for a second and regroup." Mack crouched down and grabbed Jake at the top of his legs, positioning his upper body over his shoulder. "There we go. I gotcha." He boosted him up a few more inches.

At first it seemed easier carrying Jake like a sack of potatoes, but after a while he realized he'd never make it the whole way. Not only that, he was worried about jostling Jake so much. Would it make his head injury even worse? Jake already had a concussion, and with this second blow against the windshield, it was serious.

They were well past the weeds now and on pretty solid ground. This would be a good place to stop for a break. Mack set Jake down, leaning him up against a tree on the edge of the path. He was totally out of it now. Mack was exhausted too. He stood up and bent backwards, trying to stretch out his muscles and give them a rest.

It seemed hopeless. He thought of Riley—how she could be bleeding to death in the cabin. He'd be so much faster on his own. That's what Jake would want him to do—he felt sure of it. If he left Jake here, he could run the rest of the way and bring back help.

He squatted down to tell Jake, even though he was out cold. "Okay, Jake. Hang in there, bud. I'll be back with help as quick as I can."

Something was wrong. Jake was too tranquil. *Shit!* Mack put his finger under Jake's nose. He couldn't feel any air going in or out, and fluid had run from Jake's nose onto his chin. He looked at Jakes's chest. There was no rise or fall.

"Don't you dare do this!" he yelled. He lifted Jake's wrist to feel for a pulse. It was there—it was steady. His breathing was shallow, but he had a pulse. "Okay, Jake, hang in there. I'll be back."

CHAPTER THIRTY-EIGHT

Riley was spinning as though she were on a tilt-a-whirl ride at the amusement park. Her eyes fluttered as she started to regain consciousness, her mind starting to piece things together, reconnecting the past with the present. Her eyes opened to the darkness of the cabin—the cabin with the snake!

She scrambled in a panic to get up; she needed to get off the floor. "Jaaake!" She screamed for him again and again, but he didn't answer. She was terrified, spiralling out of control, and no one there to help her. "Jaaake! Help!" She lifted one foot, then the other, high off the floor. Ahhhhh! She kept screaming, thinking any second it would wrap itself around her ankle and slither up her calf.

Her heel hit something bulky on the floor behind her. *Oh my god!* It was the man. Caleb—that was the name the woman had called out. Riley quickly stepped up onto Caleb's back—off the floor, where the snake might be. She extended one hand, feeling for the cabin wall. It was there, right behind her. That meant the door was to her left, the fireplace was ten feet ahead of her and the bedframes were on each side. Somehow, even in her state of panic, her brain had reasoned out these facts, gathering her bearings.

She'd seen the snake slither under the left bedframe toward the corner. *Is it still there? How long ago was that?*

She tried to stay calm. She tried to think. The back of her head was pounding. She reached up to touch it, but that arm wasn't moving properly. Her fingers were tingling, wet and sticky. Then she remembered. The sudden realization—she'd been shot—brought with it the excruciating pain in her shoulder. It felt like a hot poker had been rammed through the top of her arm. She started to shiver, her teeth chattering. Hysteria set in again—how much blood had she lost? "Jaaake!" She started to cry. Her shoulder was throbbing as though someone were punching it again and again. "Jaaake!"

Where are you? He wouldn't just leave her there. Maybe he'd tried to tell her he was going for help, but she'd passed out and hadn't heard him. Or maybe he was dead. She brought her good hand, shaking, up to her mouth. Maybe his body was on the floor right in front of her and she just couldn't see it in the dark. *No. No. No.* Her mind quickly ruled that out. *He went for help.*

Logical thinking came back to the forefront—she needed the flashlight. That would be the first order of business. She'd had it in her hand before she was shot. *Did I drop it? Is it on the floor?* She must have dropped it when she fell. If it was on the floor, she wasn't about to get down and feel around for it. What if she found the snake first?

Maybe the flashlight was on top of Caleb. She turned sideways, leaning her good hand against the wall, then brushed her foot gently along his upper back and torso. She nearly lost her balance when his body moved below her. *Oh my god! He's still alive!*

The flashlight was no longer the first order of business—now it was the gun. She needed to get Caleb's gun from him before he woke up. She kneeled on his back and put her right hand down on his shoulder. His body felt warm. She traced her hand along his arm, which was splayed out over his head. She couldn't reach far enough to get to his hand. She moved herself forward, putting one foot on the floor next to the wall, then stretched her arm out again. She felt his hand and the cold metal between his fingers. She lifted the gun out. She had it!

She stood up, hanging onto it tightly. She'd never held a gun before. It was heavier than she'd thought it would be. Riley aimed it down toward Caleb, her finger on the trigger. She couldn't do it. She couldn't bring herself to shoot him. Her index finger stayed firmly hinged around the trigger, ready when need be.

She wished Caleb would just hurry up and die on his own. He moved again below her, and she nearly fell off. She couldn't keep standing on his back, but she was too afraid to step onto the floor. She kept visualizing the snake. He started gasping.

It was time to move to higher ground. It was just one step over to get up on the bedframe. One step on the floor, then one big step up. The snake wouldn't be there—it would probably have curled up in a corner or someplace warm. On top of the bedframe would be safe.

She began coaxing herself. *Quickly. One step and then step up.* She raised her foot. *One, two...*

Caleb grunted as her weight shifted. *Now.* She stepped off and quickly sprang onto the bedframe. Something rolled along the wooden slats. *The flashlight!* She tried to reach for it, but a jab of pain stopped her short. It felt like her upper arm was tearing apart from her shoulder. She grimaced as she folded her arm back in and cradled it against her stomach, trying to hold it steady. She slipped her fingers inside the gaps between the buttons on her blouse. That would give her arm some support.

With the gun in her good hand, how could she pick up the flashlight? She wasn't about to put the gun down; it was staying with her no matter what. She shoved the barrel inside her waistband, leaving the handle sticking out, and then squatted down slowly, feeling for the flashlight.

It rolled as her fingers touched it, but she got a hold of it. With a huge sense of relief, Riley pressed her thumb against the switch, pushing the power bar to the on position. Her hand shook. She was terrified of what she might see.

Thank God. Jake's body wasn't there—he wasn't dead on the floor. *He got out.*

She took a deep breath and then systematically followed the stream of light back and forth across the floor. There was no snake. She shone the light into the fireplace opening; it wasn't there either. She started to think that perhaps it really did go out whenever Jake had left. She let out a deep breath.

She continued her search with the flashlight. She directed the light across to the other bedframe. Their blankets were there, one bunched on top of the other. Maybe the snake was inside—that would be a warm spot. If the snake weren't there, she could have the blanket. She wanted it. She wanted it badly. She was cold and shivering again.

A corner of the rumpled blanket hung down just below the bedframe. She stared at it intently, watching for movement. Maybe she could slowly lift the blanket by the corner and see if anything was under it? *Oh, God, no.* She scanned the floor again with the flashlight. Nothing there but the rocks that Mack had dropped down to them. That gave her an idea.

She tucked the flashlight under her chin and stepped down. She grabbed three rocks, put them on her bedframe and quickly stepped back up. She set the flashlight down, the beam of light aimed across to the blankets. She tossed a rock onto the blankets. Nothing happened. Surely if the snake were in there, that would have scared it out. She tossed another; nothing. *Okay, I can do this.* She stepped down and grabbed the corner of the blanket and gently pulled it back. Nothing. There was no snake. She quickly wrapped the blanket around herself, grabbed the flashlight and got back up on the bedframe.

Now she could focus more vigilantly on Caleb. She shone the light toward him. His head was facing away, toward the wall. Blood matted his hair and pooled around his head. She shone the light along his body. There was more blood on the floor next to him, but that was likely hers.

Caleb took in a quick snorty breath and then moaned. *Just die already.* He was making a gross gurgling sound broken by short, squeaky gasps. On and on. It was horrendous. It was making her sick. Again, she wished he would just hurry and die.

It reminded her of the time when she was eight or nine years old and they lived in a rural area near the escarpment. Her dad was away on business and her mom woke up in the middle of the night to a thumping noise coming from the kitchen. It was the mouse trap that her dad had set under the kitchen sink. The trap had snapped down on a mouse, and the poor thing was flopping around with the trap clamped onto its hind legs. Her mom wanted to put it out of its misery but couldn't bring herself to kill it. She stayed there all night long, crying—unable to help it and unable to kill it. In the morning, Mr. Glister from next door came and took it away. Riley wished someone would come and take Caleb away.

His body suddenly convulsed. He gasped and choked, his legs jerking around. It was revolting.

Riley stepped down and moved a little closer. She shone the light along his body and along the narrow strip to the wall next to him. "Ahhhhh!" She screamed and stepped back. It was the snake, uncoiling itself, raising its head up from under Caleb's neck, disturbed by his erratic movements. She screamed again.

Ignoring the pain, she held the flashlight tight in her left hand and pulled the gun from her shorts with her right. She pointed it at the snake and pulled back fast on the trigger. *Bang!* It was so loud her body shook. She missed. She fired again and again—it was still moving. She got back up onto the bedframe. Now she had a better angle. This time she aimed more carefully and squeezed the trigger more slowly. *Bang!* Part of the snake bounced back a few inches, but it was still moving, slithering behind Caleb's legs toward the door. She couldn't get a clear shot. *How many bullets are in the gun?* She didn't know how many she'd already fired or how many might have hit Caleb.

There it was, coming around from behind his feet. She aimed again as carefully as she could and pulled back on the trigger. The flashlight flickered and dimmed out.

CHAPTER THIRTY-NINE

Michelle set the alarm on the night table. She was debating whether to set it for six or seven. Across from her on the other bed, Scotty was propped up with pillows, staring at her laptop screen. "They're still on the hunt for that escaped convict," she said. "Here's a picture of his family—they're asking him to turn himself in."

Scotty spun it around for Michelle and Nick to see. "It's kind of sad—they look like a nice family."

"Hmm." Michelle still worried the pursuit for this escaped convict might undermine the search for Riley and Jake.

Nick stood at the dresser, swallowing a pain pill with a drink of water. "I guess even convicts have families." He set the glass down. "I suppose they would be worrying about him. Anything more in there about Zachary Duncan?"

"No, nothing new. Just that the police are interested in his whereabouts." Scotty plugged the laptop into the socket beside her, then rearranged her pillows for sleeping.

Is your arm sore, Nick?" Michelle asked.

"Not as sore as Hector's face is right now." He got into bed next to her. They were all exhausted. She'd never seen Nick's face looking so drawn out. From what he'd told them earlier, he'd slept maybe three hours at best out of the last twenty-four. His eyes closed as soon as his head hit the pillow.

Michelle turned out the lamp. "Goodnight. I love you guys."

"Love you too, Mom. Love you, Dad." Nick was out.

Michelle closed her eyes and silently went through her ritual. *Please let Riley be okay. Please bring them home safely.*

A loud pounding at their door jolted her upright.

Scotty bolted up in her bed. "Mom," Scotty whispered. "It's after midnight. Who could it be?"

Michelle turned on the lamp and nudged Nick, wondering how he could still be asleep through all that noise.

More banging at the door. "It's Captain Charles Adams. I need you to open up right now."

"Oh, god." Michelle's heart was pounding. *Did he have news? Had they found them?* She pulled on her robe and nudged Nick a little harder. "Nick, get up." She went to the hallway, talking through the door. "Just a minute, please."

Nick got out of bed and went to the door in his boxers and tee-shirt. He opened it up. "What is it, Charles? What's this all about?"

"How about you tell me," Charles answered angrily and stepped inside. "Y'all wanna tell me about the ransom money?"

Michelle gasped. "How did you find out? They told us no police."

"So, they've contacted you?" Charles's eye brows shot together. He raised his voice, "We've got our entire force working round the clock, lookin' for your daughter—and you're keeping us in the dark about this! What the hey-ell are you folks thinkin'?"

Michelle felt like she was falling apart. Both hands covered her heart. "I'm so sorry, Charles. We didn't know what to do."

Nick was trying to pull on his shorts with one hand. "Just take it easy, Charles. It was my decision." He nodded his head at the table, "Take a seat, and I'll show you the note and burner phone they sent us. The package arrived late this afternoon."

Charles glared at him. "Listen here, Nick. You and your family seem to think you're running this show, but if you want your daughter back, it's high time y'all start letting us do our jobs."

Scotty unplugged her phone and brought it over to the table. "I recorded the phone call when they asked for the five million dollars."

There was another knock at their door.

"Who could that be?" Michelle asked.

"Probably Andy. I told him to call you first and let you know we were on our way over." Charles sat down at the table.

Andy stepped inside. "I'm sorry ma'am. I was supposed to call, but something important came up." He approached Charles at the table. "Captain, we need to talk—we may have a possible location."

"What possible location?" Nick demanded. "If you've got a location, what are we doing sitting here?"

"We're arranging for a search party to go in at first light," Andy explained. "The area we're looking at is mostly swampland. We can't go traipsing in there in the middle of the—"

"Andy, what's this all about?" Charles said. "Where did this tip come from?"

"Was it Hector? Did he tell you something?" Nick asked.

"No, no. Just let me explain." Andy cleared his throat. "We got a tip earlier from Ben Jorden."

"Nick, he's the detective we first went to see, in Niagara Falls," Michelle interjected.

Andy continued, "Detective Jorden called earlier and said they'd received a tip from a local family who'd been driving home from Florida. They were in the Yemassee area the day Riley and Jake went missing. They saw the flatbed tow truck loaded with Jake's car. They said they recognized the Ontario custom plates."

"And you didn't think maybe you should tell me about this?" Charles snarled.

"You were out of the office, and at first it didn't seem like much of a lead." Andy went on, "They saw the tow-truck turning on to a back road, travelling southeast. Ben had them draw on a map exactly where they had seen it and he faxed it through to me."

"And?" Michelle was on the edge of her seat.

"It's a back road that connects to an access road near Ridgeview. Anyway, I asked Jan to do a search of the land registry for the ownerships of all the properties in a fifteen-mile radius. She found a small plot of land out there belonging to a Grayson Duncan—same last name as Zachary."

"Holy shit!" Nick exclaimed. "That's gotta be it."

"Well, Grayson's land is all marsh now—no land there to speak of. But the property adjacent to it used to be a hunting lodge. It burned down decades ago. The satellite map doesn't show any structures out there. Just forested wetlands."

Michelle was hanging on his every word. "There's no way we can go there now?" It was the most hopeful news they'd had yet, and she didn't want to delay another minute.

"No, ma'am. Jan's organizing a search party and lining up a guide as we speak."

"She's gonna need to bring in some off-road vehicles," Charles said.

"Definitely. First light is at six thirty-two a.m." He looked at his watch. "In six hours from now, I'll be going in with a group of officers as well as the volunteers."

Charles nodded at him. "Good work, Andy."

"Will you be going too, Charles?" Michelle asked.

An expression she couldn't read flashed across his face. "I've got a meeting first thing with our chief of police."

He glanced at Andy, who looked away, fidgeting in his seat. Michelle sensed something awkward there. Charles let out a deep breath. "I'll see about postponing the meeting.

Andy, I'll meet you there at six a.m."

"Can we go too?" Scotty asked.

"Of course we'll be there," Nick said.

Charles raised his hand. "Absolutely not. Now listen. I don't want you folks getting all excited. Sometimes a lead looks good, but nothing pans out. These swamplands can be dangerous—we'll have enough to worry about as it is." He reached for the package on the table with the burner phone and note from the kidnappers. "Now, how about you bring us up to speed on this ransom call. From what I've heard, it sounds like y'all are planning to visit a number of banks in the morning."

• • •

It was nearly two in the morning by the time Andy and Charles left their hotel room. Nick had immediately gone back to sleep. Scotty had gone to the washroom. As she headed for her bed, she said, "Mom, aren't you going to sleep?"

"In a few minutes. Do you mind if I keep the hall light on a bit longer?" Michelle was writing everything down in her log. She had a complete record of the entire investigation.

"No, it won't bother me." Scotty gave her a hug. "Mom, do you think they'll find them in the morning?"

"I hope so. I've got a good feeling about it. Now, you try and get some sleep." She gave her best attempt at a reassuring smile. "Goodnight, Scotty."

Michelle went back to her notes and finished the last section regarding the ransom money and their discussions with Charles and Andy. She didn't know why she was recording everything in such detail, but it had become incredibly important to her. It was 'one of those things,' just like the socks she'd bought in the hotel giftshop. She finished her last sentence and closed the folder. She shut her eyes and held it tightly, pressing it against her chest as though it were a lifeline to Riley. *Hang on, Riley. Just a few more hours. Please be there. Please be alive.*

CHAPTER FORTY

There were hardly any cars out on the roads. Mack tried to flag down a pickup truck as it came past. The driver blasted the horn at him and sped on by. When the next car came, Mack waved his arms again and stepped farther out into the laneway. The driver slowed, took one look at him, then drove on. Two more attempts gave the same result.

Mack hurried across the road, trying to decide which way to go. He noticed something lit up a few blocks down. He hoped it was an all-night convenience store or pharmacy—someplace that might have a payphone. Payphones were hard to come by.

As he got closer, he realized it wasn't a store at all. The sign out front said "Sudsy's 24-Hour Laundromat." A car turned in and pulled up to the front door. A couple of college-aged guys with laundry baskets jumped out and headed inside.

Mack called out and ran toward them, but they'd already gone in. He slowed down next to their car, trying to catch his breath. He could see the keys dangling in the ignition, a Big Gulp soft drink in the cupholder and a cellphone on the dash. He looked over through the laundromat window. The guys were staring out at him. One had pulled out his phone and was starting to make a call. For sure, they were calling the cops.

Now he had no choice. Nobody was really going to listen to him. Nobody was going to believe his story about the kidnapped couple. If he was going to be arrested, he might as well lead them on a chase straight out to Riley and Jake. He jumped in the car and took off out of the parking lot.

He drove to a side street and parked in a spot out of site. He made two phone calls and finished off the Big Gulp. The first call was the one he'd promised Riley.

• • •

Michelle had just drifted off when her phone started buzzing. She looked at the screen. It was an unknown caller. She pulled the sheets back and headed for the bathroom, not wanting to disturb Nick or Scotty.

"Who is it, Mom?" Scotty whispered.

"I don't know." She answered the call. "Hello."

"Hello, my name is Mack Lewis," a man said in an urgent voice. The name sounded familiar, but Michelle couldn't place it. She was groggy and couldn't make the connection. "Is this Riley's mom?" he asked.

"Yes." She pressed the phone harder against her ear.

"Riley made me memorize your phone number the first day I met her. I promised her I'd call you—she needs your help right away."

"What!" Michelle gasped. "Where is she? Please, tell me where she is."

"She's locked in a cabin. I saw the kidnappers lock her and Jake in the cabin. She needs medical help."

As he told her how to get there, Michelle scrambled to jot everything down.

"I've gotta go," he said. "I'm calling 911 right now, and I'll try to lead EMS in there myself." He hung up.

• • •

Mack had the second call on the line, recording everything in real time. "911. What's your emergency?"

"A woman's been shot—her name is Riley Marshall. Her husband is badly injured too. His name is Jake Marshall."

"What's your name sir?"

"My name's Mack Lewis."

"Okay, Mack, can you tell me the address where you are located?"

"No, I'm not with them right now."

"Mack, we show your location at 1411 Sallsberry Road. Can you confirm?"

Oh shit. They'd traced the cell phone. "No," Mack said. "Riley and Jake—they're several miles out in the bush—on the east side of the highway."

"Can you tell me exactly where they are?"

"There's a dirt road that runs southeast off the access road. It's right near the Ridgeview town line. You need to follow the dirt road for a few miles, and then it becomes a path. There're swamps on both sides. Then it's mostly weeds. It's a few more miles after that. I can meet the ambulance and show them the way."

"Mack, I need you to stay on the line. Don't hang up."

"I won't hang up. Please, they need an ambulance right away. I'll start driving now to meet the ambulance over by the access road at the Ridgeview town line."

"Ambulance and police are being dispatched."

Mack put the car in drive and pulled out, heading back toward the access road. Sirens wailed from police cars zooming down the street a block over, where the laundromat was.

"Okay, Mack. Can you tell me what's happening now?"

"I'm on my way."

"Can you provide any further information about what happened to Riley and Jake?"

"Yes. Riley and Jake Marshall were abducted five days ago. They've been locked in a small cabin. A few hours ago, the kidnappers came back and they shot Riley. Jake got hit by their car and he has a head injury—he's barely breathing."

Mack stepped on the gas and squealed off from the stop sign. He headed toward the overpass.

"So, the woman was shot with a hand gun?"

"Yes," Mack insisted." He heard sirens behind him. He looked in the rear-view mirror. Two police cars were coming up on him fast.

"Can you describe her injuries—where she was shot?"

"I don't know!" he yelled. "She's still locked in the cabin. Please, it's been hours. She might be bleeding to death—oh shit!" One of the police cars was trying to come up alongside him.

"Mack, are you injured?"

"No. Not yet."

CHAPTER FORTY-ONE

Mason was leading the pack. They were on the new section of trail that Logan found yesterday. Mason slowed down for the turn, then picked up speed once he was on the dirt path. He stood up and twisted the throttle in his hand, gunning the engine. His ATV ripped forward with a loud burst of power. He heard Logan and Carter do the same.

Mason was disappointed. The path was just too flat—boring as heck. A total waste of time. He preferred the bumpier, more rugged trails that bounced them around more. He closed his eyes for five seconds, counting in his head. *One, two, three,* a bump, *four, five.* He opened them. *Shit!* He swerved to avoid a stump at the last second. What a rush! That made it so much more interesting. He'd have to tell Carter to try that. For sure, Logan wouldn't do it. The guy was too much of a wimp.

Must be time for some brewskies, he thought. He eased off on the throttle, slowing down to let the others catch up. Standing up again on his vehicle, he looked back to see where they were. They'd stopped. Logan and Carter stood in front of their vehicles, their silhouettes lit up by their headlights.

Mason spun his ATV around and headed back. *What the Hell are they doin'?* He pulled up and cut the engine. "What the fuck!"

A man's body was slumped next to a tree. Carter kneeled down next to him. "He ain't breathin'. The dude's deader than a doornail."

"Shit!" Mason's voice was full of panic. "I mighta run over him, I don't know."

Logan's face got all screwed up. "What the fuck are you talking about?"

"I closed my eyes for fun and I felt a bump." He kicked at the dirt. "Shit! What's he doing out here anyways?"

"Why'd you have your fucking eyes closed?" Logan yelled.

"Just shut up, Logan! Let me think." Mason bent down and took a closer look at the body. He shoved it a bit. There was no response. Nothing at all. "Fuck!"

"Told ya, man," Carter said. "He's dead. We need to get out of here."

• • •

Mack headed down the access road, swerving back and forth, trying to keep the police car from passing him. More flashing lights up ahead were coming towards him. He hoped it was the ambulance, but if it was more police, he'd have to make it to the back road before they could box him in.

"Mack, are you still there?" the 911 operator asked.

"I'm here. I'm being chased by police." Mack slammed on the brakes. He'd nearly missed the dirt road. The back end of his car spun around as he turned in. "Where's the ambulance?" he yelled.

"It should be there with you now," she said. There were other voices in the background now, and her tone changed. "Mack, are you the escaped convict from Ridgeview Correctional Institute?"

"Yes."

"Mack, did you lock Riley and Jake in the cabin?"

"What? No! I've been trying to help them."

"Can you tell me what you were doing with the Marshalls?"

"I was hiding out in one of the small cabins, out in the swamplands, and the Marshalls were brought there in the trunk of a car. They were locked in a cabin by two men and a woman, who left them there. I tried to get Jake and Riley out, but I couldn't."

The dirt road was getting bumpier and the road narrower. "We'll be coming up on where I left Jake in a few minutes."

He was almost there. Finally, he'd done something right. In a matter of minutes, Jake would be saved, and they'd be able to save Riley next.

"Mack, do you have any weapons? Are you armed?"

"No! I'm unarmed!"

"I'm relaying information to responders."

Mack stopped the vehicle, scanning in all directions for Jake. He was certain this was the tree he had leaned him against. Wasn't it? *Jake, where are you, man?*

Police officers surrounded his car with their guns drawn and pointed at him. Mack was scared. He left the phone on and set it on the seat beside him. He raised his hands, keeping as still as possible.

"Keep your hands up and get out of the car, slowly!" one officer shouted.

Mack didn't want to reach down for the door handle. They'd think he was drawing a weapon. How was he supposed to keep his hands up and get out of the car? *Is this a trick?* "I'm keeping my hands up where you can see them. I can't open the door with my hands up."

There were five officers. Mack was glad. Maybe there'd be safety in numbers. One or two officers might just shoot him, but with five, it would be a harder sell to say they felt threatened by him.

An officer stepped up to the vehicle slowly. Keeping his gun pointed at Mack's head, he opened the car door and then stood back. "Now! Get out slowly and keep your hands up!"

Mack swung his legs out, one at a time, and let his feet touch the ground. In small, gradual increments, he lifted his upper body out of the car. He stood with his hands up. "Down on the ground!" they yelled.

Mack slowly lowered himself to his knees. Then a sudden forceful kick at the middle of his back thrust him forward, face down into the dirt. A second later, knees pressed against him. He was afraid they might break his back. Police grabbed his wrists, yanked them behind his back and cuffed them. They searched him for weapons and found none. They had him secured.

This was his chance to tell them about the kidnapped couple. "Officers, Jake and Riley Marshall—"

A foot pressed down hard on the side of his head. "Somebody ask you to talk?"

"Please," Mack tried again. "Let the ambulance come through. Jake is here somewhere. He has a serious head injury."

"Throw him in the car," one of them said. Two officers hauled him off the ground and dragged him to the cruiser. The back door opened and Mack was shoved inside.

"Please, they need help right away!" he begged. "Riley Marshall's been shot. Please, they need your help."

An officer swung the door shut, leaving Mack there alone. Mack tried to shout at them from inside the car. "Please, listen to me! Jake and Riley Marshall! They need help!"

The officers sauntered back to the ambulance and chatted with the paramedics. *What are they doing?* The paramedics got back into the ambulance and turned off their flashing lights.

"No!" Mack yelled. The ambulance began turning around.

The five officers continued standing there, talking. A few slapped their hands together in the air, high-fiving each other. After a few minutes, the two who had put him in the car came back and got in.

Mack started up again. "Please, let me take you to Jake and Riley Marshall. They need help right away."

The officer in the passenger seat looked back at him through the caged divider. "Likely story. Tell it to the warden."

A rage came over Mack. A rage filled with heartache and frustration. He tried to supress it. If he was going to get anywhere with these guys, he'd need to reason with them somehow. He tried to speak calmly. "Please, you must believe me. Riley and Jake Marshall were abducted. Riley's been shot, and she's locked in a cabin about three or four miles farther in. I can take you to her."

"There's only one place we'll be taking you, and you're gonna be there a long time." Both of them laughed.

"Please, I'm telling you the truth. That's why I came back and surrendered myself. I was trying to bring back help for them."

"Yah, you're a real hero, aren't ya."

Mack decided to try another approach. "You can be the heroes who saved Jake and Riley Marshall, or you can be the police officers that did nothing."

There was no retort this time—just silence up front.

"I bet social media's gonna blow up over this one. Officers could have saved the Marshalls in time but didn't. No doubt, Riley and Jake's families will file big lawsuits against you."

Still silence up front.

"And it's all recorded on the 911 call. They were on the line with me the whole time driving out here."

The driver turned, pointing his finger at Mack. "We've got orders to bring you in. Nothin' more—nothin' less."

CHAPTER FORTY-TWO

Michelle grabbed her jacket, ready to head out the door. "Let's get a move on. Andy's on his way."

Nick pulled on his shoes. He'd suggested that Scotty should wait in the hotel room, but she was having none of it. She pushed past them into the hallway. "I'll go get the elevator. Hurry up."

The three stood outside the lobby doors, waiting for Charles and Andy. Andy wheeled in first and Michelle jumped in the front passenger seat. Scotty and Nick got in the back. "Let's go, Andy!" Michelle said.

He pulled out, lights flashing, and sped down the road. He got on the ramp to the I95 south, then took the

Coosawhatchie exit. They were headed across to the access road, where Mack had told her to go.

"This must be right," Andy said. "It's the same access road where the Hamilton family spotted the tow truck."

"There's the Ridgeview sign!" Michelle called out. "Mack said the dirt road turns in somewhere near this sign."

Andy slowed down and Scotty started shouting from the backseat. "In there! I saw something way back in there. Like a flicker. Maybe headlights." She pointed her finger against the glass of her side window.

Andy made the turn, and they started up the dirt road into the woods. It was dark and eerie, and they soon lost all light from the road. Their headlights gave the forest a shadowy underglow. The Spanish moss on the tree limbs looked stretched out, like it was sagging down to them.

"Right there," Michelle blurted out. "Up ahead. Those must be the headlights Scotty saw—here they come."

Bright lights bounced towards them. It was a larger vehicle about fifty yards out. It slowed down, and so did Andy. The path was barely wide enough for one vehicle. He pulled over as far as he could and stopped the car.

"It's an ambulance. It must be them!" Michelle jumped out before Andy had his seatbelt off. *Please be okay. Oh my god.* She ran toward the ambulance, waving her arms. "Let me in!" she shouted at the driver. "It's my daughter."

The driver got out. "We don't have any patients on board. Ridgeview Police told us to turn around, and I'd advise you to do the same."

Andy walked up to her, and the paramedic directed his next words at him. "Ridgeview Police have apprehended the escaped prisoner and the situation is under control."

"Have they found Riley and Jake?" Michelle asked.

"No, ma'am. Ridgeview Police said—"

"You need to turn around and go back in. Please! My daughter and son-in-law are in here somewhere, and they need medical help right away." Nick and Scotty were out of the car now too.

"Let me handle this," Andy said to all of them. He approached the driver. They couldn't hear what he said, but whatever it was, the driver reluctantly agreed. As Andy came back, the driver shouted, "If I get stuck in here, it'll be on you."

Just then, Charles arrived, inching his cruiser past theirs, barely fitting by. His window was down. "Have they got them?"

"No," Andy said. "There's no word on Riley or Jake. Apparently, Ridgeview Police are still in there somewhere. They've got Mack Lewis in custody and told the ambulance to turn around."

"Andy, get the family back in the car. I'll lead us in from here. We'll follow their tracks."

The ambulance backed up to an area wide enough to let their vehicles get past as Charles pulled ahead.

Michelle could hardly contain herself. "Please hurry, Andy." She knew they must be close. Something about the woods and the huge trees made her feel like she'd been here before. *Hang on Riley. We're nearly there.*

Andy was giving them firm instructions. "When we meet up with the Ridgeview police, y'all need to wait in the car. I mean it, Michelle. You need to let Charles and me do the talking."

A few miles up, a Ridgeview cruiser was heading their way. Michelle was frantic. "Andy, don't you dare let them take Mack away until he leads us to Riley and Jake."

As Andy got out of his car, he turned to the family. "Michelle, you and Nick need to wait in the car."

•••

Charles and Andy walked toward the Ridgeview cruiser. Andy could see Mack in the backseat. "They've got him, Charles."

Charles spoke quietly. "We need to play it cool with these guys, use a little finesse."

As they approached, the driver got out. "Well, if it ain't Captain Charles Adams."

"Ayden, haven't seen you in a stretch," Charles said. "This here is Andy Solterra."

Andy smiled and gave him a nod. *This is great. Charles knows him. Maybe they'll cooperate with us.*

Ayden asked, "What brings y'all to these parts? Little outside your jurisdiction I'd say."

"Well, I'll tell ya what, Ayden. We're searching for Riley and Jake Marshall. Got Riley's family here." Charles motioned back at Andy's car. "They say the man you have in custody knows where Riley's being held and that she needs medical help."

Ayden said nothing.

Charles played it up. "We sure would appreciate your

assistance, for the sake of the family." He leaned in closer. "They're good people, and well connected, if you know what I mean."

"What's in it for me?"

"You'll get all the credit if we find them."

"It's gonna take more than that. Yer gonna owe me a big one, Charles." Ayden got back in the car.

Charles and Andy turned to their cars. "Guy's a real piece a shit," Charles said under his breath. "He can ask for his favour until the cows come home."

CHAPTER FORTY-THREE

Riley flicked the switch off and on, but nothing happened. She shook the flashlight violently. Still nothing. *No, no, no. This can't be happening.*

An idea came to her. She'd seen her dad do it once during a power outage. He'd switched the batteries around, and then it'd worked.

Riley shoved the gun back into her shorts and unscrewed the end of the flashlight. Carefully, she let the first battery slide out. She put it in her pocket, then let the next battery slide out. She put them back in in reverse order and screwed the cap back on.

If it worked, she didn't want to waste a second of the light. She drew the gun out from her shorts and held it ready to shoot. *Please work.* She aimed the light toward the spot she'd last seen the snake and slid the power bar on. It was still there, but it looked like it might be dead. Maybe her last shot had killed it. She had to be certain. She squeezed the trigger slowly. *Got it!* The force pushed it back a few inches. It wasn't moving.

She turned the flashlight off and leaned back against the wall. She let her body slide down slowly until she was sitting on the bedframe. She tucked her hand back into her makeshift sling, then swaddled herself with the blanket. All the emotion she'd held in check began to pour out. She sat huddled in a ball, weeping.

• • •

The Ridgeview cruiser turned around and Charles pulled up behind it, followed by Andy. Everything seemed to be happening in slow motion. "Honestly, can't they go any faster?" Michelle asked.

"Not much we can do," Andy said. "Charles is already practically pushing them from behind."

At least ten minutes went by. They'd driven a long way. Michelle squeezed her hands together on her lap. She was starting to wonder if Mack really knew where he was taking them. It worried her; if she thought that, the police would be thinking it too. She didn't want them to give up. She checked in the side-view mirror to make sure the ambulance was still following them. They had to go on.

Everyone was quiet; there was just the rustling of weeds and twigs under the car. Suddenly, a loud echoing bang rang out. A gunshot! Brake lights flared on the cars ahead. Andy wrenched the steering wheel, swerving out of the way just in time.

"Everyone, get down!" he yelled. The car scraped against some branches along the passenger side. Nick held Scotty down in the back seat.

"That was a gunshot and it sounded, close." Andy zoomed ahead. Not more than a hundred yards up, they came to a clearing. He stopped the car.

"There they are! The cabins—just like Mack had said!" Michelle was trying to get out of the car, but the door was locked.

"Everyone stay put!" Andy insisted. "Let Charles and I go first."

Nick and Scotty were also yelling at her, telling her to wait and make sure it's safe.

Andy jumped out and drew his gun. Together he and Charles crossed the clearing, heading for the cabins.

"Police! Put your weapons down," Andy shouted.

• • •

Riley heard vehicles pulling in. As soon as they identified themselves as police, she screamed as loud as she could, "Help! Please help me!"

"Riley Marshall?" one said.

"Yes, I'm Riley Marshall." She sobbed; it was finally over. Jake had brought back help. They'd made it.

The chain rattled against the door. A heavy thump, the latch was lifted, and an officer walked in.

"Riley, I'm Officer Andy Solterra." He stepped closer. "Let's get you out of here. Do you need help?"

She nodded. She was shaking again and didn't want to step down on the floor. "Is it dead?"

He picked her up and carried her out like she was a baby in a blanket. She could hear her mom calling out, "Riley! Oh my god, Riley!"

Mom. It was her! She was right there beside her, kissing her forehead. "Oh Riley, I love you so much. Thank God you're alive."

"Mom." She grabbed her hand and held it tight. "Don't leave me, Mom."

Her dad and Scotty were there too; all of them surrounding her, telling her how much they loved her.

The EMS team gently placed her on a gurney and secured her. They moved as one to the ambulance. Everyone she loved was there, except for her husband. "Where's Jake?" she asked. "Didn't he bring you here?"

Michelle squeezed her hand. "No, Mack brought us in."

The paramedic interrupted. "We need to get her to the hospital, now." They lifted the gurney into the back of the ambulance.

Riley tried to raise herself up, but the strap on the gurney held her in place. "Jake!" she yelled out for him. "Where's Jake?"

THE LOWLANDS

• • •

Mack watched from the window. He could see Riley being brought out from the cabin. She was alive. He was so thankful for that. He could hear her crying as she was reunited with her family. Tears ran down his face too.

A police officer approached the car. "Mack, I'm officer Andy Solterra with the Yemassee Police Department. Do you know where Jake Marshall is?"

"I was trying to take him out with me, to get help, but he couldn't make it. I left him by a tree, past the thick weeds, right along the dirt path." Mack tried to swallow the lump in his throat. "He was barely breathing when I left him—"

Ayden, the Ridgeview cop, cut in. "We already stopped back where he said; ain't nobody there. Can't believe a word he says."

Mack tried to continue. "Jake's head—it was hit hard, on the windshield of the kidnapper's car." Mack could hardly get the words out. "Please tell Riley I'm so sorry."

He heard her scream out Jake's name again as she was loaded into the ambulance. His heart ached. "I'm sorry, Riley!" He yelled out to her. "I'm so sorry."

CHAPTER FORTY-FOUR

She couldn't part with the pearl necklace. It was the most beautiful piece of jewellery she'd ever owned. She held up the strand, then let it slide back down into the velvet pouch. Even if she had to wait a while, someday she'd be wearing those pearls. She imagined herself at some real fancy place and everyone admiring her.

Beth-Anne tucked the pouch into her handbag and closed up Riley's and Jake's suitcases. That was everything all squared away—there was nothing else to tie her to any of this. She had wiped everything down, removing her prints, then brushed her hands together in front of herself—a job well done.

She snapped on her rubber gloves and carried everything to the side door, ready to take it out to the car. "Friggin' hell," she muttered to herself as she dragged their suitcases out. "Godamned thangs weigh a ton." She heaved them into the trunk.

Back inside, she gathered the other bags. One with her shoes and another with Caleb's burner phones. She'd seen someone get rid of their shoes on a television crime show once. The killer had to be sure there was no trace of soil that could link him to the murder scene. Beth-Anne thought this might be advisable in her situation.

After loading the car, she got in and backed out. Mindful of the neighbours, she kept the headlights off until she passed by. There were only a few other houses on their rural street. Their lights were all out. She doubted any of them would even know who she was anyway. She and Caleb had kept pretty much to themselves.

She headed for the dumpsters at the plaza. Beth-Anne pulled up as close as she could. There was an Amity clothing bin there, too. Maybe she'd donate the Marshall's luggage. She looked at the designer bags. *It ain't right for some underprivileged lowlife to get this here stuff.* If she wasn't having it—nobody was.

The top of the trash dumpster was as tall as she was. She tossed in her bag of shoes, then hoisted up the suitcases one by one and pushed them over the edge.

Next, she headed in the direction of Zachary's house, randomly chucking the burner phones out the window along the way. Everything was working out perfectly. She abandoned the car in a ditch not far from Zachary's, hoping the authorities would think it was all his doing. From there, she walked to her sister's house. It was only a couple miles to Rosalee's. She couldn't have planned this better if she'd tried.

Beth-Anne fiddled with the key in her pocket, flipping it between her fingers. Rosalee wanted her to have a key just in case. "You know, if something ever happened." The house was dark. She wet her fingers and then rubbed them all over her eyelashes, smearing her mascara onto her cheeks. Rosalee was more than likely asleep, but if not, Beth-Anne wanted to be ready.

The screen door hinges creaked as she opened it. "Frigg," she whispered under her breath. She held it steady with her knee while she put the key in and unlocked the front door. She tiptoed in, closing the door softly behind her. Everything was quiet inside. Rosalee was asleep. Beth-Anne curled up on the couch in the front room and closed her eyes.

• • •

In the morning, she awoke to Rosalee coming out of the bathroom. She'd be getting herself ready for work. Beth-Anne stayed lying on the couch, pretending to be asleep, waiting for Rosalee to spot her there.

"Goodness gracious! Beth-Anne, you scared the livin' daylights outta me. How long have you been here?" Rosalee came closer. Beth-Anne could tell she was looking at all the mascara smeared below her eyes. "What on earth?!"

Beth-Anne sat up, shaking her head in despair. "Oh, Rosalee, I'm sorry. I've been here most of the night. I had no place else to go." She dropped her head into the palms of her hands.

"You poor, sweet thang—bless your heart." Rosalee hurried over and put her arms around her. "Is it Caleb? I knew that man was trouble right from the first time I saw him."

Beth-Anne forced out a batch of fresh tears. She sniffled and then let it all out. "Rosalee, I'm so ashamed. I fell head over heels for him, and now I find out he's been seeing another woman."

"Caleb? That rotter—he's been cheatin' on you? How could that dumpy-assed scoundrel do that to you? Are you sure, Beth-Anne?"

"Pretty sure. There ain't no other explanation for it." She sniffled again and wiped hard at her tears, knowing it would leave red blotches below the mascara. "He's been actin' all secret-like—making phone calls in private and such. That's when I first started thankin', somethin's not right. Lately, he's been staying out all hours and won't say where he's been—just tells me to mind my own business." She took in a loud, shaky breath. "Oh Rosalee, I've been such a fool."

Rosalee shook her head. "No, you're not a fool. That man's slicker'n owl shit." She slapped her hands down on her thighs and stood up. "Beth-Anne, yer gonna stay right here and we'll get you all settled in, ya hear?"

"Well, I was fixin' to go back there today and get my things. Do you mean it, Rosalee? Are you sure you don't mind?" She dabbed the tissue against her eyes.

"Course I don't mind."

CHAPTER FORTY-FIVE

"Riley, you shot a snake?!" Scotty's mouth hung open.

Again, Michelle put her hands to her mouth. She was so blown away by everything Riley was telling them. She felt traumatized just listening to it.

By the time the ER doc finished up with her sutures and bandages, Riley was half out of it, her eyes barely open. Michelle wanted to tell everyone to clear out and let her sleep, but at the same time she knew how urgent it was to get as many details from her as possible. It might help the police find Jake.

Andy seemed to be wrapping things up. He made a few calls out in the hallway and came back in with an update. "I'm afraid there's no word on Jake. I'm heading back there now. I'd like to be there when the search party gets underway."

Riley was resting peacefully when the trauma surgeon came in to talk with them. Michelle picked up bits and pieces of what he was saying. "It was a clean, in-and-out shot through the pectoralis muscle." The doctor peered at her and then Nick over the top of his glasses. "Can't get any luckier than that."

Michelle agreed wholeheartedly. In her mind, it was a miracle they'd even found her. She was so grateful for everything Mack had done, risking his own life to save Riley's. "Will she be okay, then?"

"Infection is the main concern now. We've started Riley on an IV with antibiotics. It's going to be important to keep the wound clean. We've also given her something for the pain. She'll be admitted and moved to a room shortly.

"So, her arm is going to be okay—she'll have full mobility?" Nick asked.

"She'll need to take it easy for a few weeks, but there doesn't appear to be any nerve damage. As I said, she's extremely lucky. Had the bullet been a half an inch over, it would've severed an artery." He pulled back the curtain of the ER cubical to leave.

"Thank you for everything, doctor," Michelle said.

"Now, if you folks want to go to the lounge, there's a vending machine with coffee and—"

Riley's eyes bolted open. "No, Mom. Please don't leave. Promise me, you won't leave me."

Michelle squeezed her hand. "Don't worry, Riley. I'm not going anywhere." She leaned over and kissed her forehead. "You're safe."

"How about Scotty and I go and bring us back a few things?" Nick suggested. "Doctor, can Riley have anything yet? We were told earlier she couldn't have anything to eat or drink."

"That would be fine."

Riley tried to lift herself up. "Have they found Jake yet? It's been hours."

Nick tried to reassure her. "The sun's just starting to come up now. Charles and Andy promised they'd have a search party organized and ready to go in at first light. They're going to be combing the entire area." He looked at his watch. "It's almost six thirty; they'd be out there right now.

Riley started to cry. "But Mack told the police Jake was in bad shape. Dad, I'm so scared. What if they're too late? I don't know what I'd do if..." Her bottom lip quivered and she tightened her grip on Michelle's hand.

Nick came closer and joined his hand in with theirs. "Riley, honey, if there's one thing I've learned over the last few days, it's not to give up hope."

Riley nodded. "Maybe he's lost. Maybe he was trying to find his way out and got lost."

Michelle fought back tears. She looked at Nick. "I know we've been waiting on good news about Jake, but I don't think we can wait any longer. We have to phone Wendy and Rob. I don't want them hearing about this on the news. We need to let them know that Riley's been found and a search party is out looking for Jake."

Nick sighed. "I know. I'll see if I can find a quiet spot in the lounge and give them a call now."

"Dad?" Riley said. "Please tell them Jake's been thinking of them and he loves them very much." Her voice cracked. "In the cabin, we did a lot of talking—about our families—how much we love you all." The lines in her brow crumpled together as more tears flowed.

"I'll tell them," Nick said.

An orderly came into the cubical. She carried a plastic bag and held it out for Michelle. "These are the clothes your daughter was wearing when she was brought in."

"Just throw them out." Riley said. "I don't want to ever see them again." She turned her head away.

Michelle nodded at the orderly, giving her the okay to throw them out. She patted Riley's hand. "I suppose we better buy you some clean new clothes to wear out of here. The doctor said, depending on how you're doing, they might discharge you later today or tomorrow morning. How about Scotty or I go and get you a few new things."

"I don't want any new clothes, Mom." She looked at Scotty. "I'd like to wear a pair of your sweat pants, if that's okay. I just want to feel like home."

"For sure," Scotty said. "Once dad comes back, he can take me to the hotel and I'll get some things for you. I'll pick out something super comfy. Oh, and I'll bring all the fluffy socks that Mom bought for you."

Riley looked confused, and Scotty smiled at her. "That's a story for another day."

"Thank you. I love you so much, Scotty."

"I love you too, Riley. I'm so glad you're okay."

Nick came around the corner, pushing his phone into his back pocket.

"What did they say, Dad? Are they okay?" Riley asked.

Nick sat on the corner of her bed. "They're incredible. Jake has got one heck of a family. They were relieved to hear we've found you, and they asked me to send their love. Wendy apologized for not being here in person."

Michelle was in awe. "They're such wonderful people. They must be so worried about Jake. And what about Rob? How's he coming along?" She couldn't imagine being in Wendy's situation right now.

"Wendy said he's doing well. The doctors are pleased with his progress."

"That's good news," Michelle said. Now, if the police could only find Jake.

Nick wasn't finished. "There's something else Wendy asked me to do right away. I promised her I'd look after it."

"What, Dad?" Riley asked.

"I need to get a lawyer for Mack. She wants the very best that money can buy."

CHAPTER FORTY-SIX

Charles, Andy and most all of the Yemassee Police force were participating in the search for Jake. It was their number-one priority. They'd divided the search party volunteers into groups and mapped off areas for each group to cover.

Cell service was hit and miss, so group leaders wore portable police radios. Andy was with a group not far from the cabins. He had half a dozen kayakers searching the edges of the swamps; it was too shallow and weedy to bring in a motorized boat. He also had a dozen volunteers on foot. They were spread out, five feet apart, heading down the path. Charles's team was farther down, just past the weedy thicket where Mack said he'd left Jake.

Andy held the radio button down and spoke into the microphone. "They're pulling something out of the marsh now. It's a man's shoe. A loafer, I think." He was hoping it wasn't Jake's.

Charles's response came through loud and clear. "Shit—find out what size it is. I'll phone Michelle right now and get his shoe size."

"Hang on, Charles. I'll ask." Andy shouted out to the kayakers, but they were intent on bringing out something else. He walked a little closer. The ground was spongy, and his rubber boots were sinking into the swamp. The water was over his ankles.

"Charles, it looks like there's more here than a shoe." He nearly gagged as he watched the dripping limb being raised out of the water.

"I'm on my way," Charles said.

He pulled up a few minutes later on one of their off-road ATVs. He hurried over to Andy. A plastic tarp had already been laid out, and the remains sat in a small puddle on top. The shoe was there too. Andy turned away from the gruesome scene. "The shoe's a size ten, Charles."

"Michelle said Jake's an eleven, so I'm assuming this is what's left of Zachary." Charles stood with his hands on his hips, looking at the tarp. "Okay, flag the area for the forensics team. Right now, we need everyone searching for Jake. Get your crew moving farther down until they meet up with mine."

Andy couldn't respond. He wasn't feeling well and Charles was staring at him. "You look about as green as that limb on the tarp," Charles said.

That nearly did it. "Just give me a minute, Charles. I'll be fine."

The captain reached out and put his hand on Andy's shoulder. "I know it's not a pretty sight. Take a few deep breaths and get your mind on something else."

Andy started to take in a deep breath, but the pungent smell from the rotting limb filled his nostrils. He barely had time to turn away before he vomited.

Charles waited until he finished. "I've been there, Andy. I remember my second year as a patrol officer. I got called out to a fatal car crash. I was first on scene. The poor guy was decapitated—his head was dangling out the window. Now, that's something you really don't wanna see. I lost my stomach at that one." Andy turned away and puked again.

Charles's radio crackled. "This is Jerry in group one. We found some ATV tracks that aren't ours. I don't know if you want to come and take a look."

"We'll be right there," Charles looked at Andy. "You good to go?"

Andy straightened up and wiped his mouth on his sleeve. Charles had started up the ATV's engine; Andy jumped on. It was a long ride. Jerry's group was closest to the access road.

When they arrived, Jerry approached them. "I've already sent a couple of men out on an ATV to follow the tracks and see where they lead." Charles and Andy headed down after them. The tracks led to a series of trails winding around the higher ground. Charles shouted to Andy over the roaring engine. "Looks like just a bunch of trails from ATVers." They caught up with the others and cut the engine.

"There's all kinds of ATV tracks, and this spot right here looks like some sort of teen hangout," one of the volunteers said. "There's a bunch of empty beer cans and the remains of a small camp fire. We're only about a mile in from the highway access road, so I imagine it gets used a fair bit by local ATVers."

Charles nodded. "Do me a favour and check out the entire area, just in case. Maybe Jake was disoriented and took a wrong turn. He could have wandered down one of these paths."

Andy knew that was extremely unlikely. They'd driven miles outside of the area that Jake should have been in, but they were running out of options. He and Charles went back to their groups.

The search had been going on for five hours and there was no sign of Jake. Andy's crew had covered their designated section and met up with Charles's group below the weeds. It was almost noon, and they needed a short break. A volunteer in an off-road vehicle drove around handing out food and water to the various groups.

Charles and Andy took some sandwiches and sat away from the others to eat. "This isn't looking too hopeful," Andy said, letting out a deep sigh.

"Sometimes things don't turn out like you want them to, no matter how hard you try." Charles took a bite of his sandwich and a swig of water to wash it down. "Andy, if I could offer you a small piece of advice." He set the sandwich down on the wrapper. "Always trust your gut, and don't give up. Things can seem one way and turn out to be another."

Andy was feeling sick again. Not from seeing the human remains earlier, but because of what he'd done. He never should have gone to the chief about Charles. He should've just talked to the captain directly. "Charles, I know this isn't the best time, but I think I need to tell you about something I've done."

"Does it have to do with the chief?" Charles asked.

"I'm sorry, Charles. I should've come to you right away. I saw you handing a roll of cash to J.J. and arguing with him after the press conference. I was afraid it might be related to the case."

Charles stood up quickly and pulled out his gun. Andy was startled. Charles didn't even hesitate. He fired instantaneously and the loud bang echoed through the trees. There was a heavy thud in the weeds at the edge of the path. "Got him."

It was a wild boar, possibly four hundred pounds. Its bottom fangs protruded from its mouth. The carcass hide was black, with thick, wiry fur running down the back of its neck. It lay there dead, its huge snout extending onto the path.

"Holy shit!" Andy exclaimed, half in shock and half relieved he hadn't been the target. He couldn't believe it. "Look at the size of that thing."

Some of the volunteers hurried over to see what happened. One of the leaders, a man familiar with the area, squatted in the weeds to take a closer look.

"Not bad shootin', captain—got him right in the head." He straightened up and walked over to Charles and Andy. "Damn hogs are getting more and more aggressive all the time. They've been attacking horses on farms in Beaufort County."

"I've never seen one before," Andy said. "Are there many of these things out here?"

"Got them in every county of South Carolina, though most people never do see them. Their preferred habitat is the swampy lowlands. There'd be quite a few out here, I'd say."

Andy realized that was likely why there had been a hunting lodge here. "So, people hunt these wild boars?"

"You bet. They're pretty good eating." He brushed the dirt off his pants. "They're pretty good at eating everything else, too—including people. Why, a hog this size could devour a human. I've heard they go through bone like butter."

Andy was sceptical, but Charles backed him up. "It's true. Some say that the Mafia used hogs to dispose of bodies."

Andy started thinking about it. "Maybe that's what happened to Zachary's body." At first, he'd thought a gator might have pulled Zachary out into the swamp, but now he wondered if it might have been a wild boar.

"More than likely," the captain replied.

Charles instructed the group leaders to work their way back to their original positions and widen the search. He and Andy examined the map. There wasn't much dry land left to cover. "Damn it," Charles said as he folded it up. "We best get back to our groups."

Before turning away, he looked Andy square in the eyes. "And, just so you know, that money I gave J.J., it was for a gambling debt. J.J.'s been running a small gambling operation for some of the more prominent businessmen in town. I was having some financial troubles and got mixed up in it."

Charles turned away and headed back to his off-road vehicle. Andy stood there dumbfounded. Gambling was illegal in South Carolina. Charles had just admitted to committing a crime and implicated J.J.

He started piecing everything together. This corroborated well with what Sarah had told him. She said J.J. would have meetings with businessmen and even the director of the chamber of commerce. Now it all made sense—J.J. was placing bets for them.

One thing still puzzled Andy. When he saw Charles handing the roll of cash to J.J., they were arguing and Charles looked angry. Andy wondered if there might be something Charles hadn't told him.

Their radios went off simultaneously. Charles leaned against the vehicle and pushed the mic. "Adams here." Andy listened on his radio.

It was Lou, the lead investigator from the county forensics team, up at the cabins. The county sheriff's office had taken over the homicide investigation. The Yemassee police Department didn't have the manpower or forensic facilities to conduct a homicide investigation. Furthermore, the crime scene itself was several miles outside the Yemassee town line. "We're about to wrap up," Lou said. Have you got a few minutes to come back here? I've got a couple of things to go over with you before we head out."

"On our way," Charles said. "Andy, copy that?"

"Copy that." Andy jumped onto the off-road vehicle as Charles came by, and they headed back to the cabins.

CHAPTER FORTY-SEVEN

Mack was being held in a Ridgeview Police Department holding cell. He'd been charged with two felonies: Unlawful Escape and Grand Larceny, Class F for the theft of a vehicle worth between two thousand and ten thousand dollars. If convicted, he could be looking at up to five years for grand larceny and another one to fifteen years for unlawful escape, to be served consecutively to his original sentence.

None of that mattered to him. Riley was safe, and somehow that made it all worthwhile. The only thing he was desperate to know was whether Jake had survived.

An officer banged his baton against the bars of his cell. "Mack Lewis, your lawyer is here."

"I don't need a lawyer," he replied. It would just be the same as before—another public defender who had too many cases and would rather cut a deal than prepare a proper defence.

He could hear a woman's voice. "Mack Lewis, my name is Celina Barnes."

He glanced up. She was Black, middle-aged and very professional looking, dressed in an expensive pantsuit and carrying a leather briefcase. He looked into her eyes. There was something about them—something much more important than her clothes or her appearance. They were sincere and caring. "You don't look like a public defender."

"I'm not. I'm a criminal justice lawyer from Stirling, Graston and Barnes. We've been retained to handle your legal affairs. We have a lot of work ahead of us, Mack. Shall we get started?"

CHAPTER FORTY-EIGHT

Yellow tape secured by stakes contained the area around the cabins. The coroner had left with Caleb's body, and Lou and his team were packing up. Lou was an older man, probably nearing retirement. He had a reputation for being thorough. He waved at them as they approached. "How's the search for Jake Marshall going? Anything?"

"Nothing yet. Just a wild hog that had to be put down," Charles said, waving it off, like it was no big deal.

"We heard the gunshot. One of our crew went down to see what was happening."

Andy asked if they'd found more of Zachary's remains. Lou scuffed his foot along the dirt and shook his head.

"Nope, little chance of that. Unless it was floating or snagged in the weeds, it would be next to impossible to find." He stretched his arm toward the swamp. "We're talking miles and miles of swampy wetlands out there—wouldn't surprise me none if the rest of his body was dragged off or eaten by one of those wild boars." Andy couldn't help but wonder if that was what happened to Jake too.

Lou pulled out his notepad and pen. "Charles, you and Andy were the first ones here on scene. Is that right? I like to double-check my notes." Andy had heard about Lou. He was known to be a real stickler for details.

"Yes."

"And who went inside the cabin?"

"Andy was the only one that went into the cabin. The rest of us didn't come within, I'd say, twenty feet of it," Charles said.

Lou seemed pleased and put a checkmark on his pad. "Good. And I'll ask again: was the area secured until my team and I arrived?"

"Yes," Charles said flatly. "Andy escorted the ambulance carrying Riley Marshall and her family to the hospital, and I stayed here."

Lou nodded, adding another checkmark. "Just need to be sure the crime scene wasn't compromised. "So, the car tracks in the dirt outside the cabin—definitely not yours?"

Charles shook his head. "Not ours."

Andy concurred, "Absolutely not."

"Just one other question for you, Andy." Lou started to walk towards the CSI vehicle and Charles and Andy followed along. "Were you chewing any gum last night?"

"Gum?" Andy sounded surprised. "No, I don't chew gum. Why do you ask?"

"I went through the weeds with a fine-tooth comb and found a wad of chewed gum just outside the cabin door and a crumpled-up wrapper just over yonder here." He pointed to where a small flag had been put in the ground. "We'll check the wrapper for prints and do a DNA test on the gum and see what we come up with."

• • •

By mid-afternoon, Andy was beginning to lose hope. There was no sign of Jake and only a few hours of daylight left. The county sheriff's office had brought in their cadaver dogs.

"I think it's time we go to the hospital to let Riley and her family know," Charles said.

"No, I'm not giving up. We'll keep searching until the sun goes down."

Charles gave him a sympathetic look. "Okay, Andy, I'll go update the family. Keep me posted if you find anything."

He nodded, then radioed out new instructions to the search party leaders, asking them to widen the search even farther.

• • •

Riley's mom stayed close, her chair pulled up next to her bed. Scotty sat on the other side, ready to hand her sister anything she might need: her drink, more pudding, her lip balm, a tissue. Throughout the day, they'd taken turns getting some rest, but now it was late afternoon and everyone was wide awake and feeling distressed.

Riley was fidgeting, struggling to stay put. She turned her head from side to side. Her dad stood at the window, looking out, then checking his watch.

"What time is it?" she asked him.

"Nearly five." His voice was strained and his face looked stressed.

"Dad, why is it taking so long? They've been searching all day."

"Nick, maybe we should phone Andy," Her mom said. "We need to know what's happening."

There was a light tapping against the open door. Her mom jumped up. "Charles." She stepped toward him. "Have you found Jake?"

Riley could hardly breath. She gripped Scotty's hand, waiting for the news he was about to deliver.

Charles lowered his head. "I'm afraid not," he said solemnly. "I think we need to prepare for the worst."

What!? "No!" Riley cried out. "He's out there, I know it." She shook off Scotty's hand and tried to get up, swinging her legs out of the bed.

Her dad hurried over, trying to stop her. "Riley, your IV. Hold still!"

"Dad, I have to find him."

"I know. I know, sweetie." He held her back.

She felt like she was drowning, caught up in a big wave that was pulling her under. There was a terrible pain in her chest. Then her mom's voice, detached and distant.

"Charles, what are you saying?"

"I'm sorry," he said.

• • •

"No. No. No!" Riley kept screaming. Michelle rushed to her bedside. She seemed hysterical.

Nick was trying to hold on to her, but she was flailing her arms and managed to break free. The IV came out.

"Oh my god! Riley!" Michelle had never seen her like this. Scotty hurried out to call for a nurse.

"We need to go look for him! Mom, please!"

Nick got his arms around her again, trying to avoid her shoulder. "It's okay, Riley. It's going to be okay," he said, desperately trying to console her.

There was no calming her down. Michelle could see she was panic-stricken. She looked like a caged animal, frightened and fighting for its life—determined to escape, no matter the cost.

Scotty returned with the nurse who quickly took charge of the situation. She spoke calmly to Riley in short, simple sentences. "It's okay. You're going to get through this. You're having a panic attack."

"No, I don't want to get through this," Riley yelled. "I just want them to find my husband!"

"I know. I know. I understand, but first, we all need to calm down."

Riley stopped fighting for a moment. She was breathing erratically, taking in multiple short breaths, her whole body shaking. "Mommm, please!" she begged.

It was gut-wrenching. Michelle could feel her pain. "We're not giving up, Riley. I'll go out there myself if need be." She glared across the room at Charles.

"Riley," the nurse said in a soothing voice, "you need to breath in slowly. Let's all breath together." She included Nick and Michelle. "Nice and slowly now. Deep breaths."

She counted as they all breathed in and out. It worked. Riley took in deep breaths with them, and they eased her back down on the bed. Michelle kept talking to her while the nurse reconnected her IV and then promised to be right back.

From the corner of her eye, Michelle saw Charles heading out. "Scotty, please go and ask Captain Adams to wait in the hallway for us. We're not finished this conversation."

After a few minutes, the nurse returned and said they were adding a mild sedative to Riley's IV. "This should help. Riley, you'll start to feel better in a few minutes."

"I'm sorry, mom," Riley whimpered. "We just have to find him." She was rubbing her eyes with the back of her hand, her eyelids red and puffy. Michelle couldn't bare seeing her like this.

"It's okay, Riley. You've been through so much. More than any of us could ever imagine." She leaned down and kissed her forehead. "I'm going to go out to the hallway with your dad for a few minutes and talk with Captain Adams." She squeezed Riley's hand. "Trust me, I'll make sure they're doing everything possible, and then some."

She closed the door behind her and caught up with Nick and Charles in the hall. She headed straight for Charles. "What are you thinking, coming in here and talking like that?" Her tone was sharp.

Charles pulled his head back a few inches in surprise, then reasserted himself. "It might not be what you want to hear, Michelle, but unfortunately, this is where we're at." He softened his tone. "We've searched the entire area and there's no sign of Jake. You need to know: it's unlikely that we'll locate his body."

"His body?" Michelle was flabbergasted. "What are you saying? It's only been one day. I think it's too soon to give up on him." She stared angrily at Charles; he was leaving them high and dry.

"Michelle." Nick gave her a look, his way of telling her to calm down. "I think we need to listen to what Charles has to say."

She nearly snapped. "I am listening," she said curtly, "I'm not hearing any results, and I'm not hearing what the next plan of action is."

Charles carried on, his hands on his hips. "We had over a hundred volunteers out there today; off-road vehicles, kayaks and local guides, all searching for him. If Jake was out there, we'd have found him."

"So, that's it? You're just going to give up?" Michelle looked away, putting a hand up against the corridor wall.

"Michelle, what more do you want them to do?" Nick said.

Now she felt like she was up against both of them. Nick was defending Charles, backing him up instead of demanding further action be taken. She pulled back from the wall with an angry glare.

"Something," she stated brusquely. "There must be something more." She leaned in closer to Nick. "Maybe you're ready to give up, but I'm not."

She walked back into Riley's room, trying not to show her anger and frustration.

"So, what's happening, Mom?" Scotty asked.

Riley looked concerned, too, but groggy. Michelle didn't want to upset her again. "They're just sorting out the next steps."

Michelle had to get out of there. She felt like she was ready to break down crying and didn't want to put Riley into another panic attack. "Scotty, I need to get some fresh air for a few minutes. Will you stay here with Riley?"

Scotty nodded, "Sure, mom. Take your time. Riley's going to rest now."

Michelle picked up her expandable folder with all of her notes. "I think I'll go to the courtyard to sit and think for a bit." She walked past Nick and Charles in the hallway.

Charles lowered his voice as she came by. Nick held up his index finger, stopping her for a second, "Are you okay?"

She kept walking. "Just going out for some air."

• • •

"I'm sorry, Charles," Nick tried to explain. "I think we're all coping as best as we can."

Charles nodded, "Everyone processes these things in their own way." He told Nick about the wild boars and how they had to shoot one that afternoon. "We suspect this might be what happened to Zachary's body. We knew that his body was out there—both Mack and Riley said he'd been shot and dragged outside the cabin. The only thing we came up with was a shoe, along with a small piece of his remains."

Nick made the connection that Charles was leading him to. Jake's body may have been dragged off or eaten too. "Oh, god," he said. His stomach turned. *Not Jake, not like that.* He could've collapsed right there in the middle of the hallway and cried. He willed the thought away. "Maybe there's still some hope, Charles. Can they keep searching?"

"Andy's still out there, and I'm fairly certain he'll have the search party back out again tomorrow." Charles rubbed his brow. "You need to know, Nick, the county sheriff's office has brought in cadaver dogs. I'm afraid, at this point, the odds of finding him alive out there are slim. I'm very sorry."

Nick clenched his teeth, straining to keep it together. "Charles, I don't think we're ready to give up all hope just yet."

CHAPTER FORTY-NINE

Michelle sat on a bench in the courtyard. There was one spot on the end that was still in the sun. The rest of the courtyard was cast in shadows. The sun had crossed behind the west wing of the hospital, leaving a distinct line dividing the sunlight from the shade. A line always in motion, moving so slowly you'd barely even notice it, Michelle thought. *One minute you're in the sun without a care in the world; then suddenly it's gone.*

She leaned her head back and allowed herself to close her weary eyes for just a moment, her face soaking up the sun's warm rays. She took a deep breath through her nose, then let it out slowly. She wasn't angry anymore—just very tired and desperate for another miracle.

Michelle wondered how they would get through this. If she couldn't accept the possibility that Jake might be gone, how on earth would Riley? *This can't be happening.* She leaned forward, letting her chin drop down to her chest, and stared at the folder on her lap.

She decided to document what was happening in the search for Jake. She opened the folder and pulled out the notepad and pen. They'd come so far since the beginning. There were thirty-two pages of notes. She flipped through them—it seemed like so long ago that she'd written the first page. She read it over. *Ben said he would notify all police departments. Ben will check all the hospitals for identified and unidentified patients of their description.*

"Oh my god." *Had anyone checked again?* Michelle folded up her booklet and shoved everything back in the folder. *Unidentified patients in hospitals!*

She ran back inside and down the long hallway on the first floor, headed for the emergency room. She was out of breath when she got there. The triage nurse sat behind a glassed-in partition with a circular opening for people to speak through.

"Can you tell me if any unidentified patients were brought in last night or this morning?" Michelle asked.

"I'm sorry, ma'am. We can't give out any information about unidentified patients."

"You do have one, then?" Michelle persisted.

The nurse started to repeat that they couldn't give out any information. Michelle ran off toward the front of the building. She needed to find Charles before he left. If *he* asked, surely, they'd tell him.

She stopped in the front lobby at the information desk, "Has Captain Adams left yet?"

The woman pointed through the glass doors. "You just missed him." Charles was getting into his car.

Michelle reached the car just as he was pulling out. "Charles!" she shouted, her hands up in the air. "Hang on a minute."

The car jerked to a stop and Charles opened his window. Before he could get a word out, Michelle broke the news. "I think they have an unidentified patient here. They won't give me any information. Did you or Andy check for unidentified patients?"

Charles parked the car and got out. "Not sure if Andy did or not. I stayed at the cabin until forensics arrived, then at daybreak we started our search."

Michelle dashed ahead to the entrance and Charles jogged to catch up. They went together to the emergency area and this time Charles asked for information on any unidentified patients.

"We do have one—he was brought in overnight. A young man who'd been involved in an ATV accident."

Michelle lost some of her original excitement. An ATV accident didn't seem connected to Jake.

"Could you look up what time he was brought in?" Charles asked.

"No need to look it up—I was on duty when they dropped him off. It was just after two a.m. A young man came barreling in, hootin' and hollerin' at us to come outside.

When we went out, there he was—our John Doe—left lying there, right on the walkway." She put her hands deep into the pockets of her smock, indicating she was done.

"Who left him there?" Charles probed.

"Three of his friends on their ATVs—not one of them wearing a helmet. All three of them, I tell ya—as dumb as all get-out." She shook her head in disgust. "They sped off across the parking lot without even giving us his name." She paused for a second. "Probably afraid they'd all get fined or something."

Michelle's shoulders caved and her arms dropped to her sides. She'd gotten her hopes up, and it wasn't even Jake. She didn't know why Charles seemed so keen on it.

"Where is he now?" Charles asked.

"Far as I know, he's in the ICU. They had to do emergency surgery for his head trauma. Haven't heard much else."

Charles grabbed Michelle's arm and pulled her along. "Let's go."

"But, Charles, Jake wouldn't have been in an ATV accident. How could this be Jake?"

Charles wasn't talking. He hurried them along, following the directional signs posted in the corridors. They passed the radiology entrance, then took a right; the Intensive Care Unit was just ahead.

Michelle stopped. "Charles, answer me. How could this possibly be Jake?"

"Listen Michelle, I don't want you getting your hopes up, but we came across some ATV tracks this afternoon. We followed the tracks but didn't come up with anything. Maybe there's a connection."

"What?" A wave of new hope surged over her. She hurried along with him. The automatic glass doors opened like curtains as they approached the ICU. She held her breath. *Please be Jake. Please be Jake.*

Inside, there was a reception area and a small lounge over to the left. Charles interrupted the nurse who was walking by. "Excuse me. I understand a John Doe was brought here during the night."

"That's right," she said. "Hang on and someone will be right with you." As she continued on her way, they heard her talking to a colleague. "Joan, can you help some people at the front desk? They're here about your John Doe."

A registered nurse, according to the badge hanging on her lanyard, came out. "Hello, I'm Joan. Can I help you?"

"Yes, I hope so." Charles quickly introduced himself and Michelle. "We think your John Doe might be Jake Marshall. Could we see him?"

Michelle's heart was pounding. They followed the nurse past the reception desk and into the ICU where the nursing station was. Everything looked brand new. They passed by a number of private rooms, all within view of the nursing station.

Joan stopped for a moment. "The young man you're going to see has suffered a severe head trauma. He hasn't woken up yet. Straight ahead in there—room nine."

Charles walked next to her; his hand supporting her lightly under her elbow.

From the hallway, Michelle saw someone lying in a semi-upright position with bandages around his head. She wasn't sure if it was Jake. *Oh, God. Please let this be Jake.*

A few more steps.

At the edge of the doorway, she stopped. "It's him. Oh, dear God, it's Jake." She approached his bedside and dropped to her knees.

"We're here, Jake, we're here." Michelle glanced at the nurse as Charles eased her up to her feet. "Will he be okay?"

"It's too soon to know," Joan said softly. "The doctor did a procedure to reduce the pressure on his brain, but now the rest is up to Jake." The RN gave her a sympathetic smile. "The neurosurgeon, will be in shortly. If you like, I can arrange for a family consultation."

"Yes. Yes. That would be great, thank you." Michelle was still trying to catch up with reality. She sat next to Jake and took his hand in hers. "Everything's going to be okay. We're with you now."

She glanced over at Charles and caught him pressing his knuckle up to the corner of his eye. She smiled. Perhaps there was a caring side to him after all. "Charles, thank you for everything."

He gave her a nod. "Would you like me to wait while you go tell Riley and the rest of the family?

She shook her head. "No, if you don't mind, I'd like to stay right here with Jake. Would you please go and get them?"

Charles left, and Michelle asked Joan if she could make a call. "I'd like to notify Jake's parents. Are cell phones allowed in the ICU?"

"Yes, go ahead. Cell phones are permitted here."

Wendy answered on the first ring. "We found him!" Michelle said. "We've got Jake."

There was a brief pause. "They found him, Rob. They found him!" She was crying as she relayed the news to her husband. "Oh, Michelle. Is he okay?"

"He's in rough shape, Wendy. He's had a severe head trauma. We don't know much more as of yet."

"But you've found him and he's alive. Is he conscious?"

"No, he hasn't come to. They did surgery during the night or early in the morning, I presume. He's in the ICU here at Beaufort Memorial. He was listed as an unidentified patient."

"You've seen him?" Wendy sounded like she still couldn't believe it was true.

"I'm right here beside him, holding his hand, as we speak. The police captain has just gone up to get Riley and give her, Nick and Scotty the news. I didn't want to leave Jake's side. I know if things were the other way around, you'd be there for Riley."

"Oh, Michelle," Wendy sobbed. "We're so relieved. We can't thank you enough." In the background Rob asked for more information about Jake's condition.

"I can't tell you much now, but I'll let you know more as soon as I can. Jake's nurse is arranging for a consultation with the neurosurgeon. I'll call you back shortly, and perhaps you and Rob could join in by phone."

"Yes. Yes, that would be wonderful."

"Wendy, they're bringing Riley in now. I'll talk to you soon."

CHAPTER FIFTY

She leaned forward in the wheelchair, reaching out for Jake, as her dad wheeled her next to his bed. "Oh, Jake—" Her words dropped off as she got a closer look. *Oh my God.* The joy of finding him was overridden by the pain of seeing him like this. She wanted to curl up in his arms and make everything be okay.

"I'm here, Jake. We made it." Tears trickled down her face. She leaned down to rest her forehead on his hand. "I love you so much, Jake." She thought she felt him squeeze her hand. She looked up quickly to see if he was awake, but he hadn't moved. His eyes were still closed.

"I thought he squeezed my hand, but he's not awake?" Riley looked over at the nurse. "Why isn't he waking up?"

"Now that Jake's injury has been dealt with, his brain needs time to heal." She smiled gently at Riley. "That can mean shutting itself down to begin the recovery. I'm sure our neurosurgeon, Dr. Narri Jeong can better explain," she said as a woman came to the doorway.

After the initial introductions, the doctor took them to the family consultation room and Michelle got Wendy and Rob on speaker phone. They sat around an oval table in comfortable armchairs. Nick pushed Riley's wheelchair up to the table and sat next to her. She had opposed the wheelchair, but the nurse on her floor insisted it was necessary, at least until the sedative wore off.

Dr. Jeong started by explaining Jake's injury. "When Jake was dropped off at the ER, he was in and out of consciousness. An MRI showed an acute subdural hematoma."

Riley had no idea what that meant. "I wonder if you could put that in simpler terms for us?"

Wendy's voice came through the phone speaker. "We were just wondering that, too, and taking notes at our end."

The doctor nodded. "It's like a bruise or collection of blood between the skull and the brain. When that pressure builds up against the brain, it can become life-threatening and requires surgical drainage. We're lucky Jake got here when he did."

Riley could see her mom jotting down notes and Scotty cringing. "Sometimes," the doctor continued, "the drainage is accomplished by drilling what we call 'burr holes' through the skull. In Jake's case, the consistency of the hematoma was too firm to remove through burr holes alone and a craniotomy was necessary."

"Oh my god," Riley whispered. Nick put his arm around her.

Scotty looked like she might be sick. "Excuse me. I'm sorry, I just need to step outside. I'll be in the lounge." She left the room.

"I'm afraid Scotty gets a little queasy when it comes to medical terminology," Michelle said.

"What exactly is a craniotomy?" Riley asked. It didn't sound good, and she was starting to feel queasy herself.

"We opened a small part of Jake's skull and surgically removed the hematoma. Everything went very well." Dr. Jeong gave Riley a reassuring smile.

Everything went well. She focussed on that. "Will Jake be okay?"

"There are positive indicators," she said brightly. "So far, Jake's intracranial pressure has not shown any elevation. That's a very good sign and improves his prognosis. He's young, which also adds to a more positive outcome."

"So, what happens next?" Riley asked.

The doctor raised her palms slightly. "For now, we wait and see. Postoperatively, there are some inherent risks. Recurrent or residual hematoma may occur. If so, additional operative intervention may be required."

"Oh my god." Riley felt overwhelmed. Hadn't they been through enough?

"We'd like to take turns and have someone with Jake at all times," Michelle said. "I was wondering if Riley might be able to stay with him overnight. I noticed a cot set up for a family member in another room.

"Oh, could I?" Riley asked. She didn't want to leave him.

Dr. Jeong looked over at Joan. Joan nodded and smiled. "I think that could be arranged."

• • •

After the meeting, Nick went to the ICU lounge to look for Scotty, and Michelle wheeled Riley out. They were going back to Jake's room.

"I'll walk with you," Joan said.

As they passed the nursing station, Michelle couldn't help but notice how innovative the ICU appeared to be—all of the ultra-modern equipment and state-of-the-art technology.

As though she could read her mind, Joan said, "We've just had a major renovation done, thanks to a large donation from a local philanthropist."

It was karma, Michelle thought—what goes around comes around. The Marshalls had donated so much money to their local Niagara hospital. Now, nearly a thousand miles away, outside of any major city, Jake happened to land in one of the most technologically advanced ICUs in the state.

CHAPTER FIFTY-ONE

By the end of the day, Riley was officially discharged and Joan had arranged for a cot to be set up in Jake's room for her. She was so happy they were allowing her to stay with him. She needed to be by his side. Only a few hours earlier, she'd thought he could be lost forever. Now that they'd found him, she wasn't about to leave.

There'd been no change to his condition throughout the evening. When Joan's shift ended, the night nurse took over. Debbie was just as amazing. Riley couldn't believe how caring everyone was and how well Jake was being looked after. When this was all over, she'd write special thank-you cards for each and every one of them.

Her mom stayed for most of the evening and, after supper, they did a video call with Jake's parents so they could see him too. Wendy and Rob called out his name and told him how much they love him. Wendy said she thought he might hear their voices on a subconscious level.

"That's quite possible," Debbie told them, and she encouraged Riley to talk to him too.

After Debbie left the room, Riley let out a long sigh, then looked over at Jake. *Please wake up.*

It was nearly nine o'clock. Riley could see how exhausted her mom was. She was nearly nodding off in the chair. "Mom, it's late. Why don't you go back to the hotel and get some sleep? I'll be fine here with Jake."

"Are you sure? I hate to leave you, Riley. Can I get you anything before I go? Maybe a cup of tea?"

"No, thanks Mom, I'm going to try and rest now too. I'll be fine."

Michelle gathered her things but still seemed hesitant to go. Finally, she said goodnight to Jake and gave Riley a hug. "I'll be back first thing in the morning. And Riley, if you need me during the night, I'll have my phone on. Just call."

Riley held up the phone Scotty had left there for her. "Okay, I'm all set if I need you." Her mom blew her a kiss from the doorway as she left.

Riley took a deep breath. "Well, it's just you and me now Jake." She stared at his eyelids, watching for any movement, then took his hand. "I love you, Jake."

There was nothing. "You're supposed to say, 'I love you too, Riley.'" She squeezed his hand gently. "Okay, then, if that's the way you're going to be, I guess I'll have to do all the talking."

She tried to stay positive. Jake always enjoyed humour and sarcasm. Maybe that was the best approach. "Jake, maybe you just need some motivation, is that it?" She tried to think of something he wouldn't want to miss. Something that might never happen in their lifetime.

"There's a hockey game on tonight, Jake. It's the Toronto Maple Leafs, in the final game of the Stanley Cup. It's in overtime—you better wake up. Oh, no—the Toronto defence just gave away the puck. Colorado's got a breakaway. He shoots! Oh, what a save. The Leafs take it back to the other end. You're gonna miss it, Jake. It's Marner, over to Matthews; he shoots, he scores! The Toronto Maple Leafs have just won the Stanley Cup." She tried to do soft sound effects of a crowd cheering.

There was no response. "Oh Jake, I guess even on a subconscious level, you know the Leafs will never win the Stanley Cup." She kissed his hand. "Ah, well, I tried."

She decided to fill him in on everything that had happened. She told him about Mack stealing a car and leading the police and ambulance back into the wooded swamp. How he saved her. "But you weren't where Mack left you, and we didn't know what happened to you. Jake, I was so worried about you. I thought maybe…"

She started to cry and leaned in closer, whispering, "I don't know what I'd do without you. We've come so far—you just can't give up now. We've got our whole lives ahead of us. Please, Jake, you have to try. Please wake up." She let go of his hand for a moment to wipe away her tears.

THE LOWLANDS

She thought about their future together. About how much she loved him and how much she wanted a family with him. *I was afraid, that's all.* She realized now how silly she'd been. She should have told him how she felt. She'd never even given him a chance.

"And about children. I didn't want to give up my career, and I needed to know that you'd be there, that we'd be in it together, equally. I should have told you." *Please wake up, Jake.*

She started thinking about how things never seem to happen when you're waiting for them. Like how a watched pot never boils. Maybe she should let Jake wake up on his own time. The doctor said he would need a lot of rest. Perhaps the kindest thing she could do for him was let him sleep.

She squeezed in next to him and put her good arm around him. "I've got you, Jake. Everything's going to be okay." She leaned her head against his shoulder and closed her eyes.

She must have dozed off. Debbie was tapping her wrist, probably waking her up to send her back to her cot. Riley opened her eyes, but Debbie wasn't there.

"Oh, my god! It's you!" Jake was awake, drawing the infinity symbol with his finger on her hand.

CHAPTER FIFTY-TWO

Four days had passed since Jake and Riley had been found. Andy was on his way to the Beaufort County sheriff's office. Lou, the lead investigator, had called and asked him to stop by; he had an update on the Marshall investigation. Andy hoped they'd made an arrest.

Lou was standing outside, leaning against his cruiser, when Andy pulled up. He waved him over. "Hey, Andy. I'm just heading out in a few minutes. Mind if we chat outside?"

"Not at all. It sure is a nice day."

"It's a beauty," Lou agreed. "Listen, Andy. I know how invested you and Charles were in the Marshall case. I feel it's only right to keep y'all apprised of my findings."

"What have you got, Lou?" Andy was hoping they'd found the woman Caleb had been having an affair with. Whoever she was, it was a mystery.

"We got a match on the DNA from the chewing gum as well as the prints from the gum wrapper."

"That was fast. It's only been a few days," Andy said.

"Beaufort County has its own accredited forensics lab now, so we got the results back real fast."

"So, was the gum Caleb's?" Andy asked. "Or maybe the mystery woman's?"

"Well, it turns out there is no mystery woman; that much I can tell ya. Just the one and the same who was living with him—Beth-Anne Jackson. Both the prints and the DNA from the chewing gum are hers. They matched a prior assault record from eight years ago."

"Assault?"

"Oh, yeah. She's a real piece of work, this one. She attacked one of the judges at the Ridgeview Fall Fair beauty contest."

"I take it she didn't win." Andy laughed. "Then her whole song and dance about not knowing what Caleb was doing; that was all a lie?"

"I tell ya Andy, if her lips are moving, she's lying—she's quite the little actress. Anyway, we got a warrant yesterday morning to search her sister's house, where she's been staying, and found a little something you might wanna pass along."

Andy was curious. "Oh?"

Lou took a pouch out of his briefcase. "It's a pearl necklace, found in Beth-Anne's handbag." He held it up, squinting at it. "There's a small engraving inside the clasp. Says *All my love, Jake.*"

"Well, I'll be." Andy smiled and took the pearls. "I'd be happy to pass them along. You sure it's okay to release them?"

Lou laughed. "The prosecutor agreed to release them. They've got plenty of photos and they'll have testimony from Riley and Jake."

Andy looked down at the pavement, his smile fading. He couldn't help but think about Charles and wished he was there, too, to see things come to a close. If only things had turned out differently.

"Listen, Andy. I know what you're thinking—I've been around the block a few times. Don't beat yourself up about it. You did the right thing, speaking up about Charles." He gave Andy a friendly pat on the back. "I hear they're not pressing charges."

"No." Andy looked down again. "Charles gave a full statement along with his immediate resignation."

"Don't worry about it. He'll be okay," Lou said reassuringly. "I tell ya what, Andy. This Marshall case has sure turned things all cattywampus 'round here."

"How do you mean?"

"You didn't hear it from me, but word's out that three officers on the Ridgeview force have been put on leave, pending an internal investigation."

"Anything to do with Mack Lewis?" Andy asked.

"His lawyer sure is jacking things up. She's got the Ridgeview police more nervous than a long-tailed cat in a room full of rocking chairs."

• • •

Riley had Jake up and walking when Andy arrived. "Look at you," Andy said. "I'm glad to see you up and about."

Jake smiled, but kept focussed on each step until he made it to the chair. Once he sat down, he answered. "I'm walking for ten minutes, four times a day now." He grinned. "Riley's got my whole recovery plan worked out."

She sat down next to Jake. "He's doing great, isn't he? This afternoon, we've arranged for a video call with Jake's parents to show them his progress." She took his hand. "Then next week, the doctor said, they'll be taking the staples out."

"I don't know," Jake said, "I'm starting to like this zipper look on my head. It's kind of a cross between punk rock and Frankenstein."

Riley shook her head. "At least we know the head injury didn't affect his sense of humour."

Andy laughed and pulled up a chair. "I've got something that I think might belong to you." He pulled out the pouch out of his pocket and handed it to her.

"My pearls!" If there was one thing she'd wish to have back, it was those pearls. She lifted the necklace out of the pouch. "These were a birthday gift from Jake. The first gift he ever gave me."

She gave Jake a big smile, remembering that night. He'd planned an Audrey Hepburn movie marathon and started them off with *Roman Holiday*. Back when they'd first met, Riley had mentioned that Hepburn was one of her favourite actors, as well as a great humanitarian. He gave her the necklace before he started the next movie. She'd put it on right away and wore it while they watched *Breakfast at Tiffany's*.

"Thank you, Andy." Jake said. "And thank you for everything you did, trying to find us."

"You're welcome." Andy let out a sigh. "Ah, I'm sure sorry for everything you folks went through. Not exactly what I'd call our typical southern hospitality."

He was about to leave as Michelle, Nick and Scotty arrived.

"Andy!" Michelle gave him a hug. "I was hoping I'd get to see you again before I left."

"Y'all headed home, are ya?"

"Just Michelle and Scotty," Nick said as he shook Andy's hand. "Scotty's got to get back to university, but I'll be sticking around in case Riley and Jake need anything." He smiled at them. "You two aren't getting rid of me so easily."

It felt so good to be sitting there chatting with family, even if it was in a hospital. Jake squeezed Riley's hand.

Her mom thanked Andy again for everything he'd done. "I'm sorry if I was a little overbearing from time to time."

"No, ma'am. Not at all. You were just being a good mom."

He nodded to everyone. "Y'all come back now. Ya hear?"

CHAPTER FIFTY-THREE

18 Months Later

Jake poured a glass for everyone. It was their internationally acclaimed, award-winning ice wine. They didn't choose it tonight for that reason, though; it was simply because this one was their favourite. It had been bottled last year, just after they'd found out Riley was pregnant.

Scotty and Michelle were serving dessert. Everyone was there—Riley's parents, Jake's parents, their grandparents and Mack and his family. It was a celebratory dinner for Mack. His criminal record had officially been expunged and he'd received a large settlement.

Jake raised his glass to make a toast. "To Mack," he looked along the table at everyone gathered and then focused on Mack. He struggled to get the next words out. "My friend, my brother, our savior." He raised his glass a little higher. "To family, and new beginnings."

A wave of emotion came over Riley. Everything was as it should be.

"Here, here," Rob said; others joined in with the phrase.

"To family," Mack said.

After the dishes were cleared, Jake, Riley and Mack stood together on the deck, looking out at the vineyard as the sun set. Everyone had come outside to stretch their legs.

Mack's sister, Harper, was telling Scotty about the impacts of overfishing. "The fishing industry needs to be better regulated. The amount of bycatch they have is astronomical!"

Scotty nodded her head in agreement, waiting to jump in. "I know. Plus, they're destroying the coral reefs and putting critical ecosystems at risk. My dad worked on some new technology to help monitor fishing vessels and make sure their nets don't exceed regulations."

Mack elbowed Riley lightly. "Didn't I tell you Riley? These two are going to save the world."

"You did, Mack." She linked her arm through his and smiled. She was happier than she could have ever imagined.

"By the way," he said, "I'll need to get that pasta recipe. Dinner was fabulous."

"I'm glad you liked it. It's our most popular menu option at the new catering location."

Michelle interrupted them, coming outside with the

baby. "I think somebody wants to say hello."

"I'll take her," Jake said, beaming. Michelle carefully handed her over.

Jake cradled her against his chest. "Come on, Mackenzie. Let's go meet the family."

What Did You Think of *The Lowlands*?

First of all, thank you for purchasing *The Lowlands*. I hope you enjoyed it and if so, I want you, the reader, to know that your review is very important to me. It would be much appreciated if you take some time to post a review on Amazon, and share this book with your family and friends on social media.

LAUREL MARTIN lives in Waterdown, Ontario. She is married with two daughters and was previously a successful business owner in the financial services industry. *The Lowlands* is her debut novel.